ONE

Echo Lake
Twenty-five years ago ...

S he wasn't the first to die here. In 1973, a boy had gone fishing with his father, waded in too deep; his foot stuck in the muck, he had panicked. For him, it felt just like going to sleep after the terror ebbed.

A few years later, a drunk driver took the curve on Lakeshore Road just a little too fast and lost control of his Plymouth Duster. He hit the water going over seventy miles an hour, the cops said. He had struggled, trapped in his seatbelt as the car sank and silt and water filled the vehicle. They said he lived for several minutes, trapped on the bottom of the lake, thirty feet of water over his head, before he too simply fell asleep.

There were other deaths, of course. Some say the lake got its name from the cries of a lost lover. As the legend goes, a Shawnee princess, a young widow, had walked out until the water covered her head and let herself sink just a few feet from where that Plymouth Duster came to rest some three hundred years later.

They said sometimes, when the wind was still, you could hear her mournful cries echoing across the placid surface of the water.

And so it became Echo Lake.

But this time, this soul, she was the first to die here by murder.

First, she fell. If she'd had time to think of it, to remember what happened that day, she might have wondered if things could have turned out differently if only she hadn't tripped on that piece of black driftwood.

But she had, and her knee went out. She tumbled down a small incline, landing on her stomach.

Move! Run! Don't look back!

All those thoughts slammed into her brain, but for a single moment, she felt frozen. As if her legs had grown roots, tying her to the ground.

Then the air went out of her lungs as a heavy weight fell on her back.

Crack. Pop. Pain seared her side as one of her ribs snapped.

This couldn't be happening, she thought. It was a dream. It felt like that. The kind where you can't make your legs move. You try to scream but can't make a sound.

"Help," she thought, wanting nothing more than to shout it. It came out as a weak croak.

"Please. Stop!"

The weight lifted from her back. Her arm was wrenched upward, forcing her to flip over onto her back. Her hand throbbed. She'd punched her assailant. Hard. For a moment, she thought it would be enough. But it stopped nothing.

The moon was full. For some reason, that mattered to her. She could count the stars here. They were so much brighter than what she saw at home.

She had a thought toward the end. The stars were watching her. They saw. They knew. She tried to reach up as fingers closed around her throat.

So much pressure. Then the stars seemed to multiply and spin.

She kicked once. Flailed. There was something you were supposed to do. What was it? Her head smacked hard against the ground. Had it been anything harder than wet sand, it might have cracked her skull.

She tried to cough. No air. Her head filled with cotton. It hurt.

Let me go. You don't have to do this. I'll disappear. I am nothing. I am no one. I am worthless.

The stars blinked. A cold, hard, unfeeling stare. They would be there after she was gone. They would witness every other death to come just as they'd witnessed all that had come before.

I'm sorry, she thought. So sorry. For her minor sins, yes. But also for the greatest one she had yet to commit. Because at the very end, as death finally came for her in its lonely, brutal grip ... she let go.

Her pain floated away. The bruises. The broken bones. Her crushed throat. Gone. All gone. There was nothing left but stars and sand. Her broken right hand splayed out, she felt the water as it met the shore.

And then the stars went black.

I t was over. She was gone. The killer sat on her chest for seconds only. Or maybe it was hours. Every detail of her face seared into the killer's memory.

She hadn't made eye contact. That seemed strange. Instead, her now vacant eyes stared at the sky. The stars reflected in them, making them twinkle like two gemstones. Soon, the killer knew her eyes would go milky-white.

The killer touched her face. Still warm. Still beautiful. Full lips. Her smile. Her infectious laugh. Her throat was already turning black though.

"They love you," the killer said. "They all love you. They all want you. You've played them all. You stupid bitch. I love you too."

It had been so easy, in the end. The killer wondered if they would ever feel guilt. If they would ever feel anything again.

The killer felt death. The power of it. Small bones breaking. Precious breath cut off forever.

It was a rush. For that one moment, the killer had become God.

But now, as clouds rolled in, hiding the light of the moon, panic began to set in.

When they find her, they'll know.

When they find her.

There was nothing to weigh her down. No rope. But the earth was soft here. Wet sand. The killer dug using only fingers at first. But then, the killer remembered. There was a shovel in the trunk of the car.

It had been put there last winter. Sometimes, it took days for the plows to come. A shovel was a handy thing to have.

So the killer began to dig. The panic came back. When the sun came up, maybe someone might see.

But nobody lived on this side of the lake. All the houses and boat slips were further north. For years, developers had tried to buy up this land to put in condos and luxury homes. So far, the zoning board wouldn't allow it. Someday, maybe. But for now, only the lone fisherman and random hunter came back here. The woods provided the perfect hiding spot for teen lovers and underage drinkers. It was far too cold for even that now.

But it was not too cold to dig.

When it was time, the killer simply pushed the girl into the hole. She slid down the marshy wall and landed on her back with a sick, wet thud.

She was still staring up at the stars as the killer dumped the first shovelful over her face and closed her eyes for good.

Two

Echo Lake
Present day...

Today was about everything Detective Jake Cashen hated. As he stood at the far edges of the crowd, he could think of about a dozen more appealing places to be. But he was given no choice. Sheriff Meg Landry gave him a direct order to be here, so here Jake was. She stood beside him, keeping that false smile on her face. She was good at it. Only people who knew her well like Jake did would guess she didn't love this. The crowd. The ceremony. The gaggle of local reporters snapping pics and recording every word that was said.

Jake bristled. He hadn't realized he'd done it, but he made some sort of noise low in his throat. Landry, her smile never faltering, nudged him with her shoulder.

"Traffic duty," Jake said.

"Shh." Landry grew bolder and actually slapped Jake's shoulder.

"Babysitting a DOA."

"Quiet, they're starting soon."

"Seriously, put me on community services. I'll drive the Cops and Cones truck. Anything else."

She turned and looked up at him through her mirrored sunglasses. Jake's scowl reflected back at him. He pushed up his own sunglasses. Sweat made his dress shirt stick to him under his suit coat. The last week in May and the temperature had shot up to eighty. He stood on Landry's right, the sun beating down on both of them.

"Zip it," she said. "If I've gotta be here for this, you've gotta be here for this, hometown hero boy."

Jake rolled his eyes. "Trust me. I can think of at least one person here who'd rather I be out writing speeding tickets today."

They laid tarps down to keep the mud off the VIPs' shoes. The small crowd gathered thirty feet from the eastern shoreline of Echo Lake. Here, the grandest of the luxury homes would go in. The model home. Three thousand square feet of high-end, custom-built homes on one hundred feet of hard, sandy-bottom lake frontage. The builder hoped to fetch close to a million for it.

"Thanks for coming," Mayor Devlin said. The wind kicked up, blowing sand everywhere. "I'm gonna hand this over to Commissioner Arden. He's been the true champion and brains behind this project. He's assured me his remarks will be brief."

That got a laugh and a smattering of applause from the crowd. Jake's Uncle Rob Arden wasn't known for brevity at public events. Arden shook a playful fist at Mayor Devlin and stepped to the front of the crowd.

"This has been a long time coming. Long time. The Arch Hill Estates project is going to bring much-needed jobs to the county. Construction crews. Craftsmen. Fine men, all of them."

It was Meg Landry's term to growl. "Smile, Sheriff," Jake whispered.

"How can he be so bad at this?" she said through gritted teeth, better than any professional ventriloquist. "And how can these yahoos keep electing him year after year?"

"You're acting like today's your first day in Worthington County," Jake said.

Landry rolled her eyes and gave a nod to Mayor Devlin as he looked over her way. Even he was starting to lose interest in Rob Arden's rambling speech.

"This is only the beginning," Uncle Rob continued. "Over the next five years, we're going to make good on our promises to draw new business and industry to the county. This development is going to draw the most desirable people to our community. Leaders. Innovators. Business owners."

"Good luck keeping the less desirables on their side of the lake," Jake muttered. Landry smacked his arm again.

Further down the road, a small group of local protesters waved picket signs. Not everyone wanted this part of Arch Hill Township to become a gated community. They'd cut up forty acres of prime buck country and hundred-year-old oaks to break ground today.

"So," Rob Arden said, after droning on for ten minutes. "Without further ado, let's do this right."

A college-aged girl with sky-high blonde hair teetered on a pair of red heels beside Rob Arden. She wore a sash across her chest that read Miss Blackhand Hills. Smiling big, she handed Arden a golden shovel.

"Thanks, honey," Uncle Rob said. He turned back to the crowd. "Ladies and gentlemen, esteemed colleagues, honored guests. It is my supreme honor and pleasure to break ground on this exciting new project."

"Rapists!" A woman's voice drowned out Arden's. Jake turned toward it. Two of the protesters had made their way down to the shoreline. Arden glared at Sheriff Landry.

"You've raped this land!" the woman said. "Save the trees! The mute swans brood in that marshy area just over there. We have Canada geese who call this place home."

"Jake," Landry said. "Can you go over there and break that up? But ... don't draw attention to yourself."

Jake arched a brow and looked at her. "So you want me to cuff them, casual-like?"

"Jake," Landry said, her ire growing. "Just ... be cool."

"Got it," Jake said.

He broke from the crowd and started to walk toward the protesters. They were just kids. Eighteen at most. They'd probably cut school to come out here.

"I give you Arch Hill Estates!" he heard his Uncle Rob proclaim. Rob held a golden shovel high above his head. Someone had tied a big red bow to the handle. One end of it unraveled and the wind caught it, molding it to Rob's face.

"Killers! Rapists!" The protesters waved their signs and started to move closer to the front of the crowd. One of them caught Jake's eye as he came forward. He put his hands on his hips, letting his jacket pull away so they could see his badge clipped to his belt.

"We know our rights," the protester said. Jake recognized her. She went to school with his nephew Ryan. He'd seen her at his sister Gemma's house once or twice. Jake intensified his gaze on their little group. If Ryan were here, he'd kill him. Or Gemma would. Today was a school day.

"Come on, guys," Jake said to the protesters. "Let's just move back a little bit."

"You can't make us leave," the girl said. Cara? Cora? Jake couldn't quite remember her name. Jake was pretty sure her father owned the sports bar just down the road.

There was laughter behind him. Uncle Rob made some ridiculous pantomime as if he were about to dig. From the corner of his eye, he saw Arden plant the golden shovel into the ground. It hit something hard. Uncle Rob jerked backward from the force of it.

Two protesters, including Cara or Cora, started running in the other direction before Jake could get to them. He turned back to Landry.

"Let's try that again," Arden said, laughing. He raised the shovel one more time and stabbed it forcefully into the ground. Once again, Jake heard the metal hit something hard. He started to head back to Landry's side. She was now standing in the front row.

"What in the ..." Arden said. He scraped dirt away with his shovel. Whatever he saw made the color drain from his face.

Jake and Landry got closer. Clutching his chest, Rob Arden dropped the shovel.

"Uh ..." Landry said. "Jake?"

He leaned over, peering down at the same time Landry did. Phones clicked through the crowd as people started snapping pictures and taking video. Miss Blackhand Hills screamed.

A human skull poked out of the dirt, right beside Rob Arden's golden shovel.

"Jake!" Landry shouted.

Mayor Devlin ran back up beside Rob Arden. Arden stood there, holding the shovel. The idiot actually raised it again as if he were going to take another stab at the ground with it.

"Drop it!" Jake said. "Don't move. Don't touch anything."

Now everyone in the crowd seemed to have their phones out, snapping pictures and recording. They moved in a horde, knocking down the thin ropes staked in front of where Rob stood.

Jake sprang into action. He turned toward the crowd and put his arms out. "Nobody moves another inch. Back up. Just back up!"

"That's a body!" someone shouted. "That's a dead body! It has maggots all over it."

Jake looked over his shoulder. There were no maggots. Just seaweed and lots of sand. Landry had gone to his left; she too tried to push the gawkers away from the scene.

"Everyone just calm down," Rob said, grinning. He still had that damn shovel in his hand. "There's nothing to worry about. At worst, somebody's pulling a little prank. At best, we all know the Shawnee held this land for centuries before the settlers came in. Heck, if I asked for a show of hands, I bet half of you have an arrowhead you found out here when you were a kid. Just back up, like Detective Cashen said. You can take your pictures and I'll be here for interviews for a few minutes after the ceremony."

He turned, looking for Miss Blackhand Hills. She was supposed to hand him giant gold scissors so he could cut the rope separating the crowd from where he stood. But the county beauty queen was currently throwing up at the edge of the woods.

"Ceremony's over!" Jake called out. "I'm gonna need everyone to just clear out and head back to their vehicles."

"Detective Cashen," Lisa Crowley from Channel 12 Action News called out. "You're standing two feet away from what looks like a human skull."

"It's a dog," Arden shouted. "Or a beaver. Don't you print that. Don't you dare print that. It's nothing but a deer head, folks. Nothing to worry about!"

Something snapped in the man. He pushed past Jake and headed straight for Lisa Crowley, shaking a finger in her face. "I will not have these proceedings disrupted like this. You're just looking for trouble." For half a second, Jake thought Rob might actually lay hands on her.

Landry saw it too and reacted, surprising Jake. She charged over to Rob and pushed him back.

"Commissioner Arden," she said. "It's time for you to corral your people and end this. Detective Cashen and I will take things from here."

With Arden and the mayor out of the way, Jake turned and looked more closely at the bones in the ground, careful to keep his distance.

Skeletal remains weren't his expertise, but he could tell enough just by looking at the thing. The skull wasn't sun-bleached. The bones were dark brown, nearly matching the tone of the sand. If Rob hadn't had the dumb luck to plant his shovel right where he did, anyone could have walked right by and missed the thing. Though he knew better than to touch anything, Jake could see another bone sticking up a few inches from the skull. A clavicle. Next to that, the lower portion of the jaw had come away from the top part of the skull. He took out his phone and shined his flashlight right at it.

"This is good luck!" Arden said, vamping. "You'll see. It's as if the Shawnee have blessed this ground and this development. Don't anyone worry. Arch Hill Estates will proceed on schedule. We'll have our first residents moved in by the end of the summer."

"I wouldn't be too sure about that," Jake said. Arden was close enough to hear him. His face turned purple. If he could read his mind, Jake bet his Uncle Rob wished he could brain him with that shovel.

"What are you talking about?" Rob said. "I will not have you getting in my way, Jake."

Jake rose, ignoring Rob Arden for the moment. "Landry," he said. "I need you to get everyone out here."

He kept his flashlight on the jaw bone. Landry's eyes went to it. She understood.

"Whatever you need," she said.

"I need everyone," Jake repeated. "I need crews out here roping off the area. Nobody goes in or out. BCI will want to take a look at this. But we need a forensic anthropologist out here as fast as they can make it."

"Now see here," Rob said. "There's no need for any of that. Ignore all of that!" He was talking to the press, fully aware that his every word and movement was being recorded. Then, he tried to march right past Jake, practically trampling over the bones.

Jake grabbed his uncle by the shoulder and pushed him back. All of that was recorded too. In less than an hour, it would be all over the internet. Jake couldn't care less.

Rob seethed. "You're making a big deal over nothing."

"Yeah?" Jake said. "Look closer."

He didn't wait for Arden to do as he said. Jake actually turned Rob's head for him, pointing it straight at the bones.

"That's not a beaver or a dog. It's not some two-hundred-year-old Native American grave. That's a gold crown. That means there's a good chance you're now standing in a crime scene."

THREE

"It's nothing but a deer head, folks. Nothing to worry about!"

By the next morning, the clip of Commissioner Rob Arden digging up a human skull had gone viral. Someone in the front row had captured the moment by zooming in on the skull, then panning out as Arden uttered his now famous words.

"It's nothing but a deer head, folks ..."

"It's had over two million views in eighteen hours," Landry said. Jake stood behind her as she played the clip on her laptop computer.

"That's not even the funniest part," Erica Wayne said. The newest deputy of Worthington County Sheriff's Department stood on Landry's other side holding her cell phone.

A former army M.P., she had come to the department already seasoned far more than most. In just five months, she'd proven more than capable, assisting the property crimes detective on scenes, helping him clear more cases than he had in the previous two years.

For Jake, however, Erica would always be Birdie Wayne, the knock-kneed kid sister of his late best friend, Ben.

"That sound has been downloaded hundreds of times and those videos are going viral too."

"Sounds?" Jake asked. "What do you mean?"

Birdie rolled her eyes. "You're practically a Luddite. Here."

Birdie pulled up a series of videos and tilted her phone so Jake and the sheriff could see. Commissioner Arden's soundbite had been used over clip after clip showing things like car crashes, train derailments, the explosion of the Hindenburg, and various other famous disasters.

"It's just a deer head, folks. Nothing to worry about."

"What are you going to do about it?"

The booming voice came from the hallway two seconds before Rob Arden himself barged into the sheriff's office.

At fifty-eight, Rob Arden had never been physically fit. But now, his reddened face and bulging eyes made him look like he was two seconds away from a stroke or a heart attack.

"It's everywhere," Arden said. "My inbox is flooded. I got a call from a reporter at one of the cable news networks."

"Mr. Arden," Landry started.

"No," Arden said. "I didn't come here to have smoke blown up my ass. I came here to find out what *you* are going to do about this."

"Nothing," Jake said.

"I want him out of here," Arden said.

"That's not your decision to make," Landry said. "I've got what appears to be human remains out there. My priority is ..."

"Your priority is whatever the county commissioners say it is. This is a debacle. And it's your responsibility to get control of it."

"Who are you talking to?" Jake said. "Me or her?"

Since he came into the room, Arden refused to look at Jake. Now, Jake gave him no choice. He moved around Landry's desk and stepped squarely into Rob Arden's personal space until the two men stood nose to nose.

Jake studied him, looking for something he knew wasn't there. The eyes maybe. Thick brows like his mother's. But Rob had old acne scars across his cheeks. Jake recalled his mother's skin had been flawless. Like porcelain. She had worn a big straw hat in the summertime. It had been wide enough to cast him partially in shadow as he knelt beside her, weeding her rose garden.

Sonya Arden's features had been soft. A wide smile. Full lips. A dimple in her left cheek. As her brother Rob glared at Jake, he smirked, showing a similar dimple, though on Rob's face, it almost seemed a perversion.

"I will not have your screw-up be the reason that development gets delayed."

"My screw-up? You want to explain how you did that math?"

"You should have controlled that crowd. There were too many people out there with cell phones. You let them all record everything. Those phones should have immediately been confiscated or not let onto the site at all."

Jake shook his head. "It wasn't exactly an issue of national security. You're responsible for your own actions, Uncle Rob." Jake emphasized the word Uncle, knowing how much Rob Arden hated it.

"Enough," Landry said. "Arden, we've got enough on our plates right now. Jake will make sure ..."

"I don't want him having anything to do with this," Arden snapped.

"That's not your call." Landry rose. "And this? You storming into my office unannounced? That's not helping. When we know more about what we've got out there, I'll let you know. There will be a press conference once we have a clearer idea of what we're dealing with. Until then, what Jake says goes."

"We have a deadline," Rob said. "The general contractor has benchmarks he's got to meet in order to turn the keys over to the first group of homeowners by the end of the summer. He's already breathing down my neck asking for timelines."

"The timeline is when I say it is," Jake said. "At the moment, I've got a potential crime scene out there. Your precious subdivision is not my problem."

Arden sputtered. His face turned purple again. His cell phone started to ring. He put up a finger as if to silence Jake. Then he answered the call.

"Arden here. Of course. Of course. I'm on my way."

Arden pulled the phone away from his ear. "We're not done here," he whispered, directing his ire toward Landry again. Then he stormed out of the room and slammed the door behind him.

"He's his own worst enemy," Birdie said.

"Rumor is he's planning a run for the state house next year," Landry said.

"Oh boy," Birdie said. "I can see the attack ads already. They're gonna use that sound bite and these viral videos to make him look clueless about what's right in front of him. At best. At worst, they're gonna say he's advocating a cover-up."

"I don't care," Jake said. "I can't have him interfering with this investigation."

"He won't," Landry said. "I'll see to it. You let me worry about Rob Arden. But he's not the only one with people breathing down his neck. What do we know, Jake?"

"Not much. Mark Ramirez from the Ohio Bureau of Criminal Investigations is down at the scene. We've got everything blocked off. Nobody in or out. It's the work stoppage out there that's got Arden so cheesed off."

"That development was a campaign promise he made," Landry said. "Multi-millions in investment and the job creation he touted out at the site."

"Even when this is resolved," Birdie said. "Who's gonna want to live on the lot where a human skeleton was found? They're gonna say the place is cursed."

"I think they'll get over it when they see their two hundred feet of sandy bottom lake frontage through their floor-to-ceiling windows. Either way, I don't give a damn about any of that," Jake said.

"How do you even know how long those bones have been out there?" Birdie asked.

"I've got a forensic anthropologist on his way down from Ohio State. They're going to have to excavate the whole site and remove the bones to a lab in Columbus. It could take weeks before we know anything concrete."

"Terrific," Landry said. She sat down hard on her desk chair.

"Sorry, boss," Jake said. "There's no way to put a rush on this. I can't even say for sure yet that there's only one set of remains out there."

Landry put her head in her hands. "Don't say it. Lord. Don't even think it."

"You think there could be a mass grave out at Echo Lake?" Birdie said.

"I mean, it's not a bad place to get rid of a body, if you think about it," Jake said. "The south eastern shore has never been developed before. There's a marshy area. No houses around. Those that own land on the other side of the lake have been looking at nothing but trees and weeds for almost a hundred years. I mean ... other than the gorges at Blackhand Hills, that'd be where I'd hide a body if I was in a pinch."

Landry looked up. Birdie stood near the doorway, a grin spreading across her face.

"Has he always been this intense?" Landry asked Birdie.

"Yes," she answered. "My brother used to say if he hadn't become a cop, Jake would have made a great serial killer."

It was a joke. Jake had heard Ben Wayne say it at least a dozen times. But Birdie's face fell almost instantly.

"Jake, I'm sorry," she said. "I didn't mean ..."

He smiled. "It's okay."

It was. And then it wasn't. It had been nearly six months since Ben Wayne's murder. Birdie had uprooted her entire life, leaving the service so she could start over in Stanley and look after Ben's teenage son, Travis.

"Well," Landry said. "I'll let you get back to it. Like I said yesterday. Whatever you need, Jake. Arden's right about one part of this. Those bones are my top priority right now."

"Sheriff?" Birdie said. "The reason I came down. I'm sorry ... Jake, I don't want to step on anyone's toes. But ... I'd like to help. With canvassing. With anything you need."

"That's Jake's call," Landry said. "I'll let you two work it out amongst yourselves. Just get a hold of me the second you know anything from BCI or your forensic anthropologist. I need to schedule a press conference as soon as we can."

"You'll know when I know," Jake said. Landry already had her face buried in the paperwork on her desk. He held the door open for Birdie and let her walk out ahead of him.

"Sorry," she said. "I was going to talk to you first ..."

"It's okay," Jake said. Though he wasn't sure it was. He'd have preferred Birdie stay tucked away in the property room or working desk duty so he didn't have to worry about her. With Ben gone, he couldn't shake the feeling she was his responsibility now. He had to look out for her since his best friend couldn't.

"I've made a file with all the links of every video anyone's posted from the ceremony yesterday," she said. "People took shots from every angle. I know it might not be that useful. You've got bones you don't know how long have been out there. It's not exactly a pristine crime scene if it was even a crime at all."

"No," he said. "That's good. You never know where a lead might come from. That was good thinking."

"I recognized the two kids who were out there protesting. I mean, it occurred to me if you wanted to put a stop to a development like that, planting human remains out there would be a pretty ingenious way."

"Those were just high school kids," Jake said.

"Chloe Weingard and Kayla Foley. They both go to Stanley High. My nephew Travis said Chloe's actually friends with Ryan ... um ... your nephew."

Birdie showed Jake her phone again. She had a picture blown up of the two girls' faces. The girl on the left, he'd thought she looked familiar yesterday. Birdie had it right. Jake had seen her hanging around Ryan after wrestling practice last season.

"Thanks," Jake said. "That could be helpful. Don't know how yet, but ..."

"Do you want me to keep going with this?" she asked. "I can go talk to her. She might be more responsive to a female cop than the male detective who got in her face."

"She was about to trample through a potential crime scene," Jake muttered.

"No. I know. It's just ..."

Jake's phone buzzed before she could finish. The caller ID read Mark Ramirez, the BCI agent Jake had out at the lake shore.

"What do you have, Ramirez?"

"Nothing much yet on my end," Ramirez answered. "But Dr. Andre Coleman, the bones guy. He's got some preliminary findings you're gonna wanna hear. How soon can you get out here?"

"Be there in fifteen," Jake said, clicking off. Birdie stood there, grinning. He let out a grumble as he slid his phone back in his pocket.

"Fine," he said. "You can come along if you can stay out of the way."

Birdie's smile widened. She gave Jake a crisp salute then pulled out her keys. "Come on," she said. "My patrol car's closer. I'll drive."

Four

"Just about everything interesting is underground here," Agent Mark Ramirez said, leaning into Jake's open car window. "I suppose that's the good news as far as my office is concerned." As special agent for the Richmond, Ohio office of the Bureau of Criminal Investigations, Jake had relied on Ramirez's scientific expertise on several other murder scenes. Today's was shaping up to be something neither of them had ever seen before.

Jake turned off the ignition and stepped out of the vehicle. Birdie came around the other side and joined him.

"Hello," Ramirez said, extending a hand to shake hers.

"Oh," Jake said. "Mark, this is Bird ... um ... Deputy Wayne. This is Mark Ramirez, BCI."

"I got that much," Birdie said, returning Mark's firm handshake.

"Deputy Wayne," Mark said, pausing on the last name. He shot a quick look at Jake. Jake answered with a slight nod. Yes. She was that Wayne. Last year, Ramirez had the gruesome job of processing Ben Wayne's crime scene as well.

"Call me Erica," Birdie said. "It looks pretty impressive over there."

Jake tracked her gaze. In the last year, the southeast shoreline of Echo Lake had transformed from its idyllic, wild state, to a construction site, to … this. A large blue tent covered the spot where Commissioner Arden had struck his shovel. Crime scene tape blocked off a large area all the way back to the edge of the woods. Yellow numbered flags marked various spots in the sand. Four people in white jumpsuits knelt there, brushing something away on the ground.

"Come on," Ramirez said. "Dr. Coleman's been asking for you. Have you ever worked with him before?"

Jake shook his head.

"He's a bit eccentric, but he's definitely the one you want out here for this stuff. I'll introduce you."

Mark led Jake to the edge of the site. A short African-American man with glasses perched on his forehead stepped out from under the tent, his nose in a computer tablet.

"Doc?" Mark said. "Detective Cashen's here."

Dr. Andre Coleman didn't look up from his tablet. He squinted at his screen as he walked toward Jake, making Jake wonder if the man didn't realize he wasn't wearing his readers. No sooner had he thought it before Coleman took out a second pair of glasses and slid them on, leaving the original specs right where they were, defying gravity on his forehead.

"Dr. Coleman?" Jake said, extending his hand.

"Sorry," Coleman said. "I don't do that. You shouldn't either."

Jake stood there, his hand in the air. Birdie cleared her throat beside him.

"Thanks for getting out here so quickly," Jake said.

Dr. Andre Coleman was the preeminent forensic anthropologist in the Midwest. His biggest claim to fame was excavating fourteen skeletons buried under the basement slab of a house in a quiet Dayton neighborhood. His findings led to the arrest of the so-called Trash Can Butcher in the early nineties. Now, Dr. Coleman ran the forensic anthropology department at Ohio State University.

"It's a good case," Coleman said. "Light, quick strokes, Ms. Manfield!" He turned back to Jake. "Those are my doctoral students. Invaluable assets for this part of the job. My knees aren't what they used to be."

"Of course," Jake said.

"We've been lucky," Coleman said. "They're calling for rain for the next two days. That will make our job a little more complicated. I'm having lights sent in. We'll work through the night and have your skeleton out of the ground in the next twenty-four hours."

Jake walked closer to the dig site. Dr. Coleman and his students had uncovered much more of the remains than Rob Arden had. The skeleton grinned up at him, the front incisor cracked. Jake could see the entire torso, pelvis, and both arms. One of the students had nearly uncovered the skeleton's left foot.

"It's remarkable," Dr. Coleman said. "We may have a completely intact skeleton here. You got lucky. The wet sand and gravel soil helped preserved the remains. You don't usually see that."

"You're sure you can safely transport it without damaging anything important?" Birdie asked.

Coleman lifted his chin, peering up at her. Birdie wasn't particularly tall. Jake guessed five foot four or five at most. She had a good three inches on Dr. Coleman.

"It's what I do, Deputy. So yes. We'll get her out and back to my lab. It's lucky we're heading into the summer semester. Things are much less hectic for me. I should have some definitive findings for you in a week or two, Detective."

"Her?" Jake and Birdie said it together.

"I can tell a lot just on visual inspection of the bones, Detective. Enough to get you started, anyway. You'll have to wait a little longer for things like the cause of death."

"You can tell?" Birdie said, peering over the pit.

"Very often, yes," the doctor said.

"What can you tell me today?" Jake asked.

"By the shape of the pelvis, she's female. Certain features of her facial bones tell me she's likely Caucasian. Young. She could be anywhere between fourteen and twenty-five years old but if I had to guess, I'd put her at no more than eighteen or nineteen."

"You're sure?" Jake asked.

Coleman had a penlight. He shined it on the skeleton's jaw.

"She's got all four of her wisdom teeth. The upper right is partially erupted. It might have even started to cause this young lady some problems."

"You'll be able to compare dental records then," Birdie said.

"I need more to go on than just an age range," Jake said. "Do you have any estimation on how long she's been out here?"

"I have a rough guess," Coleman said. One of his students, Ms. Manfield, stood up, grinning.

"He's always right," she said, stepping away from the pit. "He's just being modest."

"Guesses don't help you out at trial though, do they, Detective?"

"Educated ones do. But we're a long way off from that."

"Exactly," Coleman said. "But I can tell you where to start. I'll have a more precise window of time after I get her back to my lab and do what we do. For now, I'd say by the condition of the bones, the surrounding topography and vegetation growth, you're looking at a burial period between fifteen and thirty years."

Jake filed it away in his brain. Caucasian female. Teenager to early twenties. Went missing sometime in the last two decades. He'd end up with plenty of hits, probably.

Dr. Andre Coleman must have read something in his face. "I said I'll have a more precise window after I get her back to the lab. Patience. She's been down here this long. Somebody may still be out there looking for her, but a few more days is nothing."

"Her dental work," Jake said.

"She's got good teeth," Coleman said. "No cavities except for one gold crown in her upper second molar. It still looks fairly smooth. Like perhaps she'd had it recently done before she died. That crack in her front incisor was probably made postmortem. Degradation from being buried in the ground for so long. But I'll have a more concrete answer for you on that in a few days."

"Thanks," Jake said. "That's really helpful. I can work with that."

"I've got more good news for you," Coleman said. He moved to the other end of the tent where he had a flimsy table set up with some equipment including a laptop computer. Coleman put his tablet down and typed on the laptop keyboard.

Jake went to join him. Birdie hung back, talking to the grad students. They were pointing out features of the skeleton to her.

"You said you had good news?" Jake said.

"We've just finished up with our ground penetrating radar. Your good news is that I don't think we're looking at a mass grave situation. No ancient Native-American burial ground that your developers would have to deal with."

Jake thought of Uncle Rob. "Well, I suppose the idea that someone's backyard was used to bury a possible murder victim is bad enough."

Coleman straightened. He raised a finger as if he were going to make another point. Then he plunged it downward and made a single keystroke. Ramirez had been spot on. Eccentric was one word to describe Coleman.

"There's nobody else down there but her," he said. "I've run scans up and down the shoreline. We went a few yards out into the water. There's nothing else in this area except some animal bones. Deer. Possum. A few feral cats. She's alone out here."

A wave of relief washed over Jake. He couldn't care one lick about the luxury homes going in. One lonely, shallow grave was bad enough. But it felt like a manageable investigation so far.

"You actually think you'll be able to determine the cause of death?"

"If it was a traumatic injury like a gunshot, strangulation, even a stabbing, there can be signs, even when we're just left with bones. If it was natural causes, that will be harder. Or a poisoning. I have no soft tissue to examine."

"But it's not … natural," Jake said, looking back at the site.

"Somebody buried that girl out here, Detective," Coleman said. "That I can tell you for sure. So no. She didn't just die peacefully in her sleep. Someone brought her out here and tried to make sure she'd never be found."

A chill went through Jake. Almost as if he could sense this girl's ghost, calling to him.

Someone dumped her out here. Alone. Hoping Echo Lake would hide that secret forever. He watched as Coleman's students continued their painstaking work, uncovering this girl bone by bone.

He hadn't made a conscious decision to walk back to the edge of the pit. But he found himself there, staring down at the vacant sockets where this girl's eyes had once been. Her jaw hung slightly open, as if she had died that way. Frozen. Screaming. But now forever silenced.

Jake knew it would be up to him to give her back her voice and bring her home to whoever was left to miss her.

FIVE

Eight girls. Jake stared at his computer screen. Eight. He'd taken the parameters Dr. Coleman had given him. Missing girls and women aged fourteen through twenty-five. Caucasian. To start, all vanished in a fifteen-year period from the early nineties to the late 2000s.

Of the eight, four were from Worthington County alone. Jake decided to start there. Ramirez from BCI was working on getting files for him on girls outside the county. Jake asked Deputy Reilly down in records to send up the cold case files from Worthington County.

But eight girls. They would be daughters, sisters, mothers, girlfriends. Children. All of them, just starting out in life. He knew their stories had broken the people who loved them. There would be runaways, of course. And maybe that's all this girl was. Jake pulled up a photo Coleman had sent him, showing a closeup of the skull at Echo Lake. He hit print.

Jake walked over to the laser printer against the wall and waited for the image to spit out. When it did, he took it to the freshly cleaned whiteboard he set up in the corner of the office. Using a magnet, he stuck the image at the very top of the board. Soon enough, he would replace it with a photograph. He would know her face. If the dental records proved a dead end, Coleman's people were working on facial reconstruction. He promised Jake a digital image by the end of the week.

"Knock knock!"

His sister's voice pulled him out of his head. Jake stepped away from the board. Gemma stood in the doorway holding something behind her back.

She didn't do this often, showing up at his office. Jake braced himself. Odds were, there was some kind of family crisis.

"Grandpa okay?" Jake said, running through which of the various simmering family crises might come to a boil the fastest. Their grandfather, Max Cashen, had lately made a menace of himself around town. Usually, innocent waitresses and cashiers drew his ire when he forgot how to use his debit card or, God forbid, picked up something off a clearance rack that didn't ring up on sale.

"Pacified for the moment," Gemma said. She didn't come fully into the room. Instead, she leaned against the door frame, hiding whatever she held behind her back. "He figured out the battery cable on his truck was loose. He's puttering with it at the moment. Trying to use it as a teachable moment for Ryan."

"Better him than me." Jake laughed. He grimaced, recalling all the times Grandpa Max had tried to teach Jake about how to fix engines. It usually ended with him swearing up a blue streak and lamenting Jake's slovenly generation. He didn't expect his seventeen-year-old nephew would fare any better.

"How long do you think it's gonna take before he figures out you're the one who loosened that cable?" Gemma asked. "Then what?"

"I'll deny it," Jake answered. The loose battery terminal cable was a temporary measure. A way to kick the can down the road before Jake and Gemma would need to have a serious talk about the old man on whether he should be driving in the first place. Jake was constantly getting calls from deputies who witnessed Gramps blowing through the stop sign at County 11 and Bent Creek Road. It had gotten so bad that all the locals knew to treat it as a four-way stop on the chance that Max Cashen was out driving.

"Is that what you came here to bug me about?" Jake asked.

"Actually, no. I came here to bug you about something else. Arch Hill Estates. That skeleton ..."

"Gemma," Jake said. "You know I can't talk to you about a case I'm working on."

"I'm not asking for insider information. Just ... give me an estimate. How long do you think there'll be a work stoppage out there?"

So there it was. Jake could add Gemma to the list of people with a financial stake in the development. For the last few years, she'd made her living as a real estate agent. Before that, she'd been a nail technician, before that, she worked at home transcribing medical data, before that, a bartender out at Winky's Bar and Grille on Route 33. He could list at least a half dozen other professions and get-rich-quick schemes she'd tried before all of that. But this ... selling houses ... she'd stuck with the longest.

"I can't tell you that," Jake said. "And you know better than to ask."

"Jake," she said. "At the lowest tier ... and I mean ... the bare bones ... those homes are going to sell for at least a half a million dollars. On the high end, five times that. I'm a buyer's agent for two clients. We just signed last week. Do you realize what the commission is on two and a half million? Jake ... in a year, Ryan will be heading off to college ..."

"Gemma, I don't have a good answer for you. Frankly, I'm getting tired of people asking about it. Our favorite uncle is raising hell for the same reason."

"He can't know I've got potential buyers," Gemma said, her face going white. He understood her fear. If there was any way Rob Arden could screw over a Cashen, he wouldn't miss the opportunity.

"He won't hear it from me," Jake said.

"Please? Are we talking weeks? Months? Or is this thing so awful it's going to kill the whole project?"

Jake sighed. "Gemma. Honest to God, I don't know."

"We talking mass grave? Native-American burial ground bad?"

She had real fear in her eyes. Jake went to her.

"No. Not that bad. But bad enough. Listen, this isn't something you can repeat. I wouldn't even say anything at all. Only ... Landry's gonna give a press conference in the next twenty-four hours anyway. I don't have all the science back. But ... yeah. It's most likely a homicide. That dead body didn't get there by accident or by itself."

Gemma's face fell. She let her shoulders drop and handed him what she'd been hiding behind her back.

"Here," she said. "Though you don't even deserve it with news like that."

The smell wafted up to him. Gemma had brought him takeout from Papa's Diner. He looked in the bag. It was Spiros Papatonis's famous gyro and his wife Tessa's cabbage soup.

"That's my girl." Jake smiled.

Gemma grumbled. "This is going to sink the whole project."

"Gemma," he said. "That's somebody's loved one out there. Someone's sister, daughter, or mom."

She nodded. "I know. I'm sorry. It's just ... am I ever gonna get a break?"

"Excuse me."

Behind Gemma, Birdie stepped into view. She was carrying a banker's box filled to the brim with files.

"Sorry," Birdie said. "Hey, Gemma!"

Gemma stepped further into the office, giving Birdie room to get beside her. Before Jake could even offer to help her with the box, Birdie walked it right over to the table in front of the whiteboard and set it on top.

"I was in the basement. Reilly was just getting your files together so I thought I'd save a step and get them up here to you."

Jake smirked. "You just happened to be down there?"

He caught Gemma's eye. She'd been studying Birdie then threw a glance to Jake. He knew that look by heart. It was her way of saying "Be nice."

"Thanks, Gemma," Jake said. "I need to get back to work. I'll deal with the old man when I get home. Ryan will be fine with him. He might learn something."

"Oh, I'm not worried about Ryan. It's about time he had his time in the barrel with Gramps."

Birdie laughed. "I got a text from Travis about an hour ago. Ryan conned Travis into heading over there too. Max has got them both out there splitting and stacking wood. In May, for Pete's sake. It's seventy-eight degrees today. Travis said Max told him splitting wood would get them *country-strong*."

Jake laughed. "That's one of the old man's favorite lines. I've heard that a million times."

"Perfect," Gemma said. "All right. My work is done here. Home in time for dinner? Gramps wants potato soup. I promised him I'd make it tonight."

"I'll try," Jake said, looking back at the files. It was already one o'clock and that would be several hours of work he didn't want to put off until tomorrow. He felt the empty eyes of that girl's skull staring at him. Waiting for the justice that had eluded her for maybe thirty years.

Gemma gave Birdie a wave then disappeared down the hall.

"Thanks for these," Jake said. He walked over to the table. Birdie had already pulled one file out.

"Evelyn Bennett. My mom was friends with her. Do you remember?"

She opened the file. The Bennetts lived in Navan Township. Lloyd Bennett had owned a tree service for fifty years.

"A real tragedy, that one," Birdie said. "Evelyn was in a car accident when she was sixteen. The day after she got her driver's license. Closed head injury that turned her into a toddler again. They had trouble managing her. She wandered off. Gosh. I was little. In kindergarten, maybe."

Jake vaguely remembered the story of the Bennetts' oldest daughter. Birdie held a picture of her. Dark-haired. Plain. But she had a warm smile.

Birdie closed the file and slipped it back into the box.

"I can help you with these if you want," she said. "With Zender on vacation, I know you'll have your hands full."

Ed Zender was technically the other detective working crimes against persons for the county. In the last year, he'd been gone more days than he'd been here. First, medical leave. Now, he was using up his six weeks of vacation. He was expected back later in the month.

"Thanks," Jake said. "I might ..."

Before he could finish, Birdie's shoulder radio squawked.

"Unit 110. We've got a property damage accident with possible injuries involved, fire is en route out on County Road Seven and Bentley Road respond Code Three."

Birdie pressed the side button on her mic. "Unit 110, copy. Responding from the sheriff's office."

Jake froze. He knew what Gemma had said. Grandpa was at home with the boys. His car wasn't running as Jake had intended. He never drove out near Bentley Road anyway. Still, in those few seconds, Jake imagined the worst.

"Darcy," Birdie spoke into her radio again. She locked eyes with Jake as if she could read his mind. "I'm here with Jake. Um ... do we have an ID on any of the drivers involved?"

Darcy the dispatcher answered back. "Hey, Jake. No worries, okay. This isn't Max. You know I'd have come to find you "

Jake exhaled. He winked at Birdie.

"Copy that," she said to Darcy. "I'm on my way."

Birdie put a hand on Jake's arm. Then she headed out of his office leaving him with the box of files.

All the missing girls from Worthington County going back fifty years. A wider net than he needed, but Jake couldn't stand just sitting around waiting to hear from BCI.

Evelyn Bennett, of course. He pulled out more of the files. Two sisters had disappeared while walking home from a dance recital in the late seventies. Grace and Joanie Hobbs. Jake knew their brother. They were young though. Grace had been ten, according to the file. Joanie, fifteen. He set Joanie's file aside. His gut told him the bones at Echo Lake weren't hers. They might have been found together.

From 1981, a young woman. Penny Garrity. There were at least a dozen reports of domestic violence by her husband. Then Penny went missing. The husband was cleared but then two years later, his second wife turned up dead.

So much violence. So much heartbreak.

Jake pulled one more file. His heart flipped as he saw the name on one.

She'd been a few years older than him. Gemma's grade, though they hadn't been friends. He opened the file. A familiar face stared back at him. It was uncanny really. In all the years he'd known this girl's sister, he hadn't appreciated how much they looked alike. How could he? This girl had been gone long before. Eons for a teenage boy like Jake was at the time.

He turned the page. Her parents had submitted her dental records when she disappeared. No cavities. Just one gold crown on the upper second molar. Jake closed his eyes. The image of the skull stuck to the whiteboard disappeared in his mind. In its place, a new face emerged. He pulled it out of the file. There would be more he'd need to do for a definitive identification. But ... deep in Jake's gut ... he knew her name.

"Nicole," he whispered. Putting his face in his hands, he dropped the file.

Six

He made it two steps out of his office door before Sheriff Landry caught him. She was TV-ready with her hair styled and heavier make-up than she usually wore. And she had on what her media liaison called her ball-buster suit. Jet-black, tailored. With it, she wore three-inch heels Jake knew she hated.

"Come on," she said. "I was hoping I'd find you down here. You might as well stand next to me during this press conference."

Jake held a file to his chest. Since he'd emailed a digital copy to Dr. Andre Coleman, he hadn't been able to put the thing down. It took him an hour to stand up from his desk and draw the strength to head up to Meg's office. He knew the moment he did, this thing would take on a life of its own. There would be a protocol set in motion. At each step, it would bring pain to people he cared about.

"What time did you tell them you were going live?" Jake asked.

Landry looked at her smart watch. "Forty-five minutes. I was hoping you'd have something to tell me."

A few deputies passed Landry in the hall. Jake waited, then motioned for Landry to join him back inside. She scowled, reading something in his own face. It was then she noticed the file he'd been clutching.

"Jake?"

He shut the door behind her and locked it. Jake didn't want to risk the thin walls or random passersby overhearing what he was about to tell her.

Landry made her way over to the table and stood in front of the whiteboard. She reached out and traced a line around the image of the skeleton at Echo Lake.

"I'm waiting for confirmation on a few things with Dr. Coleman," Jake started. "Dental records. Height. Any other identifiers they put in the file when she went missing. But ..."

"Jake," Landry said. "Are you okay? You're white as a sheet."

Jake stood at the end of the table and put the file down. He opened it and slid out a photograph. Mercifully, Nicole had just gotten her senior pictures taken. Her family had been able to provide a beautiful photograph of her standing in front of a sunflower field, the setting sun making her skin glow. Her blonde hair shimmered as it fell over her right shoulder.

"Nicole Strong," Jake said as Landry picked up the photo.

"You're sure?"

"Coleman says he's going to call me back within the hour. Her dental work was minimal. But Nicole broke her leg when she was eight years old. She fell off a jungle gym during recess. It was a compound fracture and they had to put pins in. Between that and the dental records, there won't be any doubt. It's her."

Landry finally took a seat. She covered her hand over her mouth, sensing the gravity of the revelation for Jake.

"She was Anya's older sister," Jake said. "We were twelve years old when Nicole just vanished. There was a big search. They put posters up all over the state."

"Anya," Landry said. "Anya Brouchard? As in the wife of Tim Brouchard? Our county prosecutor?"

"Yes."

"My God."

"She was seventeen," Jake said. "I didn't know Anya very well then. We got close later, when we both started high school."

Her sister's disappearance had stuck to her. The tragedy everyone whispered about behind her back when they first met her.

"Is that the girl whose sister disappeared? I heard her mom cracked up over it ..."

They said worse things than that, of course. And it had been the thing that drew him to her. Jake knew what it was like to be whispered about. To carry the mantle of family violence. His own parents had died when he was seven years old. His father had shot his mother then himself when the demons in his head took hold.

"What happened?" Landry asked.

Jake pulled out the investigative notes in the file.

"She was last seen at a class party at Blackhand Lanes. The bowling alley isn't even there anymore. Her friends said she left in her own car. It was found parked in the driveway of her parents' house."

Jake's words came from the facts he'd read in the report, but mixed with his recollections from Anya on the rare occasions when either of them talked about their family tragedies.

"She just ... disappeared," Jake said. He could hear Anya's voice in his head. He repeated her whispered words.

"It was a Friday night. She was taking the SAT in the morning over at the high school gym. Nobody knew she hadn't come home. Her car was parked in the driveway. Her mother woke up late. After nine. She made breakfast. Did some housework. She was vacuuming upstairs. When she got to the front hallway, she noticed Nicole's car in the driveway. She was supposed to be gone. Vivian ... Mrs. Strong. She went to look for Nicole in her room, thinking she'd overslept and missed her test. She wasn't there. Her bed was still made from the day before. She started yelling. Woke Anya up. It was Anya who noticed that her sister's purse was still in the front seat of her car."

"Were there ever any leads? Who was the detective assigned?"

"Adamski," Jake answered. "It was Virgil's case. They interviewed the parents. Anya's dad was a drinker back then. It got worse. Way worse in the years following all this. But there was nothing. That's what Anya always said. It was as if Nicole just vanished off the face of the earth."

"How awful," Landry said. "I guess maybe I'd heard something in passing that Brouchard's sister-in-law was dead or something. I had no idea it was something like this."

"For a while, Viv Strong walked around telling everyone Nicole was just off trying to have new adventures. She was in denial for months. It was hard on Anya."

"It had to have been hideous. Her mother was delusional, her father was drinking. Her sister was ... missing. You said she was twelve? My God. That poor kid."

"For the longest time, Anya wasn't even allowed to talk about Nicole in the past tense. It was years later when Anya and I started dating. She didn't like me coming over to her house very often. Her mother would talk about Nicole as if she were just out shopping or running late for dinner. Always in the present tense. Anya just ... bore it."

"I can't even imagine. And all this time, she was out at the lake."

"It took years," Jake said. "Her father finally started getting his act together. Went into rehab. Started following the steps. They waited years before having Nicole declared legally dead. And her dad only did that so he could finally collect on a small life insurance policy they kept on both girls. He used the proceeds to pay for Anya to go to community college."

"Dr. Coleman thinks he's going to be able to determine the cause of death?"

"He's hopeful," Jake said. "In the meantime, you've got to call off that press conference. Let me have Coleman confirm all of this."

Landry leafed through the file. Jake had added Coleman's preliminary report with the dental work visible on the remains.

"One gold crown," Landry said. "Same as Nicole Strong had. It can't be a coincidence. Damn. I suppose this will give the family closure after all this time. What kind of state is the mother in these days? Have you kept in touch?"

Jake shook his head. "I haven't seen Vivian Strong in probably eighteen years. She's kind of a recluse now. Agoraphobic maybe. Marty Strong's around some. As far as I know he's still sober."

"Were there any suspects back in the day?" Landry asked, scanning the file.

"Nothing that panned out. I've never talked to Virgil about this one."

Landry closed the file. She had a worried look on her face.

"Jake," she said. "I know Virgil Adamski had his own demons back in the day. He was also a drinker. Do you think ..."

"No," Jake said, his tone sharp. "Don't even go down that path, Meg. Virgil was a good detective. Nicole Strong was just a kid. I told you, I haven't talked to him about this case, but I know Virgil well enough. I have no doubt this is one of the ones that would have haunted him. He had his faults. But I've never heard anyone say Virgil Adamski let his drinking interfere with his job."

"That may be true," she said. "I'm not from here. I don't know the county lore the way you do. But you can be sure that somebody's going to bring Virgil's past up when this comes out. I'm not saying there's truth to it. I'm saying it's something we both have to be prepared for. And Virgil has to be prepared. Ugh. This is going to be a mess."

She took out her cell phone and called Neil Keiser, her media liaison.

"Neil? It's Meg. I need to push the presser back until this evening. Just let everyone know I'll be out there at six p.m."

There was a pause. Meg's scowl deepened as Neil apparently tried to convince her not to kill the noon press conference.

"This is what's happening," Meg said, irritated. "I know you'll get questions about whether there's a break in the case. Just tell them we're pushing things back six hours so we can share the most up-to-date information we have. Thanks."

Meg clicked off.

"Thanks," Jake said.

"Call Dr. Coleman," she said. "Get confirmation."

Jake took out his phone. It was as if Andre Coleman's ears were burning. Before Jake could punch in his number, his caller ID lit up with Coleman's face.

"Hey, Doc," Jake said, answering.

"You've got a match, Detective," Coleman said. "Dental records are exact. The fracture to the left tibia bone is evident on examination. Height matches. There are a couple other markers I'd like to compare. And I'm waiting on some more imaging ..."

"Doc," Jake interrupted him. "Are you sure enough so that I can inform this girl's next of kin?"

Coleman paused. He let out a hard breath. "Tell them," he said.

Jake squeezed his eyes shut. He knew. Of course he knew. And yet, like Nicole Strong's mother all those years ago, there was a small part of him that wanted to deny it. He knew what this could do to Anya's world again.

"You catch all that?" Jake said to Landry as he set his phone down.

Just then, Birdie walked into Jake's office. She read the seriousness on both Jake and Landry's faces. As she approached the table, she caught a glimpse of Nicole Strong's file and her picture laying in front of the sheriff.

"Is it Nicole Strong?" Birdie asked. Of course she'd read the names on all the files she brought up from records.

"Looks that way," Meg answered. "You knew her too?"

Birdie shook her head "She would have been ten years older than me, I think. But ... Anya. She's been great since my brother died. I owe her a lot. Does she know?"

"No," Jake whispered. He rose, then went to his desk and grabbed his keys. "She'll be at the Vedge Wedge now. I'd like to wait twenty minutes or so until the lunch rush clears. But I need to be the one to tell her."

"Of course," Landry said. "But Jake ... Tim Brouchard is sitting in his office across the street. He's waiting for a phone call from me too. I swore we'd tell him what we had before I gave it to the press. He should be here. We should let him know and then the two of you can go over to tell Anya."

Jake bristled. He felt his fists clench unbidden.

"Meg, I need to do this alone."

Meg came around her desk, moving closer to Jake. She peered up at him. "Jake, this is personal for you. That's going to come at me. I need your assurance that it won't be a problem."

"It's not a problem," he said. "But I need to be the one to tell Anya Strong that it's her sister out there."

"You mean Anya Brouchard," Meg said. "If you ..."

"Sheriff," Jake said. "I'm asking you for a favor on this one. Let me handle informing Anya."

Landry shot a look toward Birdie, as if the two women could share some telepathic message. "All right," Landry said. "Go see Anya. I'll handle talking to her husband."

"Thank you," Jake said.

"Jake," Birdie said. "Can I go with you? She's ... like I said. Anya's been so supportive since Ben died. If I could ..."

"I need to do this one on my own," Jake said. "But I'll tell her you'll call her in a couple of hours. I'm sure she'd appreciate hearing from you."

Birdie put a hand on Jake's arm. "I'm so sorry. I know you guys used to be close. Just ... tell her I'm ... I ... just ..."

Jake nodded. "I know. Birdie, I know."

Then he left Landry and Birdie and headed out to find Anya.

SEVEN

S he had the same blonde hair, the same wide-set eyes and easy smile as her long-dead sister. It had not brought comfort to her parents. Instead, Anya always said she could tell when they were looking at her, but seeing ... wishing for ... Nicole.

She'd tried her best all these years. She never got angry with them. Never rebelled. Was never moody or obstinate the way that teenage girls often are. From the time she was twelve, Anya Strong knew her job was to keep her parents from falling apart.

She did it by studying hard. Succeeding to the point she was class valedictorian. When her mother went to the darkest places, pulled under by a grief so strong she couldn't breathe, it had been Anya who had been her strength. Her jester. The light she could cling to when everything else went black. But most of all, Anya did the one thing her sister never could ... she stayed.

She stood behind the counter of the Vedge Wedge, Worthington County's one and only fully vegan cafe. Anya had worked here since high school. She ran it now.

Anya's haughty laugh cut through Jake as he stepped inside, trying to disappear in the corner. She seemed happy now. Content, even. This was Anya's joy. He'd always thought of her as some displaced flower-child, born in the wrong decade. She just wanted to make her small corner of the world a better place. And she did. Now … he would have to darken that corner and take her smile away.

"Jake!" Anya called out. He'd only managed to stay unnoticed for a few seconds. She raised a hand and waved it widely, making her silver bracelets jangle. Years ago, she wore them on her ankles and rarely wore shoes.

There were only three full tables at the Vedge Wedge at the height of lunch hour. He knew the place did mostly carry-out with regulars from the courthouse around the corner. Today though, there were just five patrons. Two at each of the booths along the wall. Another woman sat alone in a booth near the door. She smiled at Jake with a familiarity Jake couldn't place. He knew her from somewhere.

"Hey, Anya," Jake said.

"I knew I'd convert you," she said. "You want the taco salad, don't you?"

A few months ago, Jake had been roped into trying Anya's vegan taco salad. It had tasted far better than it had any right to. It didn't mean he was eager to try it again.

"I'm good," Jake said.

"I've got one remade," she said. "Take a seat. You didn't eat yet. I can tell."

"How can you tell?"

"I can always tell." She cleared off a space at the bar. There were no other customers sitting there. As far as Jake could tell, Anya was the only employee in the restaurant as well.

"Do you have a minute," he said. "I need to talk to you about something. We could ... can we go into the office?"

Anya put her towel on a hook behind the counter. She gave him a sideways glance, but didn't frown. Just curious, he thought. Because she trusted him.

"Shan?" she called out, directing her words to the woman in the booth. "Can you give a holler if anyone else comes in? Anybody need a refill? I'll be right back out."

"We're good, Anya," one of the women in a different booth answered. Anya untied her apron and put it on a second hook, right next to the towel. She smoothed her hair back, tightened her ponytail, and lifted the counter flap so Jake could walk through it and follow her to the tiny office right next to the walk-in cooler.

"What's up?" she said. Anya took a seat behind the cluttered desk. There was only one other folding chair in the room. She had it leaning against a metal shelf with paper products and napkin refills. Jake took the chair and stuck it in front of Anya's desk and sat in it.

"Anya," he started. "I wish there were some better way to do this. There's going to be a press conference at six. There are still a few things we have to tighten down, but I wanted you to hear everything from me."

She folded her hands. Anya took a deep breath, closing her eyes. When she opened them, Jake could already see her holding back tears.

"Echo Lake," he said. "How closely have you been following the news?"

"I've seen your uncle in a couple of viral videos. It's not good. He's a town joke. Let me guess, he's working on blaming you for that." Her voice was light. Her words came out too fast. She was stalling for time, he thought, not yet ready to hear what she had to know might be coming.

"I don't care about Rob Arden or what he may or may not try to do to me. It doesn't matter. But Anya, we found human remains out there by the lake shore. I called in a forensic anthropologist from O.S.U. He was able to match dental records and certain other features of the ... uh ... skeleton. Anya ... it's Nic."

She blinked wildly, absorbing his words. But she said nothing.

"We found her, Anya. It's her. It's Nicole."

"Features. You said features of the skeleton. What features, Jake?"

"She broke her leg. The ... um ... woman buried out the lake has the same fracture in the same place. And as I said, the dental records matched. Same height. Same ... age."

Anya pressed her hand to her forehead. She started to sweat. She was wearing a green cardigan sweater and started to pull at it. No, claw at it. Jake reacted. He went to her and helped her pull out one sleeve.

She grabbed him. Curling her fingers around the lapels of his jacket. Anya got to her feet. He put his hands under her elbows to keep her from falling down.

"She's gone. She's just ... always been gone."

"I know."

"How long? This whole time? Do you think ..."

"It looks that way," Jake said. "I don't have all the answers. I don't know what happened to her yet. But yes. I think she's been buried out at the lake this whole time."

Anya shook her head. "She took me out there. We had a little canoe. We had a picnic. I was seven or eight years old. Maybe she was thirteen. We lay out on these beach towels until some old guy chased us away. She had ... Jake ... she had her senior pictures taken out there."

He hadn't known that. He'd only seen the one with her standing against that field of sunflowers. It never occurred to him to wonder where that was. The detective in him filed that away. Those pictures were taken just a few weeks before Nicole went missing. He should talk to the photographer if he or she were still around ...

"I want to see her," Anya said.

"There isn't much to see. She's gone. It's just bones, Anya."

"I don't care. I want to see. Can you make sure I can?"

"We can talk about that later. For now, this is going to come out. By tomorrow morning, the media will have her name. Your parents ..."

Anya started to pace. "It'll kill them. I have to ... Oh Jake. I have to get to them. My mother won't believe it. You're sure? If it's just bones ..."

"I'm sure," he said. "Yes. There are still some tests that need to be run. But nothing that's going to change the outcome. We're hoping we'll be able to figure out her cause of death."

"I knew," Anya whispered. "I knew she didn't just run away. They made me say it. Over and over again, my mother made me agree with her that she was just gone. Just ... somewhere else. Of course I knew that wasn't it. She was dead. Nic would never have just left me, Jake. Not me. She was dead. She was always dead."

Then, her tears fully came. Anya let out a guttural cry that seared him. She flung herself against him. Jake wrapped his arms around her and kept her on her feet.

He let her sob. Jake knew it was the only time she would let herself give into this wave. The moment she walked out of this office, Anya would do what she'd always done. She would find a brave face. She would manage her parents' emotions. She would let them have their grief and sacrifice her own. It had only ever been Jake who saw her when she cried.

"Anya?" The woman who'd been sitting in the booth, the one Anya had called Shan, stood in the hallway. The office door hadn't completely shut. She'd heard Anya's cries. And just like that, Anya took in a great gulp of air and dried her tears. She turned and faced the woman, keeping one hand on Jake's arm.

"Jake?" she said. "This is Shannon. She was ..."

"Anya, what happened? Are you okay? Is it something at the house? Your mom's been sick. Can I take you there?"

Anya shook her head. "Jake. This is Shannon Weingard. Oh Shan. Thank God you're here!"

He let the name settle. Shannon. The bits and pieces from Nicole Strong's case file started to take shape in his mind. He hadn't yet had a chance to immerse himself in it. But there were witness statements. One name popped into his head. Her face had been familiar, and now he realized why. The Weingards. Eons ago, Anya had babysat for them.

"Shannon Murphy?" Jake asked. "You were her friend. You knew Nicole."

Shannon Murphy had been Nicole's best friend and one of the last people to see her at the Blackhand Bowling Alley. Shannon's face fell. She kept looking at Anya then back at Jake.

"What's going on?" she asked. "Anya? What's going on?"

"I have to tell her," Anya said to Jake. "I don't want her hearing it on the news either."

Shannon had already stepped into the room. She reached for Anya, pulling her from Jake's side. Shannon glared at Jake, knowing whatever had happened here, Jake had been the deliverer of news that had made Anya cry.

"Of course," Jake said. "I came to let Anya know. The remains we found at Echo Lake belong to Nicole Strong."

A tremor went through Shannon Murphy. She tightened her embrace around Anya.

"Nic," she whispered.

"Oh Shan," Anya said. "I'm just so glad you're here. Will you come with me? I've got to go home and tell my parents."

"Good," Jake said. "That's good. I don't like the idea of you being alone."

Silent tears fell down Shannon Murphy's face. "You're sure?" she asked Jake, just like Anya had.

"I'm sure," he answered just the same.

"What was she doing at the lake?" Shannon asked. "I don't understand."

"We don't know yet. We don't know anything beyond that it's her." For now, that's all Jake could let anyone know. Even those closest to Nicole.

Shannon nodded. Anya recovered enough and pulled away from her. Her tears were fully gone. Her back was straight. Anya had switched into caretaker mode. Jake knew that's all he'd likely see from now on. Not unless they were alone.

"I can go with you," he said. "To your parents' house, if you'd like."

"No." Anya sniffed. "My parents don't like cops. I'm sorry. It's still triggering for them. It's better if they hear all this from me. Shannon being there will help."

"Where's Tim?" Shannon asked. "Does he know?"

"He's probably in court. He said he was going to stop by for lunch," Anya said. "You told him too, right?"

Jake shook his head. "I wanted to tell you first. But yes. He'll be briefed before the press conference."

"I'll call him," Anya said. "My parents trust him. If some of this comes from him ... if he can answer some of these questions ..."

"Of course," Jake said. "I'll make sure Tim knows everything I do."

"You damn well better." Tim Brouchard's booming voice filled the hallway behind Shannon Murphy. As he stepped into view, he took one look at his wife and his color drained.

"Tim," Anya said, her voice steady, her eyes dry. "Jake found Nicole. She's the body they uncovered out at Echo Lake. So we know. We finally know. I want you and Shannon to come with me so I can tell my parents."

Anya went to him. Tim kept his eyes on Jake as he folded his wife into his arms. Of course he'd come straight here after Landry delivered the news.

"Thank you, Jake," Tim said as he guided his wife out of the office. "I'll take it from here."

Eight

Retired Detective Virgil Adamski lived in a manufactured home on the western shores of Echo Lake. He stood at the water's edge, sipping a cup of coffee from a chipped Ohio State Buckeyes mug as Jake pulled up. Jake hadn't called ahead, but Virgil was waiting for him.

It was pretty here. Secluded. Virgil had a prime lot that jutted out into the lake. A small peninsula with woods on either side, so he couldn't see his neighbors unless he wanted to. He'd held on to the place after two ex-wives who got tired of the hours Virgil worked, the unkept promises he made, and the solace he took from the bottom of a bottle until he put his last drink down twenty-six years ago.

Virgil didn't turn as Jake pulled up. He kept staring out at the water, sipping coffee from a chipped mug.

Jake met him where he stood. In the distance, a pair of swans paused, watching this newcomer on the shoreline next to Virgil. Between them, Jake counted five small cygnets. Four gray. One white.

"They lost one last week," Virgil finally said. "The other white one. I was hoping he'd make it. Thought the little guy was just big enough to make himself too much trouble for the snappers. Guess I was wrong."

The swans turned, swimming toward the sound of Virgil's voice. It was then Jake noticed a plastic bag on the green-and-white folding chair next to Virgil. Virgil reached in and pulled out a handful of what looked like dog food. He threw it toward the swans in a high arc.

"You want some coffee?" Virgil asked. "There's a fresh pot in the kitchen."

"No, thanks."

Virgil took another sip of his then tossed the contents in another arc, into the lake. He gripped his mug as he turned to face Jake.

"It's her, isn't it?" Virgil had bags under his eyes. His face was covered with three-day-old gray scruff. There was a second lawn chair propped against a tree. Jake grabbed it and set it next to the other one. He sat down and motioned for Virgil to do the same. He did.

"Yes," Jake said. "It's her. We've found Nicole Strong."

Virgil exhaled. He looked out at the water, squinting toward the eastern shore.

"I've owned this property for thirty-seven years, Jake. I put the double-wide up twenty years ago. It was a retirement present to myself. Promised my ex-wife I'd build her a proper house here. She didn't stick around long enough. Now, I'm kinda glad I didn't. It's what I got out of all of that. The divorce. I gave her the house on Wellman Road. She lived there mortgage-free for ten years and sold it for twice what I paid for it. But I always felt like I got the better deal with this place."

"It's a beautiful piece of land, Virg," Jake said. "You could still build a house here if you ever wanted to. If Arch Hill Estates ever does go in, your property values are gonna quadruple. You could sell it even. Move to Florida like you've been saying."

Virgil put his head down. Jake knew what he felt. He could read it in Virgil's curled posture. The shake of his shoulders. To Virgil, Nicole Strong had been the one. The case that never left him. That still haunted his nightmares.

"I've been staring at her," he said. "This whole time. She was right in front of me, just across the lake."

"Yeah," Jake said. There was no way to soften this blow. "There's going to be a press conference in about an hour. I wanted you to hear this from me."

"I do appreciate that, Jake. I truly do. But I knew. I just … knew. I've seen that awful video of your uncle maybe a hundred times. It hit me. Right here."

Virgil pressed a fist into his chest.

"I've just come from Anya's," Jake said. "She's going to take care of telling Viv and Marty."

Virgil nodded. "This thing turned them inside out. I promised them justice for her. Even then, Marty knew I shouldn't have. He told me that. You wanna know what? It made me suspect him. He seemed so calm about it all back then."

"He was far from it," Jake said. "At least not in the years I knew him."

"We looked out there," Virgil said. "I had cadaver dogs up and down that shoreline."

"It would have been hard for them to get a solid hit," Jake said. "There are all kinds of dead things out in those woods, Virgil. I've never been too impressed with their reliability except when it comes to dope. You can't beat yourself up over that."

The two men sat in silence for a moment. Virgil put his hands on his knees and sat straighter as if he were bracing himself for the next thing he had to say.

"Do you know what killed her?" he asked.

"Still waiting on a report from the forensic anthropologist. Not sure how much he'll be able to tell us."

Virgil nodded.

"It's been a long time," Jake continued. "But I need you, Virg. I want you to know, this is still your case too."

Virgil shook his head. "You don't have to do that. You don't have to worry about me."

"Well, just the same ... Did anything stick out for you? Did you have any real hunch about what might have happened to her back then?"

"I thought it was Marty for a while," Virgil said. "He had an alibi. He worked third shift at the clay mill back in those days. He was a drinker, you know that. I never had any proof that he laid hands on Nicole or her mother. But there was just something off about him. Then ... nothing. It went nowhere. He passed a poly."

Jake knew Marty Strong always harbored a grudge about that, having to take a lie detector test. In the years that followed, he mentioned it, holding it out over Vivian's head as if it made his ordeal over losing Nicole worse than hers.

"Marty came to me," Virgil said. "Oh, it was years later. I'd already retired. I took him to his first AA meeting. He asked me to sponsor him. I just couldn't. I was trying to leave that part of my life behind me. The Strong girl."

"Was there ever anyone else you looked hard at?"

"We got all sorts of kooks calling in over the years. Psychics. Then later, internet trolls. I'm glad I retired before social media was a thing. Now, you've got those armchair detectives posting crap online. Watch out for that with this one. The last thing you need is some idiot trying to make one of those podcasts about it."

"I'm aware," Jake said. "I had a run-in with one particular group during Ben Wayne's case."

"Well, then they know your number now. Watch out for it. I just had nothing. No good leads. Nobody saw anything. Nobody knew anything. She just left that bowling alley in one piece, made it all the way to her mother's front door, then vanished."

"Anya could never understand it," Jake agreed.

"She was home that night. I know it haunted her. Her bedroom was on the other end of the house. She was never in a position to see anything toward the driveway."

"I looked through the file," Jake said. "You interviewed some kid named Tom Cypher?"

"Cypher, yeah," Virgil said. "He was a production worker at Almon Steel. Got caught exposing himself to some girls at one of the truck stops off Route 33. Then one of his neighbors called the cops saying he was peeking into her window one night. She lived a couple of streets down from Nicole. I thought I had a lead. One of the clerks at that same truck stop where he flashed himself swore she saw a girl matching Nicole's description talking to Cypher the night after she was reported missing. She had some details I thought lent credibility to the whole thing. Nicole was wearing a pink fuzzy sweater and black converse high tops. And a necklace. The clerk described the high tops. And the fact Nicole had blonde hair. But nothing came of it."

"Why not?"

"Tom Cypher was a dirtbag. No doubt about that. He's doing federal time for possession of child porn now. A few years after Nicole went missing, he came back on my radar. He had some state charges on him for sexual assault of two minors out in Hancock County but those went nowhere. Two little girls. Eight and ten years old. Sisters. But the charges were dropped. The witnesses recanted. On paper, he looked good for this. Like I said. He'd been seen sneaking around looking in windows not far from Nicole's house. But the thing fell apart. Cypher got popped for a DUI in Cuyahoga County two days before Nicole went missing. When I finally tracked him down, his story was that he was still in Cuyahoga County with a couple of friends. He gave me their names. They were willing to talk to me and they backed up his story about where he was the night Nicole went missing. I'm not saying I trusted any of them, but I couldn't put Cypher in town or anywhere near Nicole the night she went missing."

"What about your truck stop witness?" Jake asked.

"She ended up being somewhat of a frequent flyer in terms of calling into the crime hotlines. If I'd put out an attempt to locate Big Foot she'd have called and said she saw him at the same damn truck stop. I knew I'd never be able to put her on the stand. Plus, one of her coworkers pretty much told me she was a total kook."

"So you think she was lying?"

"I really hoped she wasn't. But over the years, every tip she called in turned out not to be true. She's saying she saw Cypher the night after Nicole disappeared, and he's got two alibi witnesses."

"I'd like to talk to that clerk again just the same."

Virgil shrugged. "She's probably long gone. Last I heard, she developed a pretty bad drug habit. It'd be a miracle if she's still alive. But you're welcome to try. Her name should still be in the file somewhere."

"What about boyfriends?" Jake said.

Virgil shook his head. "She wasn't seeing anyone that her friends knew about. Her last serious boyfriend she broke up with at the beginning of that year. Nine months before she went missing."

"Who was it?"

Virgil pursed his lips. "That's the thing. You're not gonna like it any more than I did. She was dating Alton Bardo."

The name stopped Jake cold. "Bardo ... you mean ..."

"Yeah. Bardo. As in brother of Rex Bardo. Leader of the Hilltop Boys. I know. He would have been one of my most promising leads. Only he had an airtight alibi on account the kid had joined the army and was stationed at Fort Bragg. As far as I could tell, he hadn't seen or talked to Nicole in over six months before she disappeared. He wasn't involved."

"Still ... that's a hell of a connection," Jake said.

"I thought so too. But it went nowhere. One more dead end."

"Still," Jake said. "I'd like to talk to him too."

Virgil shook his head. "You can't. Poor kid got killed by an IED toward the beginning of Operation Freedom. He's been dead twenty years."

Jake pondered the information for a moment. Nicole Strong dating a Bardo. In all the years he'd known Anya, she'd never mentioned it. Though, they had rarely talked about what Nicole's life was like. They only talked about the aftermath of her disappearance.

"Virgil, I meant what I said. I know what this case means to you. What that girl means to you. As far as I'm concerned. This is still your case too. Any help you can give me. You can be involved if ..."

"No," Virgil said. "I don't want it, Jake. I've done my time. I can't go back to that. This case nearly destroyed me. I had a year of sobriety under my belt, and then Nicole Strong disappeared."

Sheriff Landry's concerns popped into his mind. Could Virgil's past have compromised any part of this case?

"I wanted to drink," Virgil said, though Jake had not given voice to the question. "Every week I worked that case, on Friday nights I would walk into Winky's bar. I sat at the counter and ordered a double shot of bourbon. Ned Chapin was the bartender then. He'd bring it. Set it in front of me along with an empty pitcher. I'd bring that glass to my lips. Smell it. Maybe even tasted the rim of the glass. But then I'd pour the whole thing into the pitcher and leave a twenty-dollar bill on the bar for Ned. You can ask him. He'll tell you. It took everything I had not to take that shot, Jake. I still think about it every day. Sometimes every hour. So no. I don't want back in."

"I understand," Jake said. "And I'm sorry for your loss, Virgil."

"This case? That girl? You can call me an old fool. But it's cursed. Maybe it's unsolvable. Maybe the devil himself came and scooped her up. I don't know."

"You don't really believe that, Virg."

He shook his head. "I don't know what I believe. I'm here if you need me. Anything I can remember. Anything you want to bounce off me. You know where to find me. I'll be right here, staring at that poor girl's grave. Maybe it's my penance for failing her twenty-five years ago."

"I don't believe that. But I understand. You've more than earned the right to carve out whatever peace you can for yourself."

"Peace," he whispered. "Rest in peace. I've always hated when people say that. There's no peace to it. They're just dead."

Jake rose. Virgil stayed seated. He didn't like the look on the old man's face. He couldn't help but wonder if Virgil had a bottle of bourbon waiting for him in the double-wide.

"Thanks, Jake," he said. "I do want to know what really happened to that girl if you ever find out. I have a few things here. Personal journals I kept. I haven't looked at them in decades. I don't even know what all's in them. But you're welcome to them. I'll dig them out."

"Thanks, Virg. That could be really helpful."

He put a hand on Virgil's shoulder and squeezed. He prayed that digging up old bones wouldn't unearth bigger demons for Virgil before this was all over.

Jake said goodbye and headed for his car. As he climbed behind the wheel, he got a text from Dr. Andre Coleman. A second text from Sheriff Landry came through. He read Coleman's first.

> Have some results you'll want to see. How soon can you make it to Columbus? I'll wait as long as you need.

> I'll leave now. Be there in forty-five minutes.

Landry's text made him realize Coleman had already called the office and told her the same thing. Hers read,

> Come pick me up. We'll see Coleman together. I'll fend off the press pack of wolves until tomorrow morning.

Jake put his car in reverse, and headed away from Echo Lake.

NINE

"I want to see her for myself," Landry said when Jake called her as he left Virgil Adamski's. "I don't know why it's important. This one just feels different."

He knew what she meant. So Jake swung by the station and picked her up on the way down to Dr. Coleman's lab. The next morning, Landry would have to stand in front of a bank of reporters and brief them on everything they knew so far about the bones found at Echo Lake.

Nicole. She had existed as a ghost for the entire time Jake knew Anya Strong. Her mother, Vivian Strong, had enshrined her in the den, lighting votive candles under a 20x16 canvas of Nicole's senior picture. Jake now knew the sun behind her was setting just a few hundred yards from where her body had been found.

"Thanks for getting up here so fast," Coleman said as he met them in the hallway. The place looked like any number of morgues Jake had been in. Cold. Dark. The artificial lighting made Andre Coleman look almost ghoulish. He led Jake and Landry into an exam room. A pair of Coleman's students sat in front of computer screens in the corner. As Jake entered, they quickly excused themselves, leaving just himself, Landry, and the doctor.

Coleman went to the steel drawer in the wall and pulled it open. Nicole Strong's skeleton lay there on a piece of black cloth.

"There's so much of her," Landry said, walking to the slab before Jake did. She was right. The skeleton appeared to be all there. Coleman and his students had painstakingly reassembled it and brushed away two and a half decades worth of sand, silt, and earth.

"In a way," Coleman said, "it's a miracle she was buried where she was. She was fairly well protected from the elements and predation. It's a remarkable find, really. Except for the circumstances surrounding her death."

"What can you tell us?"

Coleman grabbed a tablet off a nearby table. He opened a second drawer beside the skeleton and pulled out a large black box, resting it beside Nicole Strong's left femur.

Coleman pulled up an X-ray image on the tablet and tilted it so Landry and Jake could see it.

"Even with remains buried for as long as hers were, you can often tell a lot. With gunshots, you can often still find entry and exit wounds. If it's a stabbing, you can often find marks on the bones, usually the ribs, consistent with having been made by a sharp blade. But there was none of that here."

He zoomed in on a grainy image of the skeleton's neck bones. Coleman took a pen light and highlighted a tiny area at the top of the spine, just below the jaw.

"The hyoid bone in her neck was fractured. That's about as telltale a sign as you can get."

"Of what?" Landry said, peering closer to the image.

"She was strangled," Jake said. He made a motion, holding his hands at the skeleton's neck on the slab.

"He's got it," Coleman said. "The fracture is consistent with pressure being applied around the structures of the neck. I can't tell you exactly what the method of strangulation was. But I found no evidence of any fibrous material around the remains. No scarf. No rope. No garrote. Of course, that could have been removed by the killer. It could have disintegrated over time. But standing here today, my best estimation, we're looking at a manual strangulation."

"She was face to face with whoever killed her," Landry said.

"Yes," Coleman said. "Even without the benefit of any remaining soft tissue, this girl is telling us a lot about what happened to her. Her final moments."

"What else?" Jake asked.

"We'll be able to recover some DNA from her marrow. Though we've got a positive ID from her dental records and the break to her left tibia. I want to show you."

Coleman scrolled a few screens on his tablet and highlighted a healed fracture to Nicole's left shin bone. "You can see where the bone healed. Where it calcified. I've compared it with the X-rays taken after her surgery. This is the same leg bone. But it's not the only bone fracture she's got."

He scrolled past two more screens then zoomed in on an image of the right hand.

Jake didn't look at the screen. Instead, he walked closer to the actual skeleton. He could see what Dr. Coleman was about to point out.

"She has a small fracture to the fifth meta-carpal bone on her right hand. It shows no signs of healing or calcification."

"How do you know that didn't happen from the process of being buried?" Landry asked.

"It's a boxer's fracture," Jake said. Jake pulled his own right hand into a fist and ran his left thumb across the base of his right pinky. He could still feel the echoes of pain from when he broke that bone on Ben Wayne's head during wrestling practice when they were sixteen years old.

"Right again," Coleman said. "This girl fought someone on her last day of life."

"She punched her killer?" Landry asked. "That's what you're saying?"

"It's a theory," Coleman said. "She punched someone. And she did it within a very short time frame from when she expired. That's as much as I could testify to in court, you understand. You can infer it was her killer she tussled with. But any half-decent defense attorney will want me to admit I can't say for certain who she punched. But you're looking at a defensive wound on her. I just can't tell you within a reasonable degree of medical certainty whether that fracture happened immediately before her death or even up to an hour before. Common sense tells me she punched her attacker. But that's as far as I can go."

Dr. Coleman opened the black box on the table.

"We didn't find very much in the way of clothing or personal effects. Some fibrous material. Denim. Looks like she was wearing a cotton-blend shirt. Some pink nylon-blend fibers, perhaps from the sweater she was wearing."

"A fuzzy pink sweater," Jake said. "Fake angora, Anya said."

Coleman nodded. "We've looked at everything under a microscope. There's not much there. No other DNA or anything that could tie anyone else to that burial site. I know that's not the news you wanted to hear."

"I want to hear anything you can tell me," Jake said.

"Well, as I said. I didn't find anything that will help you put another adult at the scene. But I did find a few other remarkable items."

Coleman wore latex gloves and pulled a small baggie out of the box with a pair of tweezers. He held it up to the light.

"She was wearing this," he said. Jake got closer. It was a thin gold chain with a pendant hanging from the end of it. The pendant was in the shape of an infinity symbol, with a small, pink stone embedded into one of its loops.

"Is that an opal?" Landry asked.

"Rose quartz," Coleman said. "It's the only jewelry we found on her. There were other bits of inorganic material. Part of a plastic thong. She might have been wearing flip-flops, or they might have washed up near her sometime in the intervening twenty years."

"We know what she was wearing," Jake said. "That's not a mystery."

"This might be," Coleman said. He went to a third drawer and pulled it out. Inside was another black box, even tinier than the one before. Coleman held this one with more care, almost cradling it to his chest as he placed it on the slab next to Nicole Strong's body.

A chill went through Jake. He had a sixth sense that whatever was in that box would upend whatever theories had started to form in his brain.

Coleman opened the box. Resting on the bottom were what looked like more bone fragments. Tiny ones.

"I've got to give credit to one of my graduate students for this," Coleman said. "She found it on our last day out there, sifting through the sand near where we found Ms. Strong's pelvis."

"What am I looking at?" Landry asked.

"Those are fetal ear bones," Coleman answered.

It took a moment for Jake to process what he'd just said.

"Fetal ear bones," Jake repeated. "As in ... from a fetus."

"Exactly. Detective Cashen, your victim was pregnant the night she died."

The words thundered through Jake. Pregnant. Nicole Strong. Seventeen years old. Six months from graduating high school. Had been pregnant.

"Can you tell how far along?" Landry asked.

"Yes. By the size and developmental stage of these bones, you're looking at a fetus of about twelve weeks gestation."

"Three months," Jake said. "She got pregnant that summer."

"She probably wouldn't have been showing yet," Coleman said. "Though it's likely she would have either known or suspected."

"Detective Adamski spoke to her doctor," Jake said. "He had access to her medical records. If she knew she was pregnant, she hadn't gone to see anyone about it."

"And she hadn't pursued getting an abortion either," Landry said. "At least not through the usual routes. It's definitely a starting point."

"No one can know this," Jake said. "Meg? Dr. Coleman? That fact cannot leave this room. If it ends up on the internet ..."

"It won't come from me," Coleman said. "You have my word on that. What you choose to share with the press is entirely up to you. I'll have my full written and annotated report to you by the end of the week."

"Thank you," Landry said.

"I'm sorry I couldn't give you more. I was hoping I'd be able to find something to connect another person to that scene. It was a long shot though. We're lucky to have found what we did. This has been an incredible teaching case. I'm sorry about the circumstances, but thank you for the opportunity to work on it."

"You've been incredibly helpful," Landry said, shaking the doctor's hand. Jake went through the motions too. But his mind reeled.

He knew Coleman's instincts were accurate. Whether it would hold up in court or not, Jake knew in his gut that Nicole Strong had tried to fight off her attacker with enough force to break her own hand. And now, he knew it wasn't just her life she'd been fighting for.

Had she been thinking of her unborn child that day?

Jake stayed mute as they walked back to his car and he climbed in. He stared at the steering wheel for a moment before hitting the ignition.

"Jake," Landry said beside him. "What are you thinking?"

He shook his head. "I don't know."

"You're sure Anya or her parents didn't know Nicole was expecting?"

"Not that I know of."

"If she was three months pregnant, she would have missed at least two periods. That girl knew she was expecting. I'd bet money on it."

As Jake pulled out of the parking lot and headed for the highway, he wondered what other secrets Nicole Strong had hidden that day. And who might get hurt when he uncovered them.

TEN

"Though it's a sad day for our county and for the Strong family, I'm hopeful that the discovery of their precious daughter, Nicole, can finally bring some closure to those who loved and cared about her. I know her disappearance all those years ago has been an unhealed wound for many in this community," Sheriff Landry said. She had just finished revealing Nicole's identity to the press and reading her prepared statement. She said as little as possible but Jake knew the rumor mills around town were already churning. He stood away from the lectern, conscious of where the cameras were pointed. He would take no questions today.

"Sheriff Landry." The first reporter stood up. "Can you at least tell us whether foul play is suspected in this case?"

"Yes," she said. "It is. But I won't elaborate on that today or until this investigation is complete."

"Do you know how long Nicole Strong was buried out there?"

"I can't answer that at this time. I won't be answering any questions regarding the substance of this investigation. I can assure you that everything that can be done, will be done in order to bring this case to a timely and thorough conclusion. I want justice for Nicole as much as anyone else."

"Is there any truth to the rumor that Nicole Strong may have been another victim of the Trash Can Butcher? I have information that Dr. Andre Coleman was out at the scene. He was instrumental in identifying the remains of the Trash Can Butcher's victims in the late eighties."

"I have no information to share on that. Other than the fact that the Trash Can killer was brought to justice five years before Nicole Strong went missing. Dr. Coleman has worked on many, many cases in his capacity as a forensic anthropologist. There's no reason to suspect there's any connection whatsoever with those killings. Let's all try to share information responsibly. I'm also not going to speculate on any other potential suspects at this time."

"Is it true that body parts of other victims were found at the lake along with Nicole Strong? They just haven't been identified yet? We're hearing you have a mass grave situation out there."

Jake bristled. The questioner wasn't a formal reporter. Jake recognized him as one of the administrators of a social media page focused on solving cold cases.

"There is absolutely no truth to that!" Rob Arden stood up from his seat in the front row. He marched up to the microphone and tried to muscle it away from Landry.

Jake reacted. He was at the sheriff's side in a heartbeat. Arden put his hands in his pockets but didn't back away from the lectern.

"I can assure you there is zero truth to any of these vicious rumors of a mass grave out at Echo Lake. This is an unfortunate incident. But an isolated one. I'm sure our sheriff knows how important it is to get the truth out there to you folks. Everyone just needs to calm down."

When he stepped away from the lectern, Jake moved in, blocking him from the microphone.

"Detective Cashen, do you have any concerns about how this case was handled twenty-five years ago ... from an investigative standpoint?"

"None," Jake said. "Like the sheriff said. We're not going to comment on an ongoing case. When there's something to share, we'll share it."

"Thank you," Landry said. "That's all we have time for today. Any other questions you have you can formally submit. It's time to let my detectives do their jobs."

She pulled the microphone down and looped an arm through Jake's. Arden glowered at him. He then had the gall to follow Jake and Landry through the door and into the next room uninvited.

"This is getting out of hand," Rob said. He was bold, reaching Meg Landry in two strides. He jabbed a finger in her face.

"You need to back off," Jake said. He was a powder keg with a lit fuse. Landry was small. Maybe five two in heels. She had a tight, wiry frame and Jake knew she was stronger than she looked. But Rob Arden outweighed her by a hundred pounds and had a foot on her. Landry held her ground.

"I don't need to hear from you right now," Rob said. "You're too close to this thing now that we know whose body it was out there. Everybody knows you had a relationship with that girl's sister."

"Exactly what do you think that has to do with anything?" Landry said.

"Get somebody else," Arden said.

"You want Ed Zender on this thing?" Jake said. "Or maybe we should hand this over to BCI or the feds. How fast do you think your little development project is going to get back underway with them?"

"You're not doing enough to tamp down the rumors floating around. I'm getting calls left and right. Wild theories. People think you're hiding something. In the last week, I've had three major buyers pull out of their contracts."

"Seems to me," Landry said, "that means you've got a conflict of interest, Commissioner Arden. That's been true from the beginning."

"Just do your job and control your people," Arden said. This time, he jabbed that finger right into Meg Landry's shoulder.

Jake saw white. He moved with the force of a tsunami, grabbing Arden by the back of his jacket. He shoved him toward the wall.

"Jake!"

"You lay a finger on her again, I'll knock your damn teeth out."

"Jake!"

"You'd like that, wouldn't you?" Rob said, spittle flying out of his mouth. "This whole thing plays right into your hands. Ever since you crawled back to town, you've wanted to make things difficult for me."

Jake let go of Arden's jacket and smoothed it down with a rough hand. "You think I buried that girl out there myself just to embarrass you?"

"If you could have, you would have. As it stands now, you're doing everything you can to make sure those people out there think the worst about Echo Lake."

"I don't give a rat's ass about Echo Lake or your development," Jake said. "I care that we found a dead girl out there. I care that she's got a family who has grieved her disappearance for twenty-five years. I care that somebody out there killed her and put her in the ground. Your problems don't make my top ten, Uncle Rob."

"Get somebody else, Landry," Rob said.

"You don't have the authority to make that kind of demand. Your *nephew* happens to be one of the best investigators in the state. You should be thanking him and fate that he's here to handle this one. He's the best chance you have of this case clearing as quickly as possible."

"Thanking him? He's a Cashen. I know exactly what he is. And he'll use any chance he can to try and cross me."

Jake shook his head. "It's time for you to leave, Uncle Rob. Next time you wanna talk in private to me or the sheriff, make a damn appointment. I also better not hear you giving statements other than no comment as it relates to my investigation."

Arden pushed himself off the wall. His face had gone purple. He took a step toward Jake. Landry moved, putting herself in between both men.

"We're done here," she said to Arden. "Jake and I have work to do. I hope you do too."

"I expect daily briefings," Arden said.

Jake fumed. "I'll give you ..."

"Jake!" Landry said. She took hold of Jake's arm and pulled him down the hall. He resisted. Then Rob turned on his heel and walked the other way.

"Come on," Landry said. "He's not worth the trouble."

"You're wrong on that, Sheriff. That idiot can make all kinds of trouble. He needs to be frozen out on this one. I don't trust he won't use any piece of intel you give him to spin to his advantage. If he can manage to make me look bad in the process, he'll do that too."

"Jake," she said. "Like it or not, you're going to have to figure out a way to get along with him. At least publicly. I don't know. Start meditating. Long walks in the park. Something. You cannot let him goad you into a scene like that in front of a bank of reporters. He's wrong about you. I know that better than anyone. But if he can make it look like you're taking this all personally, he can make trouble for you. Don't help him."

Jake clenched his jaw but didn't take up the argument. Landry was right about one thing. He didn't want to waste an ounce of mental effort worrying about the idiocy of Rob Arden.

Landry followed him back down the hall. As of this morning, Landry had given him permission to convert the storage room across from his office into the war room for Nicole Strong's case. He wheeled his whiteboard in, replacing the image of her skull with her senior picture, and started drawing lines out with the principal suspects Virgil Adamski had identified and later cleared.

"Arden might not be entitled to it," she said. "But I do expect you to keep me up to speed. He's not the only one feeling the pressure of this thing. Has anything jumped out at you so far?"

"Virgil was thorough," Jake said, happy to take his focus back to the case at hand. "Without a body, he just couldn't break through."

"She was pregnant," Landry said. "Seems to me, that gives you at least one person with a motive to get rid of her. Assuming it was unplanned. And I can't think of a single seventeen-year-old girl in her situation who would plan for that. Did she have a boyfriend?"

"No," Jake said. He pointed to the picture of Alton Bardo.

"Is that …"

"Alton Bardo," Jake said. "But he wasn't her boyfriend anymore. They dated briefly the year before, when Nicole was a junior. He was a year older. By all accounts, they broke up amicably months before she went missing. He joined the army right after high school. He was in Fort Bragg that October."

"Right," Landry said. "But Dr. Coleman said Nicole was around three months pregnant when she died. So that puts conception sometime in July. Where was Bardo then?"

"It's on my list of questions," Jake said. "I want to talk to all of her closest friends about what was happening in her life that summer."

"She didn't have a boyfriend," Landry said. "But she was intimate with somebody. You have to find out who."

"According to Virgil's notes, Nicole was at that bowling alley with four other classmates. Shawn Weingard. Shannon Murphy. Brenda Pollack. Grady Thompson. Those were the people she was closest with. They'd all studied together for their SATs. All but Brenda Pollack are still local. They've all been interviewed multiple times."

"So it will be interesting to see if any of them change their stories."

"Twenty-five years is a long time," Jake said. "As far as I know, none of them have been questioned about this stuff … at least not formally … since the case went cold."

"What about Alton Bardo?" Landry asked. "You said he was army? Do you think Deputy Wayne might be an asset there in terms of reaching out to him? With her background, maybe she'd have an in or an angle that's fresh."

"Literally a dead end," Jake said. "I did some checking. He ended up an army ranger. He was killed by an IED near Kabul twenty years ago. If he had anything to do with Nicole after their break-up, we may never know."

"Tommy Cypher?" Landry said, pointing to the only other person of interest on Virgil's radar.

"He got caught peering into some houses in the vicinity. There's no doubt the guy was a creep and a pervert."

"A literal Peeping Tom? What happened to him?"

"It's a long shot," Jake said. "Virgil had no witnesses that could place him anywhere near Nicole's house the night she disappeared. Nobody saw anything. Nobody heard anything. But … it seems like Cypher's MO might have escalated in the years following Nicole's disappearance. I'm looking into him but Virgil found out he was in Cuyahoga County during the time Nicole went missing. I don't expect anything to come of it."

"But Bardo," Landry said. "As in … related to Rex Bardo?"

"Yeah," Jake said.

"Jake. Be careful. You don't think this girl could have gotten mixed up with the Hilltop Boys or anything, do you?"

"Virgil's gut said no. Alton Bardo had an alibi. He wasn't in town when Nicole went missing. But I want to pay him a visit."

"Who him? You mean King Rex? Jake ..."

"He was Alton's brother. Who else would you suggest I talk to about him?"

She sat down hard, worry lines creasing her forehead. "Just ... Jake ... tread lightly. If the press finds out you were talking to King Rex in connection with this case, this whole thing could get out of control quickly."

"Then let's make sure they don't find out," Jake said. "But tomorrow morning, I'm paying King Rex a visit."

Eleven

I f you saw Rex Bardo on the street, he wouldn't seem like anyone special. He wore his thick black hair long past his collar. His age would even be hard to place but for the peppered gray stubble covering his beefy jawline. He had hooded eyes, the left one lazier than the right, so he never quite appeared to be focused on you. He was though. Always. Then, in a brief flash, he could stare straight through someone, signaling his anger with just that one look.

Jake sat at a corner table in the common visitors' room of the federal correctional institute in Elkton, Ohio. This table was a prime spot as it was the most private you could get, far away from the other groupings of wives, and partners visiting men who were only here for doing the baddest of things. Jake suffered no delusions that his badge had earned him this perk. No. This was where King Rex held court.

Rex shuffled in, his gait and posture affected by the time he'd spent in leg chains since his incarceration, seven years ago. Rex's time hadn't always been easy. As the kingpin of the Hilltop Boys, Southern Ohio's local mob family, Rex had been a high profile prisoner. It came with perks. But it also made him a target. Today, Rex looked weary. Though it had only been a year since Jake last saw him, Rex looked like he'd aged ten.

Rex shared some words with the guard before he made his way to Jake's table. There was something dark in his eyes. Something … off.

Rex jerked his chin, acknowledging Jake before he finally sat. A small tremor went through him and Rex stiffened in a way Jake knew all too well. He'd bet his next paycheck that Rex Bardo was suffering from excruciating back pain.

"Rex," Jake said. "Thanks for making time for me."

Rex smirked. He rubbed his wrists then laid his hands flat on the table. "Not like I had a full dance card, Cashen. You wanna tell me to what I owe the pleasure?"

Jake brought a thin file folder. The guard watched from the opposite end of the room. There was only soft paper inside of it. No paper clips. No staples. And Jake would leave with everything he walked in with.

"I want to talk to you about your brother," Jake said.

"Which one? I'm the oldest of seven, Jake."

"Alton."

Jake stared at Rex. The man kept his face rock hard but for the slightest narrowing of his eyes.

"Alton's dead."

"I'm aware. And I'm sorry for your loss."

"He's been dead for almost twenty years."

"I'm aware of that too. I understand he was given a Bronze Star. He was a hero."

Rex ran a hand along his jaw. "A lot of people think he was a fool. Signing up for a war we never should have been in. And for what? We left that country worse off than when we found it."

"Maybe so. Still. His sacrifice ... your family's sacrifice had meaning. And I'm sorry for it."

"Clock's ticking, Jake. What's this really about?"

Jake opened the file folder. He showed Rex the first picture he brought. A picture of the fall homecoming dance the year before Nicole was killed. Alton Bardo looked young, dark, and handsome wearing a black suit, his arm wrapped around Nicole Strong. She was stunning in a champagne-colored, tight-fitting dress that showed off her cleavage.

"This girl," Jake said. "Nicole Strong. Do you remember her?"

"Alton had a lot of different girlfriends. He sure liked the pretty ones."

"This was his senior year. I understand he got sort of serious with this particular girl."

"Alton was my kid brother. He was ten years younger than me. I wasn't keeping track of the girls he hooked up with."

"Right," Jake said. "But you know about this one. You know what happened to her. Let's not pretend, okay? You don't miss much, Rex."

"I never knew her. I told you. I didn't give two shits about what my little brother was doing in high school, Cashen. I was running the business."

"Sure. But you know we found her. Nicole Strong. She was buried in a shallow grave at Echo Lake. She's been there for twenty-five years."

Rex shoved the picture across the table toward Jake. His cool facade slipped. "You better not tell me you came here looking to pin some shit on my dead baby brother, Jake. A thing like that might put me in a bad mood."

"They broke up a long time before she went missing. She disappeared in October. Your brother ended things with her the previous Christmas, from what I understand. What I'm trying to find out is whether they were still talking to each other. How it ended. Anything you can remember, really."

"Alton had nothing to do with whatever happened to that girl. The October she went missing, Alton was gone. Long gone. He was at Fort Bragg by then. I'm the one who drove him out there."

Jake kept his face neutral. Of course Rex Bardo knew exactly when Nicole Strong went missing. Even in here, he would have his finger on the pulse of happenings in the Blackhand Hills region.

"You're sure?"

"Go to hell, Jake. I don't like where this conversation is heading. My brother? Alton was his own man. Or trying to be. He had nothing to do with the family business. He was trying to make something else of himself."

"That's why he joined the military? It was a way out?"

"He loved his country. He wanted to serve. Said it was his calling."

"Did you try to talk him out of it?"

"He was over eighteen. He'd earned the right to make his own decisions."

"This girl though. Did he ever bring her around to meet your mother? I assume she would have wanted to see her baby boy off to the high school dance."

Rex said nothing at first. He merely sized Jake up. Finally, he cracked a smile. "I think you're too smart to assume anything, Cashen. And no. We weren't that kind of family. Alton never brought that girl or any of them up the hill."

The hill. Rex said it so casually. But the "hill" he referred to was known as Red Sky Hill, a grouping of hills deep in the southeast corner of the county. Rex's branch of the Bardo family were the only ones who had ever come down from those hills. The rest? Jake had heard rumors his whole life. Legends. They lived off the grid up there for generations. Even the census takers had no idea how many were still there. Anyone from the government usually got run off when they tried to venture up that hill.

"Rex, I'm trying to piece together what was going on in this girl's life in the days, weeks, and months before she died. Your brother was the only serious boyfriend she ever had from what I've been told. He's gone. I swear I'm not trying to dredge things up for you or your family. Do you know if she sent him letters when he shipped out? Did they stay in touch?"

"I couldn't tell you that. And if you think my mama kept some kind of shrine to her baby boy, you'd be wrong. She never forgave him for what happened. She's the one who begged him not to go. She threw him out of the house. All his stuff. Told him he was dead to her. Then ... he was. That woman never shed a single tear for the past. Not one. I can't help you."

Jake had a card to play. He knew blood mattered to Rex Bardo above all else. If he could plant the seed that Nicole Strong could have been pregnant with his nephew when she was murdered, Rex might take that personally. It could backfire though. Rex might take it upon himself to exact revenge on his own.

"What's the matter, Rex?" Jake asked, seeing Rex stiffen in his chair. The man was in pain. A great deal of it. But he said nothing. Refusing to answer Jake's simple question.

"We done here?"

Jake tapped the file in front of them. "No, Rex. There's one more thing I want to ask you about." He opened the file and took out the other photograph.

"You recognize this one?"

Jake had printed Tom Cypher's mugshot. It was a few years old, but the man had a distinctive face and neck tattoos.

Rex said nothing.

"His name is Tom Cypher. He's here at Elkton, Rex. Got popped on child porn charges a few years ago. He's serving fifteen."

Still no answer from Rex.

"Twenty-five years ago," Jake continued, "Tommy got caught looking into people's windows in Nicole's neighborhood. Taking pictures. Jacking off. No charges were ever brought, but he was doing this crap during the time Nicole Strong went missing. Then he escalated. He was suspected of hurting kids, Rex. A couple of young girls near Findlay. Rape. Charges got dropped. The girls' parents wouldn't let them testify. Back then, he was a person of interest in Nicole's case too. Only nobody ever saw anything. Heard anything. The girl just disappeared. He had a good alibi for Nicole's killing, not a great one. It hinged on the word of two of his dirtbag friends. I'd still like to know what he knows. Is he tight with anyone? Has he bragged to any cellmates about what might have happened to that girl?"

"What's that got to do with me?"

"He's here, Rex. I know you know that."

"There are twelve hundred inmates in this cage, Jake. I don't know all of 'em. Plus, they keep the kiddie touchers away from the rest of us."

"Oh, I think you could find out plenty if you put your mind to it?"

"And why do you think I'd do that? You're the one who owes me a favor, or did you forget?"

"I didn't forget. I'm just hoping you can ask around. See if this guy's ever talked about what he might have seen or done to a girl your brother used to care about. The only serious girlfriend he ever had."

"I don't even know that, Cashen."

"You need something," Jake said. "I can see it. You're in pain. What's going on, Rex?"

Rex let out a bitter laugh. "You want me to look into your boy out of the goodness of my heart? I think we're done here."

"No. Not out of the goodness of my heart. For your brother, maybe."

Rex snarled like a dog. He leaned forward. "You wanna be real careful. I think you need to keep Alton's name out of your mouth from now on."

"What do you need, Rex?"

Rex narrowed his eyes at Jake, giving him that death stare that terrified lesser men. "You want me to ask around? It's going to cost you. Not some promise of a favor in the future. Something real."

Jake knew he would regret asking. He also knew he was close to hitting a wall where Nicole Strong was concerned.

"I need you to get me out of the hole."

Jake blinked. "The hole. They've got you in solitary? Jesus. For what?"

"For nothing. For bullshit."

"Who'd you piss off, Rex?"

Rex sat back. For the first time since their meeting started, Jake sensed real need from Rex. It gave him power, but also made Rex that much more dangerous.

"There's a C.O. in here who's got it in for me. It's bullshit. It's political. He's using me to score points. See how far he can push me before I start pushing back."

"Did you lay hands on this guy?"

Rex shook his head. "Never laid a finger on him. That I can swear. It's trumped-up bullshit. But if you want me putting my ear to the ground on your grimy little pedo, I can't really do that unless I'm back in gen pop."

Jake knew he could live to regret it. At the same time, he was running out of options.

"I'll see what I can do," he said. "But I mean it. If I catch so much as a whiff that you laid a hand on this C.O. ..."

"Never even breathed in his direction," Rex said, smiling. "I've been a choir boy, Detective. Cross my heart."

Then he did. Rex looked down at Cypher's picture. Jake sensed no recognition, but knew that didn't mean anything. Even in here, Rex Bardo had eyes and ears everywhere.

"Give me a couple of days," Jake said. "I'll see what I can do to get you out of the hole."

"Time to go, Bardo," the guard said. Rex took a moment, his body stiffening as he tried to stand up. He took a breath then got his legs working.

King Rex never even looked back or said goodbye as he was led back to his cell. Jake just prayed he hadn't made a devil's bargain this time.

TWELVE

S pecial Agent Gable West met Jake at a pizza place in Greektown two days later. A Wednesday afternoon. It meant if he wouldn't agree to the favor Jake needed, he was already out of time.

Gabe was the kind of guy who looked carved out of granite. Big. Solid. Strong at six foot six, he could intimidate witnesses just by walking into a room. Today, though, he was all smiles as Jake approached his table. He got up and offered Jake a hearty handshake before the two men sat back down.

"Thanks for meeting me," Jake said.

"Thanks for asking. I've been wondering about you. Not too much news makes its way to Chicago from Backwater Hills, Ohio."

"Blackhand Hills," Jake said, knowing Gable already knew that.

"You miss it?" Gable asked.

Jake laughed. "The Bureau, ah, no. Truth is, I've barely thought about you idiots in over a year."

"The feeling's mutual. I can finally get things done now that I'm not carrying your ass."

"Saw you finally closed the case on the mayor's bribery case," Jake said.

Gable took a sip of his iced tea. Jake knew it would have been Guinness, but he was still on duty. Gable worked in the Public Corruption Unit.

"Bastard pled out," Gable said. "He'll get fifteen years, but he gave us enough to get an indictment on some mobsters running the trash hauling unit."

"That's great work. The kind of case you can retire on, Gable. When are you getting out?"

Jake already knew the answer to that question. It had been a running joke between them. Gable West would likely die with his badge still tied around his neck when he was a hundred years old.

"You've made some waves of your own," Gable said. "I was sorry to hear about your friend last year. That had to have been a rough one."

Jake nodded, but didn't want to get into it. Luckily, with a guy like Gable, he wouldn't have to.

The server came. Jake ordered a BLT with a side of pub fries. Gable ordered a Reuben. As soon as they were alone again, Gable cut to it.

"So what's this about you couldn't just ask me over the phone?"

Jake folded his napkin on his lap. "A favor," he said. "One that's a little delicate, but hopefully doable."

"I'm listening."

"Rex Bardo's serving life on a gang-related RICO charge."

"Bardo," Gable said. "Bardo. Isn't he some kind of hillbilly kingpin?"

"The Hilltop Boys," Jake said. "A family crew down in my neck of the woods. They've had their hands in just about everything over the last twenty or thirty years. Though the organization is somewhat fractured now that King Rex is in prison."

"He hasn't quite given up his crown though, has he?"

"No," Jake said. "Nobody can prove it, but Rex is still fully in charge."

"So what's he into you for?"

"This can't leave this table," Jake said. "But he's been helpful in a few cases. I don't trust him as far as I can throw him, but his information has proven useful. The problem is, he's gotten himself on the wrong side of a C.O. inside. He's been in solitary for the last month. He wants out. I'm hoping you can pull a string or two and make that happen."

Gable let out a sigh. "Jake ..."

"It's petty shit, Gable. Rex is no saint. But he hasn't laid hands on anyone if that's what you're worried about. Believe me, it's what I worried about. I checked into it. The guy's been a model prisoner. This thing? Somebody's just trying to prove a point. A new kid on the block is using Rex to make himself seem important. I wouldn't care. But like I said. He's been useful to me."

"So you made him a deal," Gable said. "Jake, it's a bad idea. I don't have to tell you, Elkton is its own ecosystem. Maybe Rex Bardo being in solitary is the best thing for him whether he knows it or not."

"Maybe. But so far, he's delivered on every promise he's made me."

Gable shook his head. "You're playing with fire."

"I know."

"Then, you've always played with fire. I see that going small-time hasn't changed that."

"Can you do it? *Will* you do it?"

"I shouldn't. I should tell you to piss up a rope for your own good. This is the same kind of thing that bit you in the ass at the Bureau."

Jake stiffened. "I was right about everything that happened back then too. Remember?"

Gable gritted his teeth. He didn't have to answer. Jake knew he understood.

"It won't be one favor with this guy," Gable said. "You know that, right? He's gonna want more."

"I can handle it."

"No. You can't. Nobody can. Not with guys like that."

"You're gonna just have to trust me that it's my problem. And I know what I'm getting into."

"You better."

"Gable. Can you do it?"

Gable sat back. The server brought their sandwiches. Gable took a giant bite out of his. Jake waited for a moment while he mulled over everything Jake had said. Finally, he put his sandwich down.

"Yeah. I can make a call. I've got my own favor to call in."

"Thank you."

"Don't thank me just yet. You might not like the next favor I ask from you."

Jake smiled. He knew Gable. By the end of the day, Rex Bardo would be back in gen pop.

"Eat your sandwich," Gable said. "And I'll need a promise from you."

"Name it."

"Promise me you'll watch your back. This guy? Rex Bardo? He'll suck you dry. He'll ruin you if it suits his needs. It won't matter whatever rapport you think you have with him. He's a devil, Jake. Through and through. Just be careful about the deals you make with him. Pray it doesn't come back to haunt you. Cuz if it does, there won't be anything I can do."

Jake took a bite out of his sandwich. Gable's warning was almost the same as King Rex's had been. They both prayed Jake's little favor wouldn't come back to bite them in the ass. As Jake thanked Gable one more time, he hoped like hell it wouldn't. But a sinking suspicion deep inside of him told him when the devil came to collect his due, it might be more than Jake could afford to pay.

Thirteen

Jake knew he had to assemble Nicole Strong's life like puzzle pieces. He would have to live in her life. Know who she knew. Today though, Jake tried to clear his mind through physical exertion. He'd taken over a corner of Grandpa Max's barn and turned it into a home gym. It was quiet here. He had free weights in one corner. He found a practice wrestling mat Grandpa had rescued from the high school gym when they renovated it after the last bond passage. Jake worked himself into a sweat rolling the 40x40 foam mat out and taping it back together.

So he came here to work out. But he also came here to think. It was better here without Ed Zender or every looky-loo in the department barging in ready with their theories of the case and latest rumors. Also, the likes of Rob Arden were far away. He'd set up a card table in one corner, and stockpiled everything he'd found from the local library on Nicole's disappearance.

Well, almost no one.

"I figured I'd find you out here." Jake could hide from everyone, but never from Gemma. The woman seemed to have radar where Jake was concerned.

She wore a suit and her three-inch red stilettos, her blonde hair teased high to heaven. Gemma closed the barn door behind her. She held a leather portfolio under her arm as she made her cautious approach.

Jake hopped down from the pull-up bar, sweat pouring down his back. He grabbed his tee shirt off the nearest folding chair and slipped it on.

"You stink," she said. "And it's too damn hot in here. You're gonna have a stroke."

Jake laughed. "I figure if I'm gonna make the boys suffer during season, I can handle a little heat myself."

"You're not eighteen anymore, Jake. And you're not cutting weight." She got close enough to give him a backhanded smack against his stomach. He flinched just in time.

Gemma walked to the back of the barn, seeing the copied photos and newspaper articles of Nicole Strong.

"The funeral's tomorrow," she said, peering up at the front-page article of the *Blackhand Hills Gazette* the day after Nicole went missing. That particular newspaper wasn't even in print anymore.

"It's so sad. Back then, it was nice to believe she just found a way out, you know? Hitched a ride to Hollywood to become a movie star. She was pretty enough. I don't expect you to tell me anything you can't. But ... how's this going?"

Jake sat down on the bench of one of Grandpa's picnic tables. For a while, he'd made a decent side hustle out of building the things and selling them from the side of the road. Gemma had offered to set up a website for him but the old man refused, saying he'd "go corporate" over his dead body. Then his eyesight went. Jake kept meaning to bring Gemma's boys out here and show them how to finish the dozen or so tables Grandpa left in varying states of production.

"How well did you know her?" Jake asked. "You were the same grade, weren't you?"

Gemma put her leather portfolio on the table as she walked closer to some of the pictures on the table. Most if not all had come from Nicole's yearbook. Jake had gotten an extra copy from the school library.

"It was Stanley High," Gemma said. "I had a hundred people in my graduating class. Of course I knew her. Only we didn't exactly hang around in similar circles."

"But what were your impressions? Of course it was big news when she disappeared. Did you have a guess back then?"

Gemma shrugged. She perched herself on a metal stool Grandpa once had at his workbench.

"I thought she ran away. She was ... I don't know. She just always seemed like she was too big for Blackhand Hills."

"What do you mean?"

"She just had every damn thing, you know? Pretty. Stylish. It's not like the Strongs were loaded or anything. You know as well as I do how little those guys make out at the clay mill. It's just, she had this quality about her. Like you always knew she was just passing through."

"You ever talk to her?"

"I mean, sure. I can't remember anything substantial. She just wasn't interesting to me. She was into all the typical high school crap. Cheerleader. Student council. She was in all the cool kid clubs. The Christian Athletes, the Future Professional Leaders Organization."

Gemma flipped through the yearbook, stopping at the index in the back. She turned the book toward Jake and pointed to Nicole's name. He'd already combed through every page the girl appeared on.

"Look at that," Gemma said. "Three rows of page numbers. See what I mean?"

Jake did. Nicole was listed as an officer of every club she was a part of.

Gemma flipped to her own name. There was only one page number beside it. He knew it didn't bother her. Gemma had always viewed high school as a means to an end. By the time she was a senior, Gemma spent half her time working at a co-op, getting her nail technician license. She was already supporting herself and part of Grandpa's household by the time she was seventeen.

"She seemed nice enough," Gemma said. "Friendly. Just ... I don't know. I always got the impression that girl was one thing to one set of people, and someone else when she was all alone."

"It wasn't great in her household," Jake said. "Her dad was volatile. Unpredictable. A drinker. Anya's mom has always just been ... I don't know ..."

"Checked out," Gemma offered.

"Yeah. She always said it was that way even before Nicole disappeared. It just got worse after the fact."

Gemma flipped to the Christian Athletes Association page of the yearbook. Her face broke into a smile as she stopped at one.

"See that?" she said, turning the book so Jake could see what page she had open. It was a group shot of the CAA. Nicole appeared in an inset photo with three other classmates. Nicole was the organization's vice president. Gemma tapped the image, pointing Jake's attention to a small gold, round pin on Nicole's sweater. He looked closer. Every student pictured had one on as well.

"It's a chastity pin," Gemma said, snickering.

"A what?"

"A chastity pin. Back in those days, these kids wore them. It was kind of a running joke in the hallways. It meant they took a chastity vow until marriage. It was all bullcrap. At least for most of them. Definitely for Nicole Strong."

Gemma put the book down. "Who the hell were they pledging this too?" Jake said, picking the book back up. He eyeballed the group's faculty advisor. It was a teacher by the name of Dennis Meacham. At the time, he'd been the vice principal.

"I told you," Gemma said. "It was all a bunch of crap. None of them were really honoring that. They just did it so they could put the stupid club on their college resumes. I think maybe two kids out of that entire group were actually virgins or abstaining."

"How do you know who Nicole Strong was sleeping with?"

"Look. Don't think I'm trying to slut shame that girl. That's not it. I'm just saying, the year before she was dating Alton Bardo. You knew that, right?"

"Yeah. I know it now. Before all this? I had no clue. I never talked about that with Anya." Jake kept his face neutral. Gemma knew him far too well. He didn't want to risk her reading anything from his expression. Exactly four people knew that Nicole Strong was pregnant the day she disappeared. He had to keep it that way for as long as he could.

"Boy, he was something," Gemma said, her eyes glazing over. "Just ... a man ... you know? A whole ass man. Dark. Brooding. Dangerous. Everyone knew who his family was. Nobody touched him. But you knew that if they did, Alton could be lethal. They seemed an unlikely pair. She was just ... good. You know?"

"Did you ever hear any rumors that he might have hurt her? Or something going on that shouldn't have?"

Gemma shook her head. "You never know about people behind closed doors. But Alton just didn't seem the type. He was a pure alpha male, sure. But honorable. Chivalrous. He protected that girl. Nobody touched her, Jake. They knew. If anyone so much as looked at her funny, they would have had Alton to answer to. He treated her like gold, as far as I could tell."

"What about after? You knew they broke up?"

"I don't think that surprised anyone. They both had that quality like I was saying. Nobody expected either of them to actually end up in Blackhand Hills. She was gonna have this big college life. He was headed for the army. God. It's so sad what happened to him. What a complete waste. At the time, I was actually better friends with Lily Bardo. She was one of Alton's cousins. Losing him just ate that family up."

"You ever get any sense from Lily that Alton and Nicole were having issues? That the break-up was messy?"

"Nope. As far as anyone knew, they were still friends. If Nicole was broken up by it, you wouldn't know it. You think Alton Bardo had something to do with what happened?"

Jake put the yearbook down. "No. He was already long gone in basic training by the time she went missing."

"Ah. I wondered about that timeline. It seemed like he was out of the picture."

"What about him?" Jake said, pointing to Mr. Meacham. Gemma peered closer. "Is he the one who wanted them all to wear those pins and take that pledge?"

Gemma shrugged. "I never had a creep vibe from him, if that's what you mean. Meacham was actually my guidance counselor. Big nerd. Well-meaning. Again, that doesn't mean I know what he was like in his personal life. But I never heard a single rumor that Meacham was inappropriate with students."

"Me either," Jake said. "But that chastity pin is just …"

"Yeah. But like I said. Nobody really took it seriously."

Gemma paused. She leaned over and flipped through the yearbook again.

"I do remember the last time I saw her."

Gemma opened the book to the social activities page. Jake looked over her shoulder. She'd stopped on a collage of photos from the fall homecoming dance. It took place just three weeks before Nicole Strong vanished.

"I remember her dress," Gemma said. "Nicole always had the most amazing dresses. Her mother sewed them, I think."

Sure enough. The layout featured Nicole Strong, front and center, wearing a black, strapless gown. She looked regal in it, her hair piled neatly on her head. She stood in a crowd of other girls. Jake recognized Shannon Murphy and Brenda Pollack. The one photo Anya kept of her sister was from this same night. It was a candid shot of her. Anya took it herself. Nicole gazed at something off camera, her smile lighting her eyes.

Gemma closed the book. "I hope you can find who did this to her, Jake. Nicole was … nice to me. You know?"

Sadness filled his sister's eyes. The kind he didn't often see in her. Gemma was as tough as women came. She never cared what people thought of her. But now, he sensed some teenage pain she was remembering. He didn't have to guess the source. She was a Cashen, after all. With the poor, tragically dead mother and crazy, murderous father. It marked them both as "other" from the moment it happened.

"Yeah," Jake said, putting a quick arm around his sister's shoulder and kissing the top of her head. "I know."

"I think I want to go to the funeral tomorrow," she said. "Pay my respects."

Jake nodded. "I'll pick you up. We can go together."

Gemma squeezed him back. "Love you," she said.

"Love you too," he answered. Then Gemma closed the book on Nicole Strong and left Jake alone among these remaining pieces of her unfinished life.

Fourteen

Every major event in Marty and Vivian Strong's life happened at Holy Cross Church on County Road Twelve. They had both been baptized there on the very same day. When the time came, they brought their daughters there. Confirmations. Weddings. And now, Pastor Patrick Hennessy would deliver a eulogy for their eldest daughter, twenty-five years after it was due.

Jake stood in the back of the church on that Sunday afternoon. It was a private service, held two hours after regular mass. Just two dozen people attended. Marty and Vivian sat huddled together in the front pew. Neither of them had the strength or desire to get up once the service had ended. Pastor Hennessy slid in beside them, speaking hushed words of comfort after Anya and Tim Brouchard had no choice but to give up trying to move them.

"Come on," Gemma whispered to Jake as the small group of mourners began to exit the church. "Shannon could probably use help back at the house. She's hosting the reception."

Gemma looped her arm through Jake's as they walked outside together. He slid on his sunglasses as they made their way through the parking lot. Jake looked to his left. Just down the street, he spotted a patrol car. As they got closer, he saw Birdie behind the wheel. She wasn't alone. Squinting, Jake recognized her passenger. Virgil Adamski.

"Why didn't he come in?" Gemma asked, spotting Virgil as he did. "The Strongs would have wanted him there."

Jake lifted a hand, acknowledging Virgil. The older man gave him a slow nod and leaned sideways, saying something to Birdie. She gave Jake a tight-lipped smile, then slowly drove away.

"I think it's too hard for him," Jake said. "This case left a mark, Gemma."

She pulled Jake closer, leaning her head on his shoulder. "Virgil got old too soon, Jake. Promise me you won't let this job do that to you too."

He kissed the top of her head but said nothing. It wasn't a promise he could make and she knew it.

The church was far too small to hold the hundreds of mourners that would have come today. Many of them were gawkers. Nicole's case had gained some statewide attention. It had been Anya's choice to keep things small here. But it seemed most of the town turned out to celebrate Nicole's life in the backyard of Shawn and Shannon Weingard's home. The two of them had stayed together after high school. Got married. Their bond maybe forged and strengthened from the loss of their friend.

At least forty cars parked along the dirt road leading to the house. It had been in Shannon's family for eighty years. After she married Shawn and her parents passed away, Shawn built on to the place, adding a thousand square feet of living space and two additional bedrooms as their family grew. They'd set tents up in the backyard for all the guests. In a way, it reminded Jake of a graduation party Nicole never got to have.

"It's like a class reunion," Gemma said as they crossed the road and walked up the driveway together. She was right. Later, Jake would learn that seventy members of Nicole and Gemma's graduating class had shown up today. It would cause the planning committee to just up and cancel their actual twenty-fifth reunion, scheduled for later that summer out at the Blackhand Hills Golf Club.

"Thank God!" Shannon Weingard's face lit up when she saw Jake and Gemma. He hadn't seen her since she was at Anya's side the day he broke the news to her about finding Nicole. He was grateful to her. Shannon had stepped in and helped Anya handle many of the excruciating details that went into planning a funeral.

"Can you help me wrangle this fried chicken?" Shannon looped her arm through Gemma's and led her into the kitchen. Gemma shot Jake a helpless look over her shoulder and disappeared into the house.

It was fine. Perfect, actually. Jake found a shady spot under a willow tree and watched the crowd.

Things would grow somber later, he figured. Once Anya showed up. There was no telling whether her parents would come. Marty Strong was frail these days. His years of hard drinking and grief had worn him down. Vivian Strong had existed in a state of denial for a quarter of a century. The service was one thing. He doubted she could handle seeing all of Nicole's old friends gathered in one place. Friends who had moved on while Nicole stayed frozen in place, her death denying the Strongs of all the milestone moments everyone else got to experience.

"Bud Light?"

Jake turned. Shawn Weingard came toward him, carrying two frosted bottles of beer. He handed one to Jake, knocking his own against the bottle in a somber cheer.

"It's nice that you've done this," Jake said. "Turning your house over to it."

"There was nowhere else, really. Marty and Viv couldn't host it. The church hall is way too small. Plus, it's not private enough. Anya was worried about that."

Jake took a sip of his beer. He wasn't a huge Bud Light fan, but anything tasted good if it was cold enough. Jake had nearly memorized Shawn and Shannon's statements given after Nicole went missing. They were her closest friends. The ones who'd been with her earlier in the night. Jake knew he'd have to have a formal conversation with both of them, but today was not that day.

Across the lawn, Shannon put Gemma to work bringing out huge trays of finger food. Shawn Weingard owned Stanley, Ohio's one and only sports bar, the End Zone. He'd taken it over from a cousin, Jake heard. Expanded it. Built an outdoor patio and a game room. They hosted fundraisers for Stanley High band, choir, and sports teams. The scoreboard in the school gym had the End Zone logo on it.

"I don't know if Marty and Viv are gonna survive this," Jake said.

"Me either. Viv's managed it all these years by pretending maybe Nicole was just off somewhere. Living some big life she couldn't get here in Blackhand Hills, you know?"

"Yeah."

"Self-preservation. I almost wonder if it would have been better for her if nobody'd ever found her. At least ... not until after Vivian passed."

"I'm worried about Anya too," Jake said.

"She's sure borne the brunt of this," Shawn agreed. "Always trying to be twice as good to make up for what happened."

Jake took another sip of his beer. He more than anyone knew what Anya had given of herself to her parents.

"She should have left with you," Shawn said. "Shannon tried to convince her to. I don't know if you knew that."

"It's a million years ago now," Jake said. The memory of his final break-up with Anya wasn't one he liked to recall. They had ended things in anger and hurtful words. Jake had told her she would wither here in Stanley if she lived her life for her parents. She had told him he would lose himself if he kept trying to run away from his own ghosts.

"We were just kids. It probably worked out for the best."

Shawn smiled. "Yeah. I can't say I've ever seen two people more different than you and Anya. Tim though … never saw that one coming either."

"She's good for him," Shannon said. She came up behind them and joined Shawn and Jake under the tree. In the distance, Gemma came back out of the house after dropping off her final food tray and went to join a group of people under one of the tents.

"He took care of her," Shannon continued. "Handled things, you know? Had a stable job. Good income. And Tim's always known how to handle Marty and Viv. Stood up to them when she needed him to."

Jake nodded. Behind him, two more people came out of the house. He recognized Shannon and Shawn's youngest daughter, Chloe, from her brief stint as an environmental protester out at Echo

Lake. She held hands with Jake's nephew, Ryan. He caught Gemma eyeing this situation from afar.

"So, that's new," Jake said, grateful to turn the conversation from his own past with Anya.

"It sure is," Shawn said. "He's a good kid, Ryan. Everyone's saying he's got a shot at the state wrestling title next year. Are you still coaching him?"

"When he'll let me."

Jake scanned the crowd. Faces and names filled his brain from Nicole's yearbook. There was Cindy Monahan, from the cheerleading squad, Randall Meacham, Mr. Meacham's son who sang in the choir with Nicole. Grady Thompson, a friend of the Weingards and one of the boys who'd gone to the bowling alley that night. He was someone Jake needed to talk to as well. Not here. But Jake couldn't help but wonder whether someone at this gathering knew more about what happened to Nicole than they had said back in the day.

"I'm glad it's you," Shannon said.

"I'm sorry?"

"I believe in fate," she explained. "You were gone a long time, Jake. Anya thought you were never coming back."

"Well, that was the plan."

"See?" she continued. "Fate. I'd like to believe that God put you here so that when they finally found Nicole, you'd be the one to handle her case. Someone who cares about her. Or ... at least cares about people who loved her. You know?"

"Shannon, stop," Shawn told his wife. "Jake's got enough pressure on him. He doesn't need you guilt-tripping him."

"It's not a guilt trip. I just mean ... I'm glad Nicole's in good hands now. That's all."

"Thanks," Jake said. He paused a moment, waiting for Shawn or Shannon to either change the subject, or move to attend to their guests. They didn't.

"You saw her that night," he said. "I know you've been asked this a hundred times. But was there anything bothering her that you knew of? Maybe a secret boyfriend? Anything out of the ordinary?"

Shannon shook her head. "I wish there was. Believe me, I've asked myself that more times than any cop ever did. She was worried about how she was going to do on the SAT. We all were. But Nicole especially. She had plans. That was the only secret she carried. She wanted to go away to school and hadn't told her folks yet. She knew they couldn't afford to send her so she was hoping she'd do well enough on that test to get scholarship money. That's what we were talking about that night. She was wound pretty tight because of that. But that was it."

"That's understandable," Jake said.

"She went home before the rest of us did," Shawn said. "That's the only thing I remember. We tried to get her to stay and finish another game. But she said she wanted to get to bed early."

"I'll see ya tomorrow," Shannon said. "That was the last thing I ever said to her. I'll see ya tomorrow. I can still see her standing under that exit sign waving back. It's just frozen in my mind like that. Her wave. Then she turned her back and she was gone."

There were tears in Shannon's eyes. Shawn put his arm around his wife and kissed her on the cheek.

"Had she been drinking?" Jake asked.

Shannon shook her head. "None of us were. Well, I guess I can only speak for the two of us. But I'd swear on my life Nicole wasn't drinking. I don't know about Grady and Brenda."

"Grady might have been. He usually brought his own in those days." Shawn pointed his beer bottle at Grady Thompson. He was huge. Six two. Probably two hundred and twenty pounds. He leaned against one of the tent poles talking to several other former members of the Stanley High football team.

"She felt like a fifth wheel that night," Shannon offered. "I do know that. She said it. Grady was with Brenda Pollack. They'd just started dating that summer. And then there was Shawn and me. But there had always been Shawn and me. We'd been dating since eighth grade. I guess that's the only thing that was maybe a little off. Nicole called herself a fifth wheel. But joking, like. I didn't get that she was truly sad about it. But maybe it was one of the reasons she wanted to leave early. I don't know. Is that even helpful?"

"Everything might be helpful at this point," Jake said. "If she was feeling lonely that night, it's useful for me to know that."

"Anya's here," Shawn said. He downed the rest of his beer and put his hand on his wife's back. Sure enough, Anya walked in with Tim. Her parents weren't with her.

"Oh Lord," Shannon said. "Marty and Viv aren't coming after all, are they?"

"Don't worry about it," Shawn said. "They'll be all right."

Shannon gave her husband a dubious glare that conveyed Jake's thoughts on the matter as well. Marty and Vivian Strong might be many things. But fine was never one of them.

Shawn and Shannon excused themselves, leaving Jake to his quiet observation under the willow tree. He watched as Anya weaved her way through the crowd, stopping at every table, hugging every guest, thanking them for coming. One by one, they all told her how sorry they were. How much they still thought of her dead sister. They asked about her parents. Anya bore up under it, saying just the right things to make them all feel better while she tucked away her own heartache.

Jake finished his beer and thought about getting a second.

"She's amazing, isn't she?" Tim Brouchard was a hulking presence beside him. Jake bristled until Tim handed him that second beer.

"She's had a lot of practice with this," Jake said, twisting off the cap and thanking Tim for it.

"She hasn't slept in days," Tim said. "She won't stop moving. Cleaning her parents' house. Answering their phones for them. Just ... going from thing to thing trying to make it all okay for everyone. She's bound to crash at some point. I wouldn't hate it if you talked to her about it."

Jake turned to him. "You think Anya's ever done anything because I told her to?"

"Come on, Jake. I know you were there for her through a lot of the bad stuff when she was growing up. If you still think of her as a friend, well, maybe she could use one."

"I'll check in," Jake said.

"Where are you on this case? You know we need it solved as fast as possible."

There was the Tim Brouchard Jake knew. "I don't have anything for you right now, Tim. When I do, you'll know."

Tim straightened and waved to someone under the tents. Even here, Jake knew Tim wouldn't miss the opportunity to campaign.

"See that you do," Tim said, keeping his politician's smile locked in place. Then he moved off, ready to glad-hand with the people here to honor his dead sister-in-law.

"You had enough yet?" Gemma said. She'd started moving in the minute she saw Tim Brouchard. Jake knew his sister was one of the few people who could really read him.

"Getting there," Jake said. He pointed his beer bottle toward the side of the pole barn. A group of the younger kids gathered there, including Ryan and Chloe Weingard.

"You knew about that?" Jake asked.

"They're talking," she said. "That's what Ryan calls it. Talking. It's some sort of precursor to dating, maybe? I'm still trying to learn all the lingo."

"You like her?"

"Well enough. She called me Mrs. Gerald. I didn't care much for that. Set her straight."

Jake smiled. Technically, Gemma *was* still Mrs. Gerald. Though she and her third husband had been divorced for a couple of years, she hadn't changed her name on account of her youngest son, eight-year-old Aiden.

"Well, I'm glad you let the girl live to tell the tale."

"This is depressing," she said. "All these people. Half of them weren't even Nicole's friends. I guess that includes me too. I don't know how Anya puts up with it."

"It helps them make sense of it, maybe," Jake said. "Makes them feel like they did something. Showed respect. I don't know."

Gemma straightened as Anya broke from the crowd. She spotted Jake, smiled, and started walking toward them.

As she approached, she opened her arms and drew Gemma into an embrace. "Thank you for coming," she said. Gemma caught Jake's eye over Anya's shoulder. It was her nonverbal way of saying "watch yourself" to him. Jake waved her off.

Gemma made some excuse about having to check on Ryan, then left Jake and Anya alone.

"I'm glad you came," she said. "It's a comfort to my parents."

"Did they head back home?"

Anya nodded. "They're just not up to all of this. These were Nicole's friends. It's hard for them to see these people. All grown up. Moved on with their lives, you know? Shannon's the only one of Nic's friends they can stand being around. Even seeing her can drive my mother into a funk for days."

"What about you?"

Anya gave him that rehearsed smile he'd seen her giving everyone else here. As she took a breath to give him what he knew would be a canned response, he stopped her.

"Don't. Don't do that. Not with me."

Her face fell. "It's all there is, Jake."

"I'm worried about you. You're going to drive yourself into the ground. When's the last time you slept? Or ate a proper meal?"

"I'm fine," she said. "I'll just be glad when today is over."

"When's the last time you slept in your own bed?" Jake asked. Anya's eyes flickered and he knew he'd hit on it.

"Anya. You've been staying with Marty and Vivian? Since when?"

She put a hand on her cheek. "Don't worry about it."

"Since when?"

"Since the day you told me you found their daughter's body buried by the lake, okay? They need me!"

This was a conversation ... an argument ... he'd had with her at least a hundred times. Anya would always put her parents' needs ahead of her own and they would always let her.

"You're going to let them kill you too," he said, then instantly regretted it. He'd said that to her before as well. In fact, it was one of the last things he'd said the day they broke up all those years ago.

"I'm not your problem anymore, Jake," she said. "And this is none of your business."

"I'm sorry," he said. A tremor went through her. He looked at her. Really looked at her. She was thin and frail. Her white blouse hung off her. He watched as hives broke out across her chest where the top two buttons were open.

It was then that he saw it. A small gold pendant in the shape of an infinity symbol. A pink stone set into one loop. Without thinking, he reached for it, pulling it out and letting it rest in his palm.

"Where did you get this?" he asked. It was the exact same necklace that had been found on Nicole's remains. This was clean though. Polished to a shine. He hadn't authorized the release of any of Nicole's personal effects and wouldn't until after a conviction was made, if even then.

"Anya, how did you get this?"

Her eyes wide, Anya stepped back. She put a protective hand over her chest.

"I've had it forever," she said. "Tim gave it to me. For our first anniversary."

"I've never seen you wear that before," he said. His brain tried to connect the dots. Tim gave it to her. How the hell had Tim given it to her?

"I don't wear it very often. He asked me why the other day. So today I put it on."

Jake tried to keep his expression neutral. He didn't want to alarm her. She seemed not to know that her dead sister had been found wearing an identical piece of jewelry.

"Well, it's very pretty. Do you know where he got it?"

"Why are you acting so weird?"

"I was just trying to give you a compliment," he covered.

"Tim designs jewelry for me all the time. He's thoughtful that way. He designed my engagement ring too."

She held out her hand, showing her pear-shaped diamond ring. "He's Roland Carmichael's best customer."

"He's worried about you," Jake said, trying to change the subject as fast as he could. "Your husband. And so am I. If ... just ... if you need anything, you know you can call me."

Anya tucked her necklace back inside her blouse. Her hives had started to recede. "I just need you to find out who murdered my sister. That's what you can do for me."

She gave him that lilting smile, then went back to join her husband. From across the yard, Tim Brouchard gave Jake a knowing nod, thanking him for whatever he imagined Jake had said to his wife.

FIFTEEN

Nestled between a Thai takeout place and the last remaining one-hour photo shop in three counties, Carmichael's Creations had the dubious honor of being the only original business in the Blackhand Hills Strip Mall on County Road Eleven. Roland Carmichael had taken the business over from his father who worked out of his home for fifty years. He'd told his son he'd ruin things the moment he went "big time." He hadn't. Instead, Roland had steadily grown his clientele over the years, surviving the pandemic, three recessions, and a bout with colon cancer that should have felled him.

Jake had been in this shop only once before. He wouldn't have remembered it at all, except it was the last road trip he'd ever taken with his father. He'd been just seven years old and his mother wanted his dad to get him out of the house for a few hours so she could wrap his Christmas presents without Jake peeking.

Jake remembered the brooch Roland designed for Jake Cashen, Sr. A Christmas tree with tiny rubies, sapphires, and emeralds for ornaments. Sonya Cashen had seen one in a store window when her husband had taken her to Frankenmuth on what served as their honeymoon thirteen years before.

Jake paused before he got out of the car, the memories flooding through him. His father had been so excited when Roland pulled the small brooch out of a red box lined with velvet. They let him hold it. Jake marveled at the way the tiny jewels shimmered under the fluorescent lighting. It had been the only piece of "real" jewelry Jake Sr. ever bought for his wife. He'd saved for over a year, taking side jobs plowing driveways and parking lots during the winter, and landscaping during the spring and summer. He'd come home bone-weary and sun- or wind-burned. All these years later, Jake wondered if his mother would have simply preferred her husband had been home for dinner more.

But that was all before "the thing" happened. Before his father stopped sleeping. Before he woke Jake up in the middle of the night wanting help painting the garage door or the wood paneling in the basement. Before Jake would find his father sitting in a lawn chair in the backyard, talking to people who weren't there.

Jake stepped out of the car just as a young couple walked out arm in arm. The woman had happy tears in her eyes. She held her hand out, admiring the diamond ring her fiancé had just put there. It would be a June wedding, just like she'd always dreamed.

Jake walked into the store. Glass display cases took up most of the floor space in squares that grew smaller toward the center of the store. The more "affordable" items were housed in the outer squares. In the center, Roland showed off his most intricate, expensive pieces. Jake went to the case where Roland had necklaces displayed on headless neck mannequins.

Birthstones for every month on fine gold chains. Large diamond teardrop pendants. There were brooches too. But it was springtime. Mercifully, Jake saw no Christmas trees like his mother coveted. He moved down the row. On one end, he saw two necklaces featuring pink quartz, not too different from the ones the Strong sisters wore. Jake clutched the small card in his pocket.

Roland Carmichael came out from the back of the store. He wiped his hands on a cloth towel, chewing the remains of whatever lunch he'd had back there.

"Is that you, Jake?" Roland asked, squinting. "Well I'll be. Look what the cat dragged in."

"Hey, Roland," he said. "Good to see you."

Roland weaved his way through the display cases and met Jake on the other side of the necklaces.

"See something you like?" Roland asked. "Those teardrops are a real stunner. You have someone special in mind for something?" Roland gave Jake a mischievous wink.

"Not exactly," Jake said. He pulled the laminated piece of paper out of his pocket and laid it on the case between them. Roland wore his reading glasses on a chain around his neck. He slid them on and peered at the paper.

"What the hell happened to it?"

The picture was a blown-up image of Nicole Strong's necklace after Dr. Coleman's students had cleaned it off. Still, some of the setting was tarnished and had dirt and sand sticking to it.

"Do you recognize this piece?" Jake asked.

Roland picked up the card and held it close to his face, scrunching up his nose.

"Sure. It's a variation of one of my more popular designs."

He put the paper down and unlocked the case in front of them. He pulled out a necklace and laid it out. It was nearly identical to the photograph, a gold infinity symbol, only the inlaid stone was an opal, not rose quartz. Also, the infinity loop was slightly larger than the one Nicole Strong had worn.

"I call it a lover's knot," Roland said. "The infinity symbol represents a lifelong commitment. A forever love. Opals represent hope. The Romans used to call it the Cupid Stone."

"So this is definitely something with a romantic meaning?"

"Most of the stuff I sell is. But yeah. For sure."

"Do you remember designing this one in particular?"

"I think so. Yeah. I usually do them with opals like this one. But I've taken requests for different stones. What's this about, Jake?"

"Roland, I need to find out who you designed this necklace for if it's for sure one of yours."

"It would help if I could actually hold the thing or see the back of it."

Roland turned the necklace on the counter. He pointed to a small engraving on the back of the setting. As Jake peered closer, he recognized the letters R and C intertwined. "That's my mark."

Jake took out his phone. He had other images of Nicole's necklace on it. He set his phone down and let Roland scroll through them.

"Yep. There it is. I recognize the thing, sure. But people copy. This is one of mine."

"Do you know how many you made using rose quartz instead of opals?"

"Not many. Most women don't want quartz. They want the opals or some other precious gem. Rose quartz is more a sentimental choice. It means unconditional love and is said to have certain healing properties. But it's also a birthstone for January."

"Roland," Jake said. "Anya Brouchard has one of these. She said her husband designed it for her."

"That's right," Roland said. "I've done several pieces for Tim over the years. He's one of my best customers. I tried to talk him out of this one. Anya would have loved a sapphire. Or hell ... even a diamond. But ... Tim was partial to this stone. It was the second time he asked me to make it for him."

Jake froze. "What?"

"He bought a few of these over the years. Maybe four or five of them. Every time he got a new girlfriend, he'd come in for another one. I teased him about it. Told him infinity means forever. He bought a couple of the opals. Then did a couple with the quartz stones. You know, I never thought that one would settle down. He had a different girlfriend every year for a long time. Then he met Anya and that was all she wrote."

"Roland, I need to ask you to do something for me. Would you happen to have records of everyone you designed this particular piece for, using that particular stone? Was it more than just Tim?" Jake tapped the picture again.

Roland's eyes narrowed. He could get a court order if he needed to. But he was hoping Roland wouldn't ask him for one. He was also hoping Roland wouldn't ask too many questions about why Jake needed to see his records.

"My girl ... Tracy ... she's been on me for years to digitize all my records. I suppose I should. But I'm old-fashioned. I like my green ledgers. Wait here."

Roland went back into his office. Jake's throat got thick. It couldn't be what he thought it was. It had to be a coincidence. There had to be an explanation. But five minutes later, Roland Carmichael came out and opened one of his green ledgers. It was heavily tabbed. Roland selected a specific yellow tab and scrolled down the page with his finger.

"Tim's been coming to me since he graduated from college. I guess that's thirty-five years now."

Roland turned the ledger so Jake could read it. He bought his class ring from Roland. Other rings, presumably for women he dated. There was a diamond engagement ring purchased thirty years ago that he paid three thousand dollars for.

"That one didn't work out," Roland said, laughing. "Story I heard is that he caught her cheating on him. Don't know what happened to the ring. He kept making payments on it for over a year after that. Tim's an honorable guy."

Roland flipped the page and showed him an entry from nine years ago. Tim had paid five hundred dollars for Anya's rose quartz infinity necklace. Jake read a notation beside it. "Copy previous design."

"What does that mean?"

"Just what it says," Roland answered. He flipped the page back and tapped an entry. Jake checked the date. It was from August 1st, twenty-five years ago. The same infinity necklace with a rose quartz as its gemstone.

"Tim had you design two of these?" Jake said, his mind reeling.

"He did indeed."

"Can you check your records and tell me how many others you sold with that stone? Can you cross-reference them that way?" At that moment, Jake desperately wished Roland had taken his girl Tracy's advice and digitized all his records.

"Don't need to," Roland said. "I told you. I usually sold that design with opals. Only had three requests for a deviation. I sold a sapphire setting to Barney Clark in 2011 for his wedding anniversary. The other two were these rose quartzes you see here."

Jake curled his hands into fists. He had to remind himself to breathe.

My God, he thought. Tim Brouchard had bought the necklace Nicole Strong was wearing when she died. Then nine years ago, he had an identical one made and gave it to his wife. The woman who had grown up to look like her dead sister's twin.

"Do you mind?" Jake asked. He took his phone back out. After Roland nodded acquiescence, Jake used his phone's app to scan the ledger pages. Then he tucked his phone in his pocket.

"Roland," he said. "Would you do me a favor? It's small, but it's kind of important."

"Shoot."

"For now at least, can you promise me you won't tell anyone I was in here and what we talked about?"

Roland scowled, but he nodded. "Sure thing, Jake. I can do that."

"Thanks," Jake said. Then he left Roland wondering, as he went back to his car and dialed Tim Brouchard's number.

SIXTEEN

"I'm glad you called," Tim Brouchard said as he walked into Jake's office. It was Monday, just after four o'clock. Detective Ed Zender had already left for the day. Something he'd been doing a lot lately since Jake joined the crimes against persons unit. It was a rare weekday when Zender would work past two o'clock. Most of the time, it worked to Jake's advantage. No more so than today. For this meeting, he wanted Tim Brouchard alone.

"I'm getting a lot of calls," Brouchard said. "I suppose you are too. It's been weeks since they found that girl. We need some progress in this case."

Jake sat at his desk, eyeing Brouchard. He was a big guy. Over six feet. Thick around the middle now, but forty-odd years ago, he'd been a defensive lineman for the Stanley High School team.

Jake thought of Nicole. It was easy to imagine her as she was the night she died. So much like Anya, but even smaller. Only five foot one. At her last doctor's appointment four months before her disappearance, she'd weighed just ninety-eight pounds. Breakable. Tiny, even. Brouchard had a foot on her and over a hundred pounds. Jake focused on Tim's hands. He had long, beefy fingers. It would have been so easy for him to wrap them around Nicole's neck and squeeze the life out of her.

"Have a seat," Jake said. He'd moved out all the items relating to Nicole's case. Tim knew plenty, but not the most critical details.

Tim complied, stopping at the coffee machine first and pouring himself a stale cup before he sat down with a thud. Jake joined him, holding a thin file folder containing a couple of photographs taken out at the lake shore dig site, and the ones he'd taken on his phone at Carmichael's Creations.

"So what's the running theory?" Tim asked. "Who have you interviewed? I wouldn't mind observing if you have a person of interest. We need to make sure everything is by the book. You get that, don't you?"

"Of course. Is there anything about me that would make you think I'd want to cut corners, Tim?"

"Oh no. No. I'm not saying that. Sorry. That wasn't the most elegant way to make my point."

"What is your point, Tim?"

"I just mean ... I'm here to help. I'm here to make sure you get everything you need with this one."

"I surely do appreciate that, Tim. If you don't mind my asking, how are things at home through all of this?"

Tim let his shoulders drop. He took a sip of his shitty coffee but made no indication it bothered him.

"It's been tough," Tim said. "But you know Anya, she'd never let anyone know that. She just does what she always does. Makes sure everyone around her is okay. I've been asking her to take some time off. I offered to take her away for a little while. She's been wanting to go on a cruise for a long time. Athens. Italy. Places like that. She won't hear of it though. Says she can't leave her parents right now."

"She'll never leave them," Jake said. "I wish she would."

Tim sat back. "Yeah. She's told me that over the years. She told me that when you came back to town. That you resented how attached she was to Marty and Viv."

"I never resented it," Jake said. "It was just hard to watch her put the oxygen mask on everyone but herself."

"That's exactly it," Tim said. "That right there. She runs herself ragged for those two. And God bless her, but Viv counts on it. You know, last month, she called Anya in the middle of the night. Like two a.m. Wanting her to come over because she couldn't find her purse. And off she went. Anya is up by five every morning. She's at the Vedge Wedge by six to open. Every single day. But she went. Never even had the thought to tell Vivian she'd help her later. It's ridiculous. And there's no talking her out of it. My wife is just hard-wired to help other people. It's one of the things that drew me to her."

Jake felt his whole body go stiff. One of the things …

"Tim," Jake said. "How well did you know Nicole Strong?"

Tim didn't meet Jake's stare at first. He kept his gaze soft, his expression unreadable. Would he try to lie? Say he never knew her at all? Or was Tim smart enough to catch on to the fact that Jake might already know something different?

"I knew who she was," Tim answered.

"She was seventeen when she went missing. So you were what? Thirty-one, thirty-two?"

"Sounds about right."

"Already a lawyer. Already established."

"I had my own practice then," Tim said. "Criminal defense. Started out taking court appointments. Then got hired in as an assistant prosecutor after about ten years of that."

"You gonna run for judge? I heard Larraby isn't interested in running to keep Judge Rand's seat."

Tim smiled. "The bench has never been my ambition. But I can't say it wouldn't be nice. It's political, but it's above the fray from where I am now. I don't know. Anya's been on me to start thinking about retiring. I told her I'd do it if she did. That pretty much ends the conversation right there."

"I bet it does."

Jake waited, letting a heavy silence fall. Tim Brouchard was a lot of things. Stupid wasn't one of them. He knew. The bastard knew this wasn't just a casual update on the case.

Jake took one photo out of his file and slid it in front of Tim.

"She was wearing this," Jake said. "That hasn't hit the internet. But Dr. Coleman's people found this tangled in her bones."

Tim looked at the photo. The only sign of stress he displayed was the contraction of his throat as he swallowed. Brouchard was still wearing his suit jacket. The ventilation in the office was awful. The man would sweat, Jake had no doubt.

"Do you recognize it?"

Tim's eyes flicked to Jake's. He put his palm flat on top of the picture then began to tap it.

"Tim, I'm gonna need you to level with me. You knew that girl well enough to give her that necklace." Jake pulled out a second item from the file. It was the scanned copy of Roland Carmichael's ledger page showing Tim's order history. Jake had highlighted the two entries, fifteen years apart. One for the rose quartz necklace found on Nicole Strong, the second, for the one he'd given Anya.

Still, Tim said nothing.

"Roland's only had two custom orders for that particular necklace. He usually sells them with opals. But you came in asking for versions with that pink quartz. Twice. I've got the first one in an evidence bag. The second, I saw around your wife's neck, Tim."

Tim Brouchard gave Jake an icy stare. Jake could feel Brouchard's hatred of him starting to fill.

"What the hell are you doing?" Tim asked.

"I'm trying to find out what happened. What was your relationship with Nicole Strong?"

"You son of a bitch," Tim said. "This? This is what you have?"

"You commissioned an expensive necklace for a seventeen-year-old girl when you were a grown man. Tell me why."

"What are you accusing me of?"

"You know how this goes," Jake said. "I'm not going to insult your intelligence, Tim. Don't insult mine."

Tim sat back. He gripped his coffee cup. Then he downed the last of it, grimacing at the lousy taste.

"You want something stronger?" Jake asked. "Pretty sure Ed keeps a bottle of hooch in his desk drawer."

"You can go to hell. I'm done talking to you." He said it, but he made no move to leave. Jake could guess exactly what was going through Tim Brouchard's mind. He knew he didn't have to sit here. But he would also desperately want to know what Jake had. Soon enough, Jake planned to tell him.

"You saw her in town? Or maybe at the diner on Flanders Road. She waited tables there back in the day. Is that how you first met her? Tim, I'm gonna find out. You know I'm gonna find out. So why don't you do us both a favor and give me a reason to get you out from under this."

Tim stayed silent, but still didn't get up from his chair.

Jake reached behind him and pulled Nicole Strong's yearbook off his desk. He had it tabbed to the CAA page. He pointed to the picture of Nicole wearing her gold pin.

"Gemma told me it was a chastity pin. She had a good laugh about that. Said everyone in this club wore them. That it was almost a private joke among them. My sister didn't come out and call Nicole a slut or anything. But I got the impression the girl got around. She was young, yeah. But seventeen. Just over the legal age of consent. If you were screwing her, it wouldn't have been a crime, Tim."

Tim shook his head. "I don't know about any pin she wore, Jake."

"No. Just the necklace you gave her. Roland told me that quartz symbolized unconditional love."

"I was an advisor," Tim said. "FPLO. The Future Professional Leaders Organization. I had my own practice then. I gave some talks at the school. There was a mentoring program. Nicole came to my office a few times with a couple of her classmates."

"Which classmates?" Jake asked.

"I don't even remember," Tim said. "But Nicole was different. She asked good questions. Seemed genuinely interested."

"And you took an interest in her."

"I wasn't looking to screw her," Tim said. "That wasn't it. But she was hungry, you know? Eager to get as far away from home as she could once she graduated. She asked me if I'd write her a letter of recommendation for college. She wanted to get out of Stanley. I got the sense she didn't really have anyone to talk to about all that. Her parents wanted her home, going to community college. Getting some dead-end job here but always within sight of them. Nicole wanted other things. She didn't know how to get them. I tried to help her."

"Then it got physical?"

"I never said that," Tim said. "I was her mentor. That's all."

"You never told anyone this. Christ, Tim. Have you ever told Anya this?"

Tim's face went hard. "It never came up. I don't care what you think. But Anya and I didn't start dating ... I didn't even know she existed ... until hell, ten years after Nic went missing."

"You were close enough to her that you felt compelled to get this girl a token of your affection. You paid three hundred dollars for it. That's a pretty extravagant gift."

No answer.

"We're done here," Tim said. "I've done nothing wrong. Not back then. Not now. And you? You've been waiting for something like this, haven't you? Ever since you rolled back into town with your tail tucked between your legs. You had no choice. I don't care what story you cooked up and fed to Meg Landry. I know you were canned by the FBI."

"This isn't about me, Tim."

"The hell it's not. Boy. I bet you got a bona fide hard-on when you found that necklace. What are you planning on telling my wife?"

"That's up to you, Tim," Jake said, leaning forward. "Are you sticking to your story that your relationship with her dead ... no ... her murdered sister was platonic?"

"Screw you, Jake."

"She was pregnant, Tim."

Tim Brouchard blanched. In that split second, beads of sweat formed above his brow.

"How the hell do you know that?"

"Dr. Coleman found fetal ear bones among Nicole's remains. She was three months pregnant, Tim."

"You think it was mine?"

"I don't have to think anything. In about a week, Dr. Coleman will have a DNA profile from them. I expect a cheek swab from you. Then we'll know for sure."

The sweat on Tim's face went from beads to a slow trickle. Jake was bluffing. There would be no DNA. He hoped Tim wasn't sophisticated enough to call him on it.

"I'm done with this."

"It's not done with you, Tim."

Brouchard finally got up from his chair. He glowered at Jake.

"Figure out what side of this you wanna be on," Jake said. "For the moment, this stays between us. But that's not a long-term promise. You know why it can't be."

"I've done nothing wrong. I've broken no laws. And I had nothing to do with whatever happened to that girl. Whatever relationship we had, it was over. Way over by the time she went missing. You've got nothing, Jake."

"I've got your DNA. So why don't you tell me where you were the night Nicole disappeared. Start there."

Tim threw his hands up. "You're asking me to tell you where I was on some random night twenty-five years ago?"

"It wasn't a random night. A girl that you had a relationship with … an inappropriate one. I don't care if she was of the legal age of consent. She was seventeen. She was a high school student. And you were in a position of power over her. You know how bad that looks. You knew it then. Her disappearance was big news. And you said nothing. Not a word. You didn't tell Virgil Adamski what you knew. That makes you look guilty. As much as that necklace or anything else you've done."

"I did nothing wrong," Tim said, straightening his jacket.

"So prove it," Jake said.

"That's not my job," Tim said, turning to go. "It's yours."

Jake rose. He grabbed Tim by the shoulder and made him face him. The two men glared at each other. White-hot rage poured through Jake's veins.

"Here's what's going to happen now," Jake said. "Your very next phone call when you leave here is to the A.G.'s office. You tell them you need a special prosecutor appointed to this case. You tell them you have a conflict of interest. Your wife is the sister of the victim. If I don't get a phone call by the end of the day with that special prosecutor's name, I'm gonna call the A.G.'s office myself. Trust me, you don't want that. Are we clear?"

Tim said nothing. A vein bulged in his neck. Jake let him go, pushing him away.

"She looks just like her," Jake said. "You sick son of a bitch. You preyed on that girl. Then you preyed on her sister. Whether you killed her or not, that's always going to be true."

Tim took a large step backward. There was fear in his eyes, but he kept his mouth tightly shut.

"Go to hell, Jake," he said. When he left, he slammed the door behind him.

Seventeen

On a Tuesday morning, retired detective Virgil Adamski would only be one place. Jake knew he'd find him in the back room of Papa's Diner in downtown Stanley. Spiros and Tessa Papatonis, the restaurant's proprietors, served a special breakfast only for their favorite patrons, the Wise Men. Or so they called themselves. It was an ever dwindling group of retired law enforcement officers who met twice a month to tell their war stories and get unlimited cups of Tessa's strong coffee and Spiros's heavenly cooking.

"Jake!" Tessa called out as Jake entered the restaurant. She always lit up and got teary-eyed when Jake showed up. She made a beeline for him, pulling him into a motherly embrace. A little over a year ago, Jake had become an honorary part of her family as far as Tessa was concerned. He'd delivered justice for her own daughter.

"Come sit. Come eat," Tessa said. "Those wise asses are in the back. I suppose you already knew that."

"Thanks," Jake said. "I'll just take a cup of coffee today if you don't mind."

Tessa waved him off. Jake knew she'd bring him a heaping plate of bacon and eggs no matter what.

Thankfully, there was nobody else in the restaurant at the moment. Jake had waited until after nine for that exact reason. He trusted Spiros and Tessa to mind their own business, but no one else from town. He walked to the back room. It was just Virgil, Chuck Thompson, and Bill Nutter today. Jake wondered if they'd invite Ed Zender if and when he ever retired. Or him, for that matter.

"Hey, Jake," Chuck said. "We were just talking about you. Wondering when you were gonna grace our presence and rub the lamp."

The older he got, the more Chuck Thompson spoke in riddles. A former shift lieutenant detective, he'd been acquainted with his grandfather back in the day. Jake had recently learned there was a rumor Chuck had even vied for his Grandma Ava's affections when she was still single. However it ended, they'd remained friends, so Jake had to assume Chuck had been good to both of them.

Virgil was the only one of the men who didn't smile as Jake approached. He knew. It was a cop thing, but Jake sensed Virgil already guessed this wasn't just a social visit.

As predicted, Tessa sat a steaming plate in front of Jake then poured his coffee. As the rest of the table grew quiet, Tessa's smile faded. She understood this might be a business breakfast too and excused herself, shutting the double doors to close this part of the restaurant off from anyone else who might get nosey.

"What's the word, Jake?" Virgil said.

"I wanted you to hear it from me," Jake said. It went without saying this couldn't leave the table. Though it was hard won, he'd grown to trust these men. Among them, they had a wealth of knowledge about Worthington County and crime solving in general. Though they might not be the oracle they fancied themselves, Jake valued their collective wisdom, nonetheless.

"I may have a break in Nicole Strong's case," he said. He pulled out the pictures he had of Nicole's necklace and the ledger sheet from Roland Carmichael. He laid them both on the table. The men peered closer, confused by what they saw.

"This hasn't been in the press," he said. "And it won't be. But she was found with that necklace and now I know who gave it to her."

Virgil sat back. "I never saw that on her. I pored over the most recent pictures her mother and friends had of her. But I've never seen that."

Jake took a breath. "Tim Brouchard gave it to her. Roland had the records. And Brouchard admitted that much to me. Says he mentored her through this young professionals group."

"Christ," Virgil said, throwing his napkin on the table. "He was banging her?"

"He hasn't admitted that part, but yeah. I think it's safe to say."

"He's almost sixty," Bill Nutter said. "He would have been what, in his early thirties back then? She was seventeen."

"I'm sure he thinks that matters," Jake said. "That she was of the legal age of consent. That's as close as he got to admitting a sexual relationship."

"I'd say that's a pretty clear admission," Virgil said. "That son of a bitch. Dammit. Jake."

"As near as I can figure," Jake said, "they probably started seeing each other early in the year she disappeared. He commissioned this necklace from Roland late that spring and gave it to her in June. She had already broken up with Alton Bardo by then."

"What was he doing back then?" Chuck asked.

"He had his own law practice," Jake said. "Doing mostly defense work. That's how he got involved with this FPLO organization. They solicited local business owners. He said Nicole was one of the only ones who seemed serious about what he had to say. It grew from there."

"She was a kid," Virgil fumed. "He's married to her sister. God."

"I know."

"She looks like her," Virgil said. "I can't even go into that vegan place because of it. Not that I would anyway. But … Jake, they could be twins."

"I know that too. Tim's claiming that's just a coincidence. He started dating Anya years after Nicole's death. Only he never told anyone about his relationship with her. He never came forward after she went missing. And he's never told his wife he had a romantic relationship with her dead sister."

"Does she know?" Nutter asked.

Jake folded his hands and rested them on the table. "No. At least, not from me. I haven't told her."

"Are you planning on it?" Virgil asked.

"I honestly don't know. Not yet anyway. Brouchard's a creep. But so far, that's all I can prove."

"She could be in danger," Virgil said. "You think he killed Nicole?"

"I think he's just moved to the top of my list of suspects. Only I don't have anything other than this necklace right now. Being a creep isn't a crime."

"He's a liar," Chuck said. "He's kept this secret for twenty-five years. From his wife, even."

Jake locked eyes with Virgil. Nicole Strong also had one big secret. Virgil knew it now, but Jake hadn't spoken of it to anyone outside the department other than Virgil yet. Virgil gave him a quiet nod.

"She was pregnant," Jake said. "I've got physical proof of that. But no way to prove paternity."

"Brouchard doesn't need to know that," Virgil said.

"No, he does not. I've got him convinced I'm waiting on labs that'll give me a DNA profile on the baby. I just wish like hell that were true. I'm hoping the threat of it will be enough for Brouchard to do something to help himself."

"He's a weasel," Chuck said. "I've always thought that. A smarmy, self-important asshole. He said nothing. All these years. That's not the act of an innocent man."

"Does he have an alibi?" Nutter asked.

"Says he can't be expected to remember where he was on a random Friday twenty-five years ago," Jake said.

"His girlfriend went missing!" Virgil said, nearly shouting it. He pounded his fist to the table with enough force to levitate his silverware.

"Easy," Jake said. "I trust Spiros and Tessa. But there's no point putting them in an awkward position. This is strictly Cop's Code. I know you all know that."

"Consider this your sanctuary, Jake," Chuck said. "But we know *you* know that."

"I do."

"None of her friends knew," Virgil said. "They all told me she hadn't been seeing anyone since she and Bardo ended things. I never got any indication that was anything other than amicable. And that kid was long gone by the time she went missing. I told you that."

"She got pregnant in the middle of the summer," Jake said. "That we know. But that's it. And now I know she was sleeping with at least Tim Brouchard a few months before that."

"She could have made things awkward for him," Virgil said. "If she told him she was carrying his kid, it might have ruined things for him. He's always had political ambitions. How would he explain getting a seventeen-year-old girl pregnant?"

"A seventeen-year-old girl he was supposed to be mentoring through a school-sponsored program. Twenty-five years ago, that would have been a slam-dunk career-ender."

"But you can't prove it," Nutter said. "I mean, how can you prove it at this point? You've got no physical evidence linking him to the murder. Nobody saw anything the night she disappeared, right?"

"Not that anyone's come forward to admit," Virgil said. "What do you need, Jake?"

"I don't know," he said.

"What's your gut telling you?" Nutter asked. "You think Brouchard was capable of doing this?"

"Of course. Nicole Strong was a hundred pounds soaking wet. She cared enough about Tim Brouchard to be wearing the necklace he gave her on the night she died. If that was the most disturbing piece of this, that would be enough to make me think he's guilty. But I haven't told you how I figured out he gave her that jewelry. I saw Anya wearing an identical one at Nicole's memorial service.

Brouchard had a second one made for her after they started dating years ago."

"My God," Virgil said. "Jake."

"I know," he said.

"You can't tell her," Virgil said. "Christ, Jake. She's married to the guy who might now be your main suspect. If this were any other case, you know you can't say anything."

"I know," Jake said.

"She was wearing his necklace when she died," Chuck whispered, still processing it.

"And he went after her sister ... just in time for her to grow up looking exactly like Nicole," Virgil said. "Jake, I don't like it. Not one bit."

"He's got to know this is going to come out," Nutter said. "You think he told his wife himself by now?"

"Honestly? No," Jake said. "When we talked, he was actually trying to spin it that he's done nothing wrong. Anya isn't going to see it that way when she finds out. Though I'll admit, even before all of this, I couldn't understand what she saw in him."

"The girl's got Daddy issues," Virgil said. "Sorry, Jake. I know you have a history with her. But it's true. It's been a long time. But Jesus. For years, I'd pay a visit to the Strongs. To let them know I'd never forget about Nicole. Jake ... once or twice, Tim was there at the house when I talked to them. After he married Anya. It's been years. But the last time I went over there, it was the twentieth anniversary of the night she went missing. They made me dinner. We talked about the case. Brouchard was there. He was there!"

Jake felt Virgil's anger. It was as if it had risen up and hovered over the table like a specter, choking the air from Jake's lungs.

He knew. All this time. He knew. But did it make Tim Brouchard a murderer?

"I need more," Jake voiced his thoughts. "I need to understand Nicole better. I need to reconstruct the last days and weeks of her life. Maybe she confided in someone. There had to be something. A tipping point. What made her leave with someone that night just hours before she was going to take a test that would partly determine her future?"

"Anya might hate you forever," Virgil said. "Are you prepared for that?"

"What do you mean?"

"You've got information that'll explode that woman's life. And for right now, you can't say a damn word. But she's going to find out eventually. Even though you're not the cause, you've got your own history with Anya Brouchard. She might resent you just for being the messenger. Just ... be prepared for it."

Jake knew. The last thing he wanted to do was hurt her. But this was a bomb he knew he couldn't save her from.

Two seconds later, his phone buzzed with an incoming text. His blood froze as he read it. It was from Anya herself. If there was any doubt whether her husband had filled her in, Anya's message dispelled it. The text read:

> Hi. I got the keys to the storage unit from my mother. If you'd like to look through what's left of Nicole's things, can we meet out there first thing in the morning? It's the U-Store out on Grace Church Road. Meet me at nine. A.

Jake hovered his thumb over the message. He let out a breath as he answered with a simple.

K.

He filled the others in on what she'd said.

"How are you gonna get through that without saying anything?" Virgil asked.

Jake pocketed his phone. "I don't know. I honestly don't." He'd have exactly twenty-four hours to decide.

Eighteen

Each garage door at the U-Store lot off Grace Church Road was painted in alternating rainbow colors. Unit number 242 had a red door. Inside of it, Jake could only hope he'd find some answers.

He waited ten minutes before Anya pulled up in her blue Prius. She was alone. Two calls Jake had made to Tim Brouchard went unanswered. Anya's bright smile and wave answered one big question for him. Brouchard had not yet told her about what Jake knew. Now he'd have to decide if he would break protocol and tell her himself.

"Sorry I'm late," Anya said as she got out of her car. "Michelle was supposed to spell me at the Vedge Wedge but her babysitter fell through. I had to wait for LeeAnn to get there."

"It's fine," Jake said. "I just got here myself. Does that mean you have to hurry back?"

"No. I told LeeAnn she could close right after the lunch crowd. I'll go back tonight to do prep for tomorrow morning."

The late spring sun beat down on Jake's head. Anya had to shield her eyes as she walked up to the keypad on the right side of the red garage door. She punched in a code and the door automatically slid upward in great, screeching fits.

"It's been a while since I've been out here," she said. "Actually, I haven't since the day we moved everything in here."

Anya flipped a light switch and Jake followed her into the 10x20 bay.

There wasn't much to see. In one corner was a garment rack with dresses hung in plastic bags. A dresser drawer stood beside that. Then, stacked against one wall were five plastic storage tubs. Red ones with green lids. The kind you use to store Christmas decorations.

"Lindy Potter gave me a deal when I rented this unit," Anya said. "I probably should have just taken a smaller one. But we were going to maybe put Nicole's car in here."

"What happened to it?" Jake asked. "Her car."

Long ago, Jake remembered the cobalt-blue Dodge Neon parked behind Anya's parents' house. Her parents wouldn't let anyone drive it. They'd kept Nicole's room as a shrine for as long as he could remember back then. A locked door no one but Anya's mother would ever go into.

"Finally ended up donating it," Anya said. "When I moved my parents into the condo six years ago, this unit was a compromise. I wanted to donate, sell, or pitch most of this stuff. Maybe it's cold of me, but I couldn't see the point in hanging on to all of it. I wanted my parents to keep one or two mementos. They flat out refused. It turned into a major drama and they were gearing up to use it as the excuse not to move altogether. They got to the point they just couldn't maintain that house anymore. My dad's had both hips replaced. My mother's not nearly as strong as she was before her stroke. So, this was a compromise. We saved all of Nicole's things. I told them they could come out here and sit with this stuff whenever they wanted. It's silly, maybe. But it's the closest thing we've had to a grave all these years. Until ..."

"I get it," Jake said. "And I know how Marty and Viv were ... are ... This makes sense."

"Only they never did come out here," Anya said. "Not even when Tim and I brought everything here. They just watched us drive away. My mom said it's enough just knowing this stuff is here if and when she wants it. Now that Nicole's finally been laid to rest, I'll probably start lobbying to get rid of everything once and for all."

"Can I ask you to hold off on that? Just in case ..."

"Oh, of course. Everything here is yours, Jake. But after..."

Jake walked over to the garment rack. One by one, he slid Nicole's dresses down the rack.

"She was a bridesmaid a couple of times," Anya said, pointing to two pink, puffy-sleeved dresses. "This was her prom dress for her junior year. I loved this one. I wanted to wear it when you took me our junior year. My mother wouldn't hear of it. We got into a major fight."

"She threatened to throw you out of the house," Jake said. "I forgot about that until just now."

It was a black, strapless dress with a short skirt. Jake was surprised Marty and Viv let their daughter leave the house in something that covered so little. The dress was certainly modest compared to what he'd seen high school girls wearing these days. But he supposed that just meant he was getting old.

"She went with Alton Bardo that year," Jake said.

"Yeah."

"Do you remember much about him? You never talked about him. Until I got into this case, I had no idea that's who she was dating. Why didn't you tell me?"

"I was eleven years old when my sister dated him," Anya said. "Back then, I didn't even know his last name. It wasn't like Nic confided things like that to me. I was a nuisance to her then. And after? It was just easier not to remember. Not to talk about any of that."

"It's okay," Jake said. "But whatever you can remember now might help."

"He didn't come to the house very often. Only once or twice when he picked my sister up. My parents were furious she was dating him. Said he was just going to amount to a criminal like his brothers and father. At the time, I had no idea what they meant by that. To me he seemed so mysterious. Like James Dean in *Rebel Without a Cause* or something. Definitely sexy. But they were broken up long before Nic went missing. Almost a year."

Jake walked over to the Christmas-colored bins. They were labeled with sharpies. Clothes. Pictures. Jewelry. Nic's Schoolwork.

"May I?" Jake asked as he went for the bin labeled "Pictures."

"You don't have to ask," Anya said. "Seriously, Jake. Whatever you need."

He picked up the bin and set it on the ground by itself. Some dust had collected on the top. Jake pried open the plastic lid. There were hundreds of loose photos. He picked a couple up at random. One was a picture of Nicole and Shannon Weingard standing beside a mall Santa. They were probably thirteen or fourteen years old. In another photo, Nicole and Anya sat in rocking chairs outside a Cracker Barrel, a checkerboard in between them. Jake's breath caught. Anya was probably ten or so years old. Nicole, at fifteen, looked exactly like Anya had when they started high school.

"I forgot about that one," Anya said, peering over his shoulder. "She had a big cork board on her wall. I remember that one was tacked in the top corner."

Sure enough, several of the pictures Jake held had small tack holes in them. There were other items too. Award ribbons from various school contests. First Place at eighth grade Field Day. Best Trot at Happy Day Horse Camp. Buried further down in the box, Jake saw yearbooks. He pulled one out. It was from Stanley Middle School, Nicole's seventh grade year. He flipped through a couple of pages. Every blank space was covered with her classmates and teachers' signatures.

"She made sure everybody signed her books," Anya said. "She'd spend like a month on it."

"To a great girl I met this year," Jake read, smiling.

"Detective Adamski looked through all of that too," Anya said. "Not here, obviously. But back at the house. That was tough on my parents. My mother kind of went off on him at one point. Made a big scene. She accused him of defiling Nicole's things."

"I can't imagine how hard it was for her back then," Jake said. "I'm sure Virgil didn't take it personally."

"They're pretty angry with him. That's something I wanted to give you a heads up about. I think I've talked them both off their ledges for the time being. But my mom wanted to go to the local news. She knows Detective Adamski lives out at Echo Lake. She feels like her daughter was right under Adamski's nose and ..."

"Trust me. Virgil blames himself plenty for all of that. But I have to tell you. So far, I think he did the best he could with what he had."

"I know. I don't blame him at all. I know this case affected him. He's told me as much over the years. I just wish …"

"Yeah," Jake said. "Me too."

He put the lid on the bin and opened another one. It was filled with plastic baggies containing Nicole Strong's jewelry. Mostly earrings, but quite a few necklaces and bracelets too. Some looked homemade.

"She went through a phase," Anya said. "She made beaded bracelets and necklaces for everybody. My dad would get so angry finding these tiny plastic beads all over the house. They'd make an awful noise when they got sucked up in my mom's vacuum cleaner."

It wasn't lost on Jake that every story Anya told seemed to end in some screaming match between her parents. It was happening even before Nicole went missing. After? Things had gotten almost untenable. Anya grew up in a war zone.

It would take Jake some time to go through the rest of the baggies. He wanted to see if anything else bore Roland Carmichael's mark. Was there anything else Tim might have given her?

Tim. Anya had moved over to the tall dresser against the wall. She opened the top drawer and took out a tie-dyed tee shirt. Anya wiped a tear as she held the shirt against her own chest.

"This is why I never come out here," she said. "It just makes me sad. For so long, my mom said she could still smell Nicole on all these things. I never could. But then, one day … I was maybe sixteen or so. I found her sitting in the middle of the floor of Nic's room crying. I mean wailing. She said it was gone. Like overnight. She said the smell was just gone. She never went into my sister's room after that. She kept the door locked. As far as I know, it stayed that way up until Tim and I moved all this out and brought it here."

"Tim," Jake muttered. His chest felt tight. "So he went through all of this with you?"

"He helped me pack it up," Anya said. "That was a fight even. My mom and dad didn't want anybody but me to touch this stuff. They wouldn't have even allowed that but the two of them weren't really in the best physical shape to do it themselves. We sent them out to dinner then Tim and I packed it up. We loaded the stuff into the back of his car and we brought it all here."

"Who else has the code to that keypad?" Jake asked.

Anya gave him a curious look. "Do you think someone would want to mess with this stuff? Do you think there's really anything in here that will help you find who did this? I told you. Detective Adamski ..."

"I don't know," Jake said. "Maybe not. Can you remember whether anyone else came to look at her things? I mean, beyond your parents or Virgil? Any of her friends that came to the house back then?"

Anya shook her head. "Not that I remember. But I was twelve. That said, my parents wouldn't have allowed it. My mother in particular. It's like I told you. She was protective of it. That smell she said was there for all those years. Then her anger at Adamski for "defiling" it. So no. I don't think anyone else has ever been through this stuff."

"The code though," Jake said. "In the six years this has been out here, who has access to it?"

"Just me," she said. "And I wrote the code down for my mom and dad way back when. I just don't think they've ever used it."

"Does Tim know you were planning on meeting me out here today?"

Anya put the tee shirt back in the drawer and closed it. "I told him. He's on his way to Columbus today. He's speaking at a trial practice seminar. He'll be gone for a couple of days."

Jake's heart settled with relief. The longer Tim Brouchard stayed away from Anya, the better.

"Jake, what aren't you telling me?"

She came to him. Before Jake could answer, she put a halting hand up.

"You know what? Don't. I don't want to know. I don't even know if I want to know if you find something damning in all this stuff. I know it's silly, but I don't think I'm ready to hear all Nicole's sordid secrets."

"What makes you think she had any?"

"I don't. I don't know. In some ways, that's the hardest part of all of this. I've managed to just put my sister in this compartment. Almost like she's not a real person anymore. She's just been this ... spirit. Or an idea. She can be whatever I make of her. Now ... it's just all so real. I hadn't realized how much keeping her on a pedestal of sorts has made this easier to bear for me. I know it sounds crazy. But there's a part of me that wishes nobody had ever found her. Ugh. Now that I said it out loud, it sounds so awful. That's not what I mean. Not exactly."

Did she know? On some level, had Anya suspected some of her sister's dark truths and how they might impact her? One thing was clear: he could not let her stay in the dark about Tim's possible role in this forever.

"I'd like to take these bins with me," Jake said. "Get them back to the office so I can organize these things."

"Of course," Anya said. "Between the two of us, I think we can get them loaded into your car. They're not very heavy. Tim and I had no trouble when we did this the last time."

"When's Tim coming back again?" Jake said. "Um ... I may need to brief him."

"Saturday," she said. "There's an outing for the instructors at the seminar on Friday night. He always stays for that then comes home the next morning."

Three days. It was as long as Jake could allow Anya to remain in the dark. Then he'd have to play a hand in possibly destroying her entire world.

NINETEEN

By noon the next day, Jake had the contents of Nicole Strong's short life dumped out on three folding tables he'd wrangled from the union hall. Sheriff Landry had let him take over an old storage room two doors down from his office. Jake spent the better part of the morning turning the place into his bigger, more private war room for the duration of this investigation. Now, he just had to figure out how to make sense of it all.

"Will you be able to use any of it?" Landry asked. Her voice startled Jake out of his own head. He hadn't even heard her come in.

"I don't know yet," he said. "Anya said her mother kept everything. I mean, there are twenty-five-year-old candy wrappers in here."

Landry stepped forward. She picked up one of said candy wrappers. It came from banana-flavored taffy with a joke written inside. "What kind of shoes do frogs wear?" she read. She turned the wrapper over. "Open toad."

"Ouch," Jake said.

"You think any of this is more than garbage?"

"I don't know. I can't assume anything at this stage. But that's not my biggest problem."

"What is?"

"Oh ... I'm sorry ..." A new voice came from the hallway. Jake turned. Birdie Wayne stood there looking a little sheepish. She had her hands on her hips, her gun belt snug around her small waist. He was still getting used to seeing her in her brown deputy's uniform. She wore her hair pulled back in a tight bun.

"Were you looking for me?" Landry asked.

"Sort of," she said. Birdie stepped into the room, eying all of Nicole Strong's things. Landry handed her the candy wrapper. Birdie read it and smiled at the corny joke.

"She was a teenage hoarder, I think," Jake said.

"Maybe not," Birdie said. "Girls save things for all sorts of reasons. A friend might have given her this. Or it could have been part of a Valentine from somebody she cared about."

Landry smiled. "She's right. When I was a kid, I had an old cigar box filled with Dum-Dum wrappers. I saved them every time I went to the doctor. You used to be able to send them in and get prizes."

"Great," Jake said. "So you're telling me I just have to think like a teenage girl to make sense of this."

"Or ..." Birdie said. "You could get some help from someone who's been there."

"That's a brilliant idea," Landry said. "You can fit it in?"

"Wait, what?" Jake said.

Landry had an arm around Birdie. "I like it. Jake, I like what Erica did compiling the cell phone footage from the ground-breaking ceremony. She knows a lot of the same players you do. We're shorthanded on the streets so I hate pulling her, but this is important too. Erica, do you mind working a split shift for a while?"

"What? Um. No. Of course not. Whatever you need, Sheriff. That is ... if Jake's all right with ..."

"Of course he is," Landry said. "Aren't you, Jake?"

"Sure," he said. It wasn't a bad idea. Landry was right. When it came to speaking girl-ease, he was lost. Birdie might have some useful insights. He also didn't mind her not working out in the field as much. It'd be safer for her.

"Great. That's settled. Erica, you do what Jake needs from say nine to noon every day. Then you're back on field ops for the rest of your shift. Get with Sergeant Hammer to work out the logistics. Now ... what's your biggest problem, Jake? You were saying?"

"This," Jake said. "Even if we find something useful, we're gonna have an evidentiary hurdle. Anya told me Brouchard was the one who helped her pack all this stuff up and take it to the storage unit six years ago."

Landry's face fell. "Things are looking worse and worse for him, aren't they?"

Jake didn't answer. Birdie came farther in the room and started picking up some of the items from the bin containing photographs. She pulled out three VHS tapes. Their labels had begun to yellow and peel off.

"Junior Prom. Senior Homecoming," she read.

"Do you have anything else besides that necklace and his admission that they were friends?" Landry asked.

"Just the bluff I told him about getting DNA from those fetal bones."

"He's too smart for that," Landry said. "He's probably talking to his own DNA experts as we speak."

"He's in Columbus for the rest of the week at some legal education seminar. You're probably right."

"Well, get something concrete. As soon as you can. In the meantime, no leaks, okay? Nobody else needs to know Brouchard's a person of interest."

"They won't hear it from me," Jake said.

"Or me," Birdie answered. She was still holding the VHS tapes.

"Good. Talk to Darcy. We should still have a VHS player somewhere in the building."

Birdie nodded.

"In the meantime, I've got the ball rolling on getting a visiting prosecutor to take over. Regardless of Tim's involvement in the actual case, he's the brother-in-law of the victim. We needed to go outside the county for this anyway. You'll be dealing with Roger Bernicki from Marvell County. We're putting out a joint statement on that today, citing Brouchard's relationship to Anya, nothing more."

"That's good," Jake said. "The longer we can keep things under wraps, the better. Once Tim's name hits the news as a person of interest, this thing is going to go more high profile."

"Hallo, there!" A booming voice came from the hall. "Jake?"

Landry was closest to the door. She poked her head out then turned back to Jake.

"I think your grandfather is looking for you. Hi, Max," she said. "He's down here."

Grandpa Max stood in the hallway, hands on his hips. "You're late, kid."

"How did you get down here by yourself?" Jake said. "You're not supposed to be driving."

"It's a beautiful day," Grandpa Max said. "A man can walk."

"Not all the way from Poznan Township," Birdie muttered.

"Good to see you, Max," Landry said. "Have the fish been biting?"

"Caught a six-pound bass just yesterday."

"Phil's been itching to have you take him out on the lake yet this spring," she said.

"Well, if you can get his ass out of bed before nine, he's welcome to pick me up anytime."

"I'll tell him," Landry said, smiling. "Good to see you, Max. It's Wednesday, isn't it? I'll leave you to it."

Jake and Grandpa Max had a standing lunch date every Wednesday afternoon. Grandpa liked to go to the Coney Island on Fifth Street. It wasn't Jake's favorite, but Gramps had been going there for forty-odd years, ordering the same hot roast beef sandwich with mashed potatoes and gravy.

"Is that little Erica?" Grandpa Max said.

Erica went to him. She hugged Max Cashen. "Look at you," he said, squinting to see her. Jake really did worry how Max managed to get downtown by himself. He damn well better have been dropped off by Gemma. That was a different conversation he'd have to have with his sister.

"Nice to see you, Mr. Cashen," she said. "I'll let you and Jake have your lunch."

"Enough of that," Grandpa said. "Nobody calls me Mr. Cashen. Call me Max, kiddo. And you're skin and bones. Come on. I'll get one meal into you at least. You'll come with us. Plus, you're better lookin' than my grandson."

"I'm better lookin' than you at least," Birdie teased. Oh boy, thought Jake. The quickest way to Max Cashen's heart was to dish out bullshit as well as he did. Max put his arm around her.

"Well I've got a date," he said. "Come on if you're coming, Jake."

"I'm coming," Jake said, sighing. He gave Birdie an apologetic look. She waved him off with a wink.

TWENTY

Grandpa liked the back corner booth at the Coney Island. The thing was a six-seater you had to practically crawl across to get to the middle. Jake let Birdie get in first. Max took the opposite side and quickly ordered for all three of them.

"How are you settling in, honey?" Max asked Birdie.

"Well enough," she said.

"You planning on staying at Ben's place or getting something new?"

Birdie's eyes flicked downward. Jake winced. It wouldn't have been his choice to invoke Birdie's dead brother and his best friend before they even got their drink orders. But Max Cashen suffered under no such etiquette. He said what he thought when he thought it.

"Travis and I are still trying to figure that out together. He's had a lot of upheaval in the last few years after losing both his parents. I want it to be his choice."

"You've had your own upheaval," Max said. "Wasn't your plan to leave the army when you did."

"Gramps," Jake said. "Birdie knows all of this. Lord. Let her just eat her salad before the inquisition."

"It's okay," Birdie said. "Everyone else is afraid to bring Ben up to me. Travis says the same thing. It's not like he likes to talk about it. It's just nice sometimes knowing people care."

"They care," Jake said.

The waitress brought their drinks and salads. Grandpa tucked his napkin into his collar and dug in. It allowed Jake a few merciful minutes to breathe. Then, he started right back in.

"You gonna find out who killed that girl?" Max asked.

"That's the idea," Jake said. He looked around the restaurant. There were only two other tables at the very front. Far out of earshot. The lettuce on his salad was wilted. He knew the burger he ordered would come overcooked. He'd tried to get Gramps to bail on this place for years. The food was terrible. But today, it worked to his advantage. Jake felt comfortable talking without any eavesdroppers.

"Maybe you can help," Birdie said, as if she could pick up on Jake's thoughts. "I don't remember much about it. I was only like seven or eight years old when Nicole went missing. But I know it was big news. What do you remember, Max?"

Jake realized he was curious to hear his grandfather's answer. Max paused, chewing on his own wilted lettuce.

"It was a shocker all right," he said. "We searched everywhere for that girl."

"You were part of the search team?" Jake asked, surprised his grandfather failed to mention that before. He only had vague memories of that time period himself.

"Oh sure," Grandpa said. "Pretty much every able-bodied man in town was. They even came onto my property, searched out the back fifty acres where the swamp comes in."

"Why didn't you tell me that?" Jake said.

"You didn't ask," Max said. "She did."

"They thought you had something to do with it?" Birdie said.

"Nah. It wasn't that. It was just everybody was looking in every nook and cranny in the county tryin' to figure out where somebody'd be able to hide a body."

"Who'd you search with?" Jake asked.

"Your dad for one," Max said, pointing his fork at Birdie. "Couple of the guys from the mill. I don't know why nobody thought to drag Echo Lake."

"It wouldn't have mattered," Jake said. "She wasn't technically in the lake."

"What were people saying back then?" Birdie asked. "There had to have been rumors. What was the chatter among the search parties?"

These were good questions. Jake was impressed Birdie thought to ask them.

"All sorts of crazy stuff," Grandpa said. "But the main one ... we all thought it had something to do with that Bardo boy she was dating. Like some kinda retribution for stuff his family was into. Damn shame though. Alton was a good kid. He was nothing like the rest of that bunch. You know, he actually came to talk to me before he enlisted with the army. He knew I served in Vietnam. He came into the Veterans Center one time. Sat and played chess with me. Beat me, too."

Jake knew that was no small feat. He'd only ever beaten his grandfather at chess twice in his lifetime.

"You helped him," Birdie said, smiling. "Like you helped me."

Jake did a double take.

"Shows how much you know," Grandpa said, picking up on Jake's shock. "Lots of people come to me for advice. I'm not just some old fart."

"I've never once thought of you as just an old fart," Jake said. "A windbag, maybe."

The waitress came with their meals. As expected, Jake's burger could have doubled as a hockey puck. Birdie's too. But out of respect for his grandfather, she ate it without complaint.

"Nah," Grandpa said. "I knew Alton had nothing to do with whatever became of that poor girl. But a lot of 'em were saying maybe they helped her start a new life. They would have had the means and methods to get her fake IDs and that sort of thing. It just seemed pretty far-fetched to me. Marty Strong had his issues. But I never got the sense he was abusing those girls. Did you?"

"No," Jake said. "Not physically. And Virgil did a good job chasing down all those leads. It amounted to nothing. I trust his detective work on that."

"Me too," Grandpa said. "It's just a shame. I know this thing's been eating at him all these years."

Birdie's shoulder radio went off. "Unit 110, Unit 110. Are you in the vicinity of Maudeville?"

She spoke into it. "I'm at Fifth Street and Canton." She gestured to Jake. He scooted out of the booth so she could exit and take her radio call in private.

"That was a bad time," Grandpa said. "Every parent of a teenage girl in the county was scared to death something would happen to theirs."

"I figured," Jake said.

"Your grandma most of all. Ava had a hell of a time. Your sister was a hellcat back then. Always breaking curfew. Defying any rule we laid down. Your grandma thought for sure she was gonna be next."

"Sorry about that," Birdie said as she came back to the table. "I hate to eat and run but I've gotta go."

"Anything you need?" Jake asked.

"No. Just a domestic situation out in Maudeville. The Bloom place."

"Christ," Jake muttered. "Dusty's at it again. Be careful. And watch out for raccoon shit."

"Um ... what?" Birdie asked.

"Just trust me," Jake said. "You want me to head out there with you?"

Birdie smiled. "I think I can handle it."

Jake found himself more worried than he probably should have. Dusty and Arlene Bloom were generally harmless. Arlene had just let Dusty back into the house after kicking him out last year. But domestic violence calls could easily go sideways.

"Good seeing you, Max," Birdie said. She leaned down and kissed Grandpa Max on the top of his head. She got the old man to blush.

Birdie said goodbye to the waitress on her way out the door.

"I like that one," Grandpa said as Jake watched Birdie leave. A patrol car pulled up with Deputy Chris Denning behind the wheel. Birdie climbed into the passenger side. Jake caught Denning's eye through the window. Denning waved at Jake as he waited for Birdie to climb in.

"I just wish she'd have taken a job down at the post office or something," Jake said. "Ben's gotta be rolling in his grave at her wearing a badge."

"She's a combat veteran, grandson," Max said. "I think that girl can handle herself against Arlene Bloom's rabid raccoon."

As Birdie's patrol car sped out of view, Jake turned back to his grandfather.

"You got anything else you wanna know?" Grandpa said. "Finish your burger. Is it not to your liking?"

"It's just fine," Jake lied.

"Liar," Grandpa said. "It's a damn charcoal briquette."

Jake choked on a French fry.

"This town needs you to find out who killed that girl, Jake. You know that, dontcha?"

"Yes," he said, taking a sip of water. "I know it."

"Good," Grandpa said, throwing down two twenty-dollar bills. No matter how long they'd been coming here, Grandpa refused to let Jake pay.

Jake thanked him. "Come on," he said. "You got time to drive me home?"

"Sure thing," Jake said, sliding out of the booth. He held out a hand for Grandpa. The old man had a trick knee on top of everything else.

The two men made it as far as the parking lot before Jake's phone blew up. Jake looked at the screen. It was a text from Sheriff Landry, reading simply ...

> Open your news app. Then get back here as fast as you can.

Jake opened his app.

"Son of a bitch," he muttered.

"Trouble?" Grandpa asked.

Jake pocketed his phone. "The worst kind," he said. "Let's go."

TWENTY-ONE

B y the time Jake dropped his grandfather off and got back to the station, the place was swarming with press. By the labels on a couple of the live trucks, this thing had gone national.

Jake managed to sneak in through the service door and make a beeline to Landry's office. He got there just in time to hear her yell at the dozen or so people crowding in to clear out. When she spotted Jake, she set her jaw in an angry line.

"This is a mess, Jake," she said.

He pushed past the outgoing command officers and closed the door behind them. Landry had a remote control and clicked on her television. The local station was in the middle of a live broadcast right outside Landry's window.

"Details are still emerging," the reporter said. He vaguely knew her. Kirsten Smith. She managed to get herself demoted from a station in Cleveland and now covered the crime beat in the tri-county area.

"Sources say prosecutor Timothy Brouchard has emerged as the main person of interest in the twenty-five-year-old cold case murder of Nicole Strong. At the time of her death, Ms. Strong was a seventeen-year-old high school senior here in Stanley, Ohio. It's unclear when her relationship with Mr. Brouchard began. At the time of her disappearance, Mr. Brouchard was a local attorney in Worthington County. We spoke to two of Ms. Strong's classmates who remember him acting as a mentor for the Future Professional Leaders Organization. The group participated in several field trips including a visit to the state capitol. Based on the information we have, Mr. Brouchard never came forward to disclose his inappropriate relationship with a minor, nor was he ever interviewed by the police. Mr. Brouchard has so far declined to comment. Interestingly, as it stands right now, should an arrest be made in this case and charges brought, it's Tim Brouchard himself who would likely be assigned to prosecute the case. Obviously, that presents a huge conflict of interest at the very minimum. My calls to the prosecutor's office have also gone unanswered. We're waiting for a statement from the Worthington County Sheriff. A press conference is scheduled for later today. We'll of course bring that to you live ..."

Landry clicked off the television. "Wall-to-wall coverage," she said. "CNN and Fox have picked it up as well. I've got a call to return to the attorney general."

Jake sat down in one of the large leather chairs along Landry's wall.

"What sources?" he said. "Who the hell tipped them off?"

"I don't know."

"Nobody has this," Jake said. "It's you, me, Deputy Wayne. Virgil ..."

"Jake, you don't think ..."

"Absolutely not," he said. "Whatever's going on, this didn't come from a law enforcement source."

The moment he said it, Jake knew there was one other person who knew he'd inquired about Brouchard's involvement.

"Roland." Landry and Jake said it together.

"Son of bitch," Jake muttered. "Someone must have gotten to him."

"What did Roland know?"

"I never told him my questions had anything to do with Nicole Strong," Jake said. But he knew it didn't matter. The whole town knew Jake had been assigned to investigate Nicole's murder. Roland also knew Jake's interest in the commission of that necklace twenty-five-years ago. It would have been easy for him to connect the dots.

"That weasel," Jake said. "I'm gonna kill him."

Landry shook her head. "We were going to have to go public with it soon enough. Where's Brouchard now?"

"Still in Columbus teaching a continuing legal ed class. Anya said he was due back in a couple of days."

His heart turned to ash. "Dammit. Anya."

Meg Landry's face was drained of all color. She sat down on the edge of her desk. "Oh Jake."

"I didn't tell her. I was trying to protect her and the integrity of this case. Whatever Brouchard's involvement with Nicole was, I don't have anything close to probable cause to arrest him. He knows it. I wanted something more concrete before I blew her life up."

"Well, consider it good and exploded now," Landry said.

"I've got to find her. I've got to try and explain ... something."

"Jake," Landry said. "I'm not sure I agree that's your business at this point. What on earth would you even tell her?"

"I don't know. Maybe that I'm sorry?"

"Are you? What for exactly?"

"I'm sorry she had to find out like this. Sorry her husband is the creep I always thought he was."

"Yeah. Neither of those things are your fault."

"That's not how she's gonna see it."

"Look. You two have a history together. I'm as angry this thing leaked as you are. But if you'd come and asked me whether you should tip off the wife of your most viable murder suspect before you've had a chance to build a proper case against him? Well, I would have told you not to. You couldn't tell her. Besides, are you absolutely certain she didn't already know about all of this? You said yourself, Brouchard was the one who helped her move Nicole's things out of her parents' house. Tim and Anya have been married for almost a decade. You have no idea what she knows. If you didn't have a relationship with her, there's no way you would have told her any of this. If it were any other case ..."

Anger swept through Jake. Landry's words made sense, but they didn't make him feel any better. He knew in his soul that Anya had been in the dark about Tim's past connection to Nicole. White-hot rage flooded through his veins. Before he knew what he was doing, he was on his feet, barely able to breathe. He needed to do something. He needed to ...

He took one step forward and smashed his fist into the plaster, denting it. He split the skin and fire spread across his hand. For that one instant, it felt good to have the pain crawling across his flesh, matching the anger burning through his heart.

"Feel better?" Landry asked, not even so much as flinching.

"Yeah, actually."

"Good. Glad you got that out of your system. Now. Whether you like it or not, there's not a whole lot you can say to Anya Brouchard."

His phone rang. He slipped it out of his jacket. He showed the screen to Sheriff Landry. It was Anya.

"Jake," she said. "You might hate me for this. But you're going to have to treat that woman just like she were any other wife of a potential murder suspect. You can't discuss the particulars of an ongoing investigation. Roger Bernicki is about to be appointed the visiting prosecutor anyway. I'll coordinate with his office and figure out some kind of statement. As far as Anya goes ..."

"She's not just the wife of a suspect, Sheriff. She's the victim's sister. That's how I've treated her. It's how I'll continue treating her."

"You cannot talk to her about what you have on Tim. You know that."

"That isn't going to be her question," Jake muttered. "That is going to be her question." He pointed to the television.

"Yeah. I suppose it would be mine too." She rubbed her brow. "We're both in it now, Jake. I'm going to have to figure out what to say at this press conference."

"You say what we always say. Same thing you want me to tell Anya. We can't comment on anything specific. I need to pay Roland Carmichael another visit though. I'd like to wring his damn neck."

"I'd like to help you. For now though? You need to step things up with Brouchard. Find a way to either clear him or charge him. We don't have the luxury of time anymore."

"Yeah. Sorry about your wall. Take it out of my paycheck."

"Oh no. You're going to fix it yourself. You know how long a maintenance request is gonna take? Bring some spackle and paint tomorrow, buddy."

Jake found a hopeless smile for her. He was about to excuse himself. Her door opened and her new civilian assistant, Justine, poked her head in.

"Sorry to disturb you. Hey, Jake. I just wanted to let you know. We've got a minor situation."

"Minor?" Landry said, then shouted through the open doorway. "That's an understatement, Neil!"

"Oh. No," Justine said. "I don't mean the press conference and the Brouchard mess. Um ... we just got a call into dispatch. A couple of the deputies were out on a domestic disturbance call. They just called for an ambulance. We've got an injured officer."

The air went straight out of Jake's lungs. He knew exactly which two deputies had gone out on a domestic violence call this afternoon.

"How bad?" Landry asked.

But Jake was already on the move.

TWENTY-TWO

"Where is she?"

"Jake ..."

"Where is she?" Jake stormed past the nurses' station at the Stanley Hospital. Nurse Candy Sims had known Jake since he was in kindergarten. She'd been a friend of his mother's and had been one of a daisy chain of concerned mothers who had brought meals to the house and offered to sit with him in the weeks after his parents died. Though he hadn't seen her in ages, Nurse Sims had seen Jake's temper before.

"Jake!" she shouted as he slipped through the security doors as a different nurse came out.

A third nurse came out from behind a pink curtain. That's where Jake headed.

Jake flashed his badge. "You have an injured officer?"

The nurse gave him a blank stare. "Are you family?"

"Where is she?" he asked, his anger growing.

"Detective, you can't be back here. I haven't ..."

"It's okay." A familiar voice came from behind the pink curtain. Birdie pulled it back. She was holding a blood-soaked cloth to her head.

"Deputy," the nurse said. "I'm going to need you to get back in bed. I'm not done assessing ..."

"I'm fine," Birdie said. But she respected the nurse's glare. Jake advanced on Birdie, making her take two steps backward toward the bed.

"I'm fine," she said again. "It's just a little cut. See?"

She pulled the gauze away, revealing an ugly gash on her forehead just above her left eye.

"I'll be the judge of that." Behind Jake, a doctor in blue scrubs stood. Her name was Dr. Sue Chaudhry.

"Have a seat, young lady," Chaudhry said. "You her husband?"

"I'm her ... coworker," Jake said.

Chaudhry went to the nearby sink and washed her hands. She then put on a pair of blue latex gloves from a box on the wall. She went to Birdie and shined a pen light on her wound. Birdie hissed slightly as Chaudhry palpated the cut.

"It's not so bad," she said. "You'll need a few stitches. I don't think I can close that one up with glue."

Jake shifted his weight on his heels, anxious, bracing himself for more bad news. Dr. Chaudhry asked Birdie a series of questions, ruling out whether she'd need any more tests.

"You want to tell me what happened?"

"It's embarrassing," she said. "I got hit in the head with a ceramic coaster."

"How the hell did that happen?" Jake asked. "Where was your partner?"

"Relax, Jake," she said. "Denning and I got called to a domestic disturbance out at the Blooms. Arlene said Dusty threw a bowl of soup at her. I mean, the actual bowl. She was dripping in chicken noodle when we arrived. We got them separated. Arlene had bruises on her cheek. Dusty more or less admitted to it all. So, I was in the middle of arresting him. All of a sudden, Arlene got agitated. She yelled at me not to take her man away from her. Next thing I know, there's a purple ceramic coaster sailing through the air. Her son made it in art class. Heavy sucker. I turned just in time to get it right here."

Birdie pointed to the gash on her head.

"Where was Deputy Denning?" Jake asked. Chaudhry and Birdie exchanged a look.

"It happened lightning fast, Jake. It's nothing. Stuff happens. Everybody was calm. Civil even. Then when Arlene saw the cuffs, I don't know. She just lost her mind for a second. Now she and Dusty get to spend the night in lockup until her brother can post bond. You ask me, it might be good for them."

"Well, I don't think you need anything more than stitches," Chaudhry said. "But if you start to feel dizzy or nauseous, you call me. All right? I'll get you stitched up ..."

"Does she need a plastic surgeon?" Jake asked.

"Look here," Dr. Chaudhry said. "The lucky part, when this heals, it's going to blend right into the natural crease of your forehead. You'll be good as new."

"You're saying I'm wrinkly, Doc?" Birdie teased.

"Just enough," she teased back. "Let me go get what I need and we'll get you sorted out, Deputy. You planning on staying with her, Detective?"

"You don't have to ..." Birdie said.

"Yes," Jake answered.

Chaudhry put a friendly hand on Birdie's shoulder then excused herself.

"That could have been way worse than it was," Jake said.

"It wasn't. Geez, Jake. It was nothing. I told you. Stuff happens. Nobody's more sorry about it than Arlene Bloom. What the heck are you doing down here anyway? I, uh ... saw the news."

Jake looked behind him to make sure there was no one listening. He pulled the pink curtain shut.

"Bad day, huh?" she asked.

"It's a mess," Jake said.

"Who do you think leaked the news about Brouchard?"

"I'm not one hundred percent sure, but odds are it was Roland Carmichael."

"Ugh. Great. Do you have any recourse? Can you charge him with obstruction?"

"That might do more harm than good. Up until a few days ago, he was cooperating with me. When the time comes, if the time comes ... he'll have to be called as a witness for the prosecution."

Birdie whistled. "Only the prosecutor is your main suspect. I don't know. I still have a tough time believing Brouchard's a murderer."

"We already know he's been lying all this time."

"He's been lying to his wife most of all," Birdie said. Then her face registered a new shock. "Wait a sec. This means Anya Brouchard got to hear about all of this on the news? Do you think her slime of a husband had the decency to tell her himself before Roland opened his big mouth?"

"I doubt it," Jake said.

"You can't talk to her," she said. "Jake ... you can't. She's a witness now. Her husband's the suspect in a capital murder case."

"That about sums it up."

"I'm starting to think even with getting bashed in the face with a homemade coaster, I'm having a better day than you are." Birdie smiled when she said it, then laughed at her own joke. Jake couldn't. She wasn't wrong.

"What is taking that doctor so long?" Jake asked.

"Where's Brouchard now?" Birdie asked.

"I don't know. Columbus, last I knew."

"You think he's a flight risk?" she asked.

"I don't know what to think anymore. But this whole thing has accelerated the urgency of this investigation. I need to figure out how to prove where Tim Brouchard was when Nicole disappeared."

"I'd like to help with that," she said. "Why don't I head to the courthouse in the morning and see what cases he was an attorney of record for during that time frame. We might be able to piece together something from whatever hearings he had scheduled that week."

"That's a good idea," he said. "You should be on light duty anyway after this."

"For the love of ... Jake. It's barely more than a scratch. Quit big-brothering me."

The second the words were out of her mouth, Jake watched as a wave of grief went through her. Birdie blinked away tears before they had a chance to fall. She stiffened her back and found a quick smile. It happened so fast. But Jake knew. Grief can be like that.

"Jake," she said. "You can do one thing for me. Do you think you could scare up some Coke for me from the vending machine?"

"Sure," he said.

Dr. Chaudhry slid the curtain aside and walked in carrying a tray of suturing supplies. Nurse Sims came with her. Jake was glad of it. He guessed Candy Sims could stitch even better than a plastic surgeon if given the chance.

"She wants a Coke," Jake said to Chaudhry. "Is that all right?"

"It's perfect," Nurse Sims answered for the doctor. "Besides, she doesn't need you hovering over her shoulder like some gargoyle."

"Good point," Birdie said. "The woman's about to thread a needle through my face. Take a walk, Jake."

Grumbling, Jake did as he was told. He'd seen a vending machine near the elevators and headed for it. He made it halfway there when Deputy Denning appeared, heading in the opposite direction toward Birdie.

"Hey, Jake," he said, nodding at Jake.

Unbidden rage flared inside of him. "What the hell happened out there, Denning?"

Denning's face fell. He recovered quickly though. Anger flashed through his eyes.

"What are you talking about?"

"What I'm talking about is why you thought it was a good idea to turn your back on Arlene Bloom and fail to protect your partner."

"What? Jake, you don't know what you're talking about."

Denning took a step forward. Jake blocked his path. Denning held his hands up. "You need to step aside," he said.

"I don't think I do. I want an answer, Denning. You were on a domestic call. You've been in field ops for what, ten years? You should know better than to leave your partner exposed like that."

"You should know better to mind your own damn business, Cashen. Now I asked you to step aside."

"She could have lost an eye. It could have been something worse than a ceramic coaster. Did you pat Arlene Bloom down?"

"She wasn't the one under arrest," Denning said. "Now, I've had about enough of this. You weren't there. Nobody did anything wrong. I'm real sorry you can't keep control of your own cases so you feel the need to step all over mine."

"Fuck you, Denning. That girl could have been seriously hurt because of you."

"That girl ... did two tours in Afghanistan. She doesn't need you babysitting her."

"No. She needs a partner she can depend on, not one that'll get her a trip to the ER."

"You are way out of line! Now step aside!"

Chris Denning advanced. He laid his hand flat on Jake's chest and tried to shove him backward.

Jake reacted. He threw an arm bar and pushed Deputy Denning into the wall.

Just then, the elevator doors opened. Meg Landry walked out. Her face turned sheet white when she saw Jake and Chris Denning.

"Jake!" she yelled.

Jake could only hear his own pulse pounding inside his head. He could only see the fear in Denning's eyes.

"Jake!" This time, the shout came from Birdie. She was already stitched up and walking toward the elevators.

Jake looked from her to Landry, then back at Denning. His nostrils flared. Jake gave him one more hard shove, then released his grip. Landry grabbed Jake by the arm and pulled him back into the elevators.

"Listen to me. I have no idea what that was about. I'm going to assume you've just had a very bad day. I need you to go home. Get some sleep. Watch some baking shows or something. Whatever you do to unwind. But do it fast. I cannot have you losing your temper like that."

Jake fumed, but said nothing more. Landry rode the elevator all the way down to the lobby with him.

"Tomorrow?" she said. "Don't even bother coming into the office unless you've had eight full hours of sleep and a proper meal in your belly. You understand?"

"Meg ..."

"Do you understand?"

Jake gritted his teeth by way of an answer. Landry raised a brow but didn't press him further. Finally, he turned his back on her and headed out to his car.

It took him a few minutes to stop seeing white spots as he gripped the wheel. Slowly, Jake felt his blood pressure start to drop to less homicidal levels. Even so, he punched the steering wheel before he put the car in gear and drove south to Poznan Township.

Despite Landry's edict, he knew sleep would never come tonight. It might not come at all until he knew what to do about Tim Brouchard.

His route home took him past the southern edge of Echo Lake. He thought about turning toward it. Maybe standing on the shores, just feet from where Nicole Strong had lain for a quarter of a century, might give him answers. As if her ghost could whisper something to him. Help him find his path forward.

In the end, he decided to simply take the road north until he turned up the hidden drive onto his grandfather's sprawling property.

Gravel crunched under his tires as he made his way to the small, two-bedroom cabin he called home. Maybe he was wrong. Maybe he would sleep.

It was full dark now. As Jake got out of his car, he heard the near-deafening chorus of the spring peepers hidden in the reeds of the pond just past the trees.

He took two steps toward the house then froze. Someone was there. His hand went to his weapon, holstered on his right hip.

She stepped out from the shadows, setting off the motion light on the porch.

Jake's very bad day was about to get worse. Her face swollen from crying, Anya Brouchard stepped off the porch and came to him.

Twenty-Three

He didn't know what she would say. Jake half expected Anya to slap him in the face. Maybe he would have deserved it. He would have preferred it. Instead, the hurt look in Anya's eyes cut through him and he had no earthly clue what to say to her.

"Anya ..." he started.

She put a hand up. "Don't. Just ... don't."

So he stood there on the gravel path leading up to the cabin porch steps, waiting for her to make the next move. She didn't though. Anya simply swayed on her feet as if she were about to keel over, as the weight of all the lies she'd been told settled into her bones and ripped at her soul.

Finally, she found the strength to meet Jake's eyes again. "Why?" she whispered.

"Anya. I'm sorry. You weren't supposed to find out like this. There was a leak. I have an idea who, but ..."

"Did he do it?" she asked.

"I don't ..."

"Tell me!" she shouted, and the dam within her burst. She rushed toward Jake; raising her fists, she pummeled Jake's chest. He let her, the first time. When she drew her hands back again, he caught her by the wrists.

"If it will make you feel better to beat the crap out of me, go ahead."

She wrenched herself out of his grip. "I wish it would!"

"Come on inside," Jake said. "I could use a drink. So could you."

It was then Jake noticed the bottle of cherry vodka sitting on the porch step. He understood now why she swayed on her feet. Anya had already gotten herself good and drunk.

"Come on inside," he said again. "I'll put on a pot of coffee."

"I don't want to go inside," she said, but Jake didn't listen. He went in without her. A moment later, Anya followed. She slammed the screen door shut behind her and plopped down on the leather couch against the wall. She had the vodka bottle in her hand and took another swig of it.

"You want a glass for that at least?" Jake was already planning a strategy for getting her home safely. One or two more shots of that stuff and she'd pass out on his couch.

He set up the coffee maker then went to the far cupboard. Vodka wasn't his drink. Bourbon was. He poured himself a single shot of Jim Beam and joined her in the living room, picking the chair across from the couch.

"I'm sorry," he said.

"When," she said. "How long have you known?"

"Not long," he said.

"Did you know when you met me at the storage unit?"

Jake took a sip of bourbon. "Yes."

"Did you know at Nicole's memorial service?"

He took another sip, letting the smooth liquid warm his stomach.

"No."

"Tim was sleeping with her."

"I don't know for sure," he said. It was true enough.

Anya abruptly stood. Her skin turned gray. Jake started to rise. Anya lurched forward, then took a staggering left turn and made it to Jake's bathroom around the corner. She dropped to her knees and threw up into the toilet.

Jake stood over her, amazed at how much liquid poured out of such a small woman. When Anya finally got back to her feet, he knew she was already half sober.

He gave her a wide berth as she made her way back to the couch. She held the vodka bottle to her chest, but didn't drink anymore. Jake poured her a glass of water and handed it to her. He figured it would go down better than the coffee.

"Did he do this?" she said, her voice hoarse.

Jake sat on the couch beside her.

"Jake? Did Tim kill my sister?"

"I don't have a good answer for you yet," he said.

"He said he didn't," she said. "I was just standing there in the middle of the cafe. I was flipping through the channels. The early dinner crowd likes to watch the news. It was there. Right at the counter. That's how I heard it, Jake. That's how I heard you think my husband killed Nicole."

"He's a person of interest," he said.

"No." She shook her head. "Don't do that. Not with me. I need you to tell me the truth. All of it."

He ran his finger along the rim of his glass, then raised it to his lips. He downed the rest of the bourbon.

"This was never meant to come out like this," he said. "I'm going to get to the bottom of how this was leaked. It never should have happened. I'm sorry."

"I don't care," she said. "My God, Jake. You think I'm mad at you because somebody in town has a big mouth? I'm mad at you because you didn't tell me. I'm mad because Tim didn't tell me. All this time ... all this time! Have I been married to a murderer?"

"I don't know. Not yet. But you've been married to a liar."

She barked out a hard laugh.

"Anya, where's Tim now?"

"I don't know. He called me from the road. He's on his way back from Columbus. I told him not to come home."

"He probably will anyway," Jake said. "Anya, I don't want you going back to that house. Not like this. Not until things settle down a bit."

"When's that going to be, huh?"

"Let me help you," he said. "I'll call Gemma. You can stay with her for a day until you figure out ..."

"Gemma never liked me," she said. "Not since you left for college."

"A hotel then," Jake said. "If you need money ... I can talk to Sheriff Landry. We can make arrangements to put you in protective custody."

She started to unscrew the bottle of vodka. Jake reached over and took it from her. "Stick with water for now."

"You think I'm in danger? God. Tell me the truth. Did Tim do this? What else do you know?"

"Anya, I can't. I know it's not the answer you want, but I can't talk to you about any evidence I have against your husband. But I don't want you staying under the same roof as Tim right now."

"You were fine with me staying under the same roof three days ago when I left that storage lot. You knew?"

Anya's face went from gray to white. "Oh my God. He ... I told you ... Nic's things. Tim helped me bring all of that stuff over. He ... do you think ..."

"Let's not do this," Jake said. "Not right now. I promise you. When I can tell you something ... when I know something ... we'll figure this out. For now, we need to find you someplace safe to stay."

Anya rose to her feet. "My parents have a spare room at the condo. I can go there."

Jake wasn't sure that would be good for Anya's sanity, but knew it wasn't his place to say it. Still, it was a better idea than her sharing a roof and a bed with Tim Brouchard for the time being.

"I'll call them," Jake said.

"There's no need," she said. "They're already on their way."

"Here?"

No sooner had he said it than headlights filled the window. Marty Strong drove up in his giant Suburban. Jake realized he didn't know what to say to them either.

"Anya?" Marty called. Jake went to the front door and opened it. Vivian Strong came out and stood next to her husband. He put an arm around her as their daughter came out and met them.

"I'm okay, Daddy," Anya said. Marty gathered his daughter into his arms. Anya handed her mother her car keys.

"I'm sorry," Jake said. And he was. But Marty and Vivian Strong had nothing to say to him. Vivian simply walked to Anya's car, slid behind the wheel, and slowly drove away.

"Did you ask him?" Jake said to Anya. "When you talked to Tim. Did you ask him?"

Marty turned to his daughter. Jake realized the man was eager to hear her answer as well.

"He told me not to believe anything you say," Anya said.

"I'm gonna kill him!" Marty said.

"Marty." Jake stepped forward. "I know you're angry. I know you have a lot of questions. So do I. But promise me you're not going to make a bad situation worse. Let me do my job. Please. I told Anya. When I have something concrete to tell you, I will. I swear to God."

"She was seventeen," Marty whispered. "She was just a baby."

Anya started to weep in earnest. Marty pulled her against his chest. He and Jake locked eyes. Then Marty walked his daughter back to his car and helped her get inside. As they drove away, Jake knew no matter what else happened, the already fractured Strong family might not survive this at all.

TWENTY-FOUR

"Mr. Brouchard is eager to cooperate with the authorities and put this matter behind him. He has nothing to hide."

Jake stood in Meg Landry's office as he watched a live press conference taking place on the courthouse steps directly across the street.

"He's been hiding everything for twenty-five years," Jake muttered.

"Close the door," Landry barked, not taking her eyes off the television screen.

"Mr. Edwards," one reporter asked. "Was Tim Brouchard involved in a sexual relationship with Nicole Strong?"

"We have no comment," Malcolm Edwards said.

"Who is that guy?" Jake asked.

"He's about a thousand dollars an hour," Landry said. "He's the guy I'd hire if I could afford it and somebody I cared about got charged with murder."

"Did Tim Brouchard kill Nicole Strong?" another voice shouted from the television. Jake peered closer.

"That kid's not even a reporter," he said. "That's Tyler Tobin. He runs that website, the Dark Side of Blackhand Hills."

"My client is innocent," Edwards said. "And he has not been charged with any crime. What he is, is a victim of a bungling detective who is in over his head. No one wants the truth to come out about what happened to Mr. Brouchard's sister-in-law more than he does."

"Wanna bet?" Jake muttered. Landry clicked off the television.

"Sit down," she said, her tone sharp.

"Sheriff..."

"Sit down," she said, even more firmly.

He did.

"Jake?" Landry pressed her fingers to the bridge of her nose. "The last thing we needed was for this case to get away from us."

"It hasn't," Jake said.

"That's not what the mayor and county commissioners think."

"Since when do the mayor and county commissioners dictate police procedure?"

"Jake," she said. "They want you off this case. And they're not the only ones suggesting it."

"What are you talking about?"

"The Strong family has hired their own lawyer. Roger Bernicki, our visiting prosecutor, has also expressed concerns."

"Sheriff ... tensions are high. This mess? We didn't create it. Tim Brouchard's the one who's been lying to the cops and obstructing justice for a quarter of a century."

"And you haven't been doing me or yourself any favors, Jake."

"What do you want? You want Ed Zender handling this case? Be my guest."

"What was that at the hospital yesterday, huh? You and Chris Denning. Ten people saw you put him into a wall."

"That was nothing," Jake said.

"That was you letting your emotions get the best of you."

"So I'll ask you again. What do you want? Zender?"

"No. God, no. I've gone to bat for you before. And I'll do it again. I'm just getting damn tired of having to."

"Who's this coming from? Rob Arden? Sheriff, I don't have to tell you what that's all about."

"No. But you do have to get a hold of yourself."

"I've done nothing wrong."

"Yes, you have! Things are starting to spiral out of our control. If Tim Brouchard did kill that girl, he's already laying the groundwork for reasonable doubt. All he's gotta do is bring up your history with his wife."

"I haven't done a damn thing wrong!" Jake shouted.

"Yeah? So you wanna tell me Anya Brouchard wasn't at your house last night?"

"Who told you that?"

"Doesn't matter. Was she?"

"She showed up," he said. "She was upset. She was drunk. I sent her home. Though it killed me to do it, I told her I can't talk about the case with her anymore. Not while her husband is a suspect. And I told her not to go back home to him."

"You know how certain people are going to interpret that."

"I could care less."

"I need you to care," she shouted. "That's the problem."

"I'm doing my job. Rob Arden, Tim Brouchard, Malcolm Edwards, they can all go to hell. I care about one thing. Finding out who killed that girl. I don't care who ends up ruined because of it. I don't even care if I'm the one who ends up ruined because of it. She was seventeen, Meg. She was pregnant. And she died alone, in a hole, left to rot there."

Landry sat back down behind her desk. "I know. But you're too close to it."

"Damn straight I am. I'm close to all of them, Sheriff. That's how this works."

She lifted her head and stared at him. "Jake. I will fight for you. But you have to promise me. No more side shows. No more working out whatever big-brother complex you have over Deputy Wayne while you're on the job."

He opened his mouth to protest, but Landry held a finger up to silence him.

"And no more letting whatever torch you might still carry for Anya Strong into this."

"There's none," he said. "That's been over since high school."

"You sure?" she asked.

"Completely."

"Well, that is not the impression I get from her. You get that, right? I've seen how she looks at you. Everyone has."

"That's my fault?"

"No. But it's your problem. As long as you're working on this case, it's my problem too. So please. Promise me. You keep your shit straight, Jake."

He gripped the chair back and gritted his teeth.

"Jake."

"I've got things handled," he said.

"I hope so. Because I need you. And Nicole Strong needs you."

Jake nodded. But he'd rather have punched another hole in Sheriff Landry's wall. Instead, Jake's phone vibrated. He pulled it out and checked the caller ID. It was a number he didn't recognize.

"I'd better take this," he said. "But we're on the same page. That's a promise."

"Good," she said. As Jake turned to head into the hallway, she stopped him.

"I'm leaving anyway. Take your phone call. You can stay here."

She excused herself, leaving Jake alone. He answered the phone.

"Cashen," he said.

"You someplace you can talk?" A gravelly voice cut in and out, but Jake recognized the man instantly. Jake went stiff. It was Rex Bardo. He had to have called from a burner phone from somewhere inside the prison. It meant Gable West had pulled the right strings. Rex was out of solitary.

"Rex?"

"I'm a man of my word," Bardo said. "I've got something I think you'll be interested to hear."

"Keep talking," Jake said.

Twenty-Five

J ake closed the door to Meg Landry's office and locked it. He walked over to the window and looked out across the street. Tim Brouchard's press conference just broke up. His lawyer ushered him into a black SUV.

"Jake?" King Rex's gravelly voice broke through.

"I'm here," Jake said.

"Seems like you're still hell-bent on making as many enemies as you can."

"You're talking about Brouchard?" Jake asked. "He didn't need my help to make his own enemies."

"He's always been a worm. So now maybe he's a murderer."

"Whatcha got, Rex? I'm assuming from the fact you're calling me on a phone you shouldn't have, you're out of the hole. So ... you're welcome."

"Let's not pretend this was a favor, Jake. But I told you I'm a man of my word. I've got something for you," he said. "Check your department mail. And don't say I never did anything for you."

Jake went to the door and made his way down to his office. Ed Zender and Gary Majewski sat at their desks, barely acknowledging Jake as he walked in. They each had metal inboxes bolted to the wall. Jake looked in his. A single manila envelope had been stuffed in it. His name was written in a scrawling hand in blue ink. There was no return address. No stamp. Which meant it had been delivered by a courier.

"I have it," Jake said.

"Good. This one cost me. My mother didn't want to part with it."

"Your mother?" He went to his desk, grabbed a letter opener and sliced open one end of the large envelope. A smaller one spilled out. It had been torn open but taped shut. Jake's pulse quickened as he read the recipient's address. It had been sent to Alton Bardo at Fort Bragg, and it was postmarked August 13th, 1997. The return address practically stopped Jake's heart. It was from Nicole Strong.

"Where did this come from?" Jake said as he sank into his chair. Gary and Ed had left their desks and went to the door. Gary gestured to Jake. The two were on their way to lunch. Jake shook his head and put a hand up. Zender and Majewski left the office without him.

"Rex?"

"My mother kept a box of mementos," Rex said. "She burned most of Alton's things. I told you. She never forgave him for leaving her and getting himself killed. But ... she kept a few things in a box. It was in there."

"Does she know why you asked for it?"

"That's none of your business," Rex said.

"I appreciate this," Jake said.

"Understand one more thing, Jake. You don't use this to hurt my family. Are we clear?"

"I think you're smart enough not to give me something that has the potential to hurt your family, Rex."

"I'm going to hold you to your word, Cashen. Bet on it. But you still owe me."

"How do you figure?" Jake asked. "You're sitting there talking to me. Which means you know I'm a man of my word."

"I've got some information on the other thing you asked me about. Your pedo. Tom Cypher. I'm gonna need you not to ask me how I know. But he's not your guy. You can take that one to the grave. Trust me. He had nothing to do with whatever happened to Alton's girl."

Jake felt a cold chill go through him. "Rex. What happened? What did you do? How do you know?"

Silence. Jake could only just hear Rex let out a breath. It was the only answer he would get.

"Thank you for the letter at least," Jake said, though he wasn't sure if he should be grateful yet. Every cell in his body told him he'd come to regret having Rex check into Cypher. The letter though. It could be gold. Even without reading it, he knew Rex wouldn't have sent it if he didn't think it might be useful to him.

"I don't want your thanks. I'll let you know when I need something from you next."

It was a veiled threat, of course, but Jake knew King Rex didn't care. He was already in federal prison. In his world, the worst had already happened. And Jake knew how dangerous that made him.

Rex clicked off without saying goodbye. Jake tossed his cell phone on the desk. Steeling himself against what he might find, Jake sliced through the scotch tape and read Nicole Strong's letter.

> Alton,
>
> I'm sorry I didn't answer the phone when you called. I was being petty. You were right. I wasn't ready to admit it. But I want you to know I've been thinking about every single thing you said.
>
> You're right. Okay? There. I said it. I CAN admit when I'm wrong. I know I screwed up. Big time. But I don't agree that I'm trying to sabotage myself again. I'm just trying to figure out what's right. That's all. There aren't any easy answers despite what you say.
>
> Easy, would have been us staying together. I know that now. I'm sorry for how angry I got when you told me you were leaving. That was mean of me. What you're doing is noble and dangerous and that's why I reacted the way I did. I'm scared for you. I can't bear to think about not having you in my life. I hope you find what you're looking for. I really do. I just wish you could have picked something safer. Ha ha. I wish one of us could have won the lottery or something

and we could have sailed off into some magical sunset away from our screwed-up families and lived together on some island. I could learn how to cook. We could lie naked on the beach together and watch the waves all day.

I don't know. I'm rambling. I just miss you, that's all. Don't worry. I'm not trying to make you feel guilty for anything that's happened. I'll figure this out. I'll be all right. Somehow.

Please don't stop writing me letters. Please don't give up on me. Please! I know I've made the stupidest of mistakes. But I didn't make it alone. That's the thing you have to understand. I made it out of love. Maybe that's hard for you to hear. I'm sorry if it is. It's the thing I couldn't say to your face. So maybe I'm a coward now for saying it in a letter you'll probably never answer. I wish you would.

Wow. So I can't believe I said that out loud. Or ... well ... wrote it down in words. Love. I fell in love, Alton. That's been my biggest downfall in my seventeen years on this planet. I give my love too easily, maybe. I'm an optimist. An idealist. A dreamer. A fool.

But that's the heart of it. My heart. I love. He might not love me back anymore. He might not be able to. I know I took something that didn't belong to me. But I have something that belongs to him whether he wants it or not.

I know what you think. You said I'd be throwing my life away. That maybe it means you and I can never go back to how things were. That makes me sad. I'm crying now just thinking about it. But I can't kill something inside of me just for the chance you might love me more. Or that you might wait for me.

Why does this have to be so hard? I'll tell him. I promise. I'm scared though. He has the power to hurt me. Just like you do. You men. Don't you understand that power? I wish you would. I need so little to be happy. Just a smile. A word of encouragement. An I love you. Or hell, maybe just send me a postcard once in a while. I would live off that.

I'm sorry. I'm sorry. I'll be sorry for the rest of my life where you're concerned. I can drown in all the what-ifs.

Okay. Enough of all that. I know you hate when I get melancholy. That's getting worse. Hormones. Gross. I'll do the right thing. I promise. As soon as I figure out what that is. I'm just so scared. That's really all this is.

I'm scared for you. Terrified, actually. And I'm scared of what he'll say when I finally get brave enough to tell that asshole the thing that will change his life forever too. Thank you for not overreacting. Thank you for not going over there and ripping his nuts off. There was a part of me that wanted you to.

Ugh. Enough. I'm even sick of me now. I love you, Alton. Forever and always. Never forget that. I'll see you at Christmas. I promise I'll be nothing but smiles for you.

Love you, love you, love you.

Nic

Jake folded the letter and slid it back into its envelope. It would take him days to unpack everything Nicole wrote. She knew she was pregnant. Was it Alton's? Was it Brouchard's? Or someone else's? Only one thing was clear. There was another man in her life. One she was in love with. One whose life she knew she had the power to destroy.

Was that enough of a motive to silence her forever?

TWENTY-SIX

"He's in the interview room," Darcy said as Jake tried to get to his office the next morning . "I told him you weren't in yet. I told him you'd need him to make an appointment. He won't leave. He came here initially to see the sheriff, but she's out of town at that seminar and he wouldn't leave … and …"

"Darcy," Jake said. "It's okay. Might as well get this over with. Did Bird … has Deputy Wayne made it in yet?"

"She's set up in your war room."

"K. Thanks. Can you let her know I'll be down as soon as I finish with Brouchard's mouthpiece?"

Darcy still looked upset. Jake could only guess what Malcolm Edwards said to her. Jake put a comforting hand on her shoulder, then went to the interview room to face Edwards.

Edwards wasn't sitting. Instead, he stood leaning against the far wall, his battered briefcase on the table. As soon as Jake walked in, he pushed himself off, unsnapped his briefcase and pulled a thick file out of it. He lobbed it across the table.

"About time you bothered showing up," Edwards said. "This how you conduct a murder investigation? With part-time hours?"

Jake didn't take the bait. He didn't sit either. He closed the door behind him and took his own post on the opposite wall.

"You have something you wanna share with me? Or did you just come down here to scream your head off? If it's that last thing, you don't need me for this. I'm sure you can scare up a few reporters who might be interested in your speech."

"I came here to apparently do your job for you, Detective Cashen. A job that you won't have for very much longer once I'm through with you."

"Here we go," Jake sighed.

"You have bungled this case from the beginning. So here I am, fixing it for you."

Edwards grabbed the file folder, opened it, and took out two stacks of stapled paper. He set them down and pounded his fist on one.

"Tim Brouchard has an airtight alibi for the night Nicole Strong disappeared. If you'd bothered to do your job, you'd have this figured out already. As it stands, you've worked to ruin his reputation, not to mention make it that much harder for Nicole Strong's real killer to be found."

Jake picked up the papers. They were old photocopies of what looked like college transcripts. He looked closer. They weren't from any institution of higher learning. Instead, they bore the letterhead of the Worthington County Bar Association. Jake thumbed through them.

"You're aware that members of the Ohio bar are required to complete a certain number of hours of continuing legal education each year."

"Okay?" Jake said. He ran his finger over the dates in the far left column on each page. There were entries and credit hours listed. Topics included Professional Ethics and Responsibility, Trial Practice, Criminal Defense Seminar, and so on.

"Nicole Strong disappeared on Friday night, October 17th, 1997. That's been established," Edwards said.

"It has," Jake answered. He noticed a red sticker tab toward the back of the stack of papers. He went to that page.

"See it now?" Edwards said.

Jake saw the entries for 1997. Tim Brouchard had twenty-five credit hours of continuing education. Highlighted in orange was a Federal Practice Seminar.

Edwards grabbed a second stack of papers from the desk. He shoved them toward Jake. Jake took them. It was a photocopy of what looked like a course pack. It bore the title Federal Practice Seminar, Washington D.C. The Watergate Hotel. October 14 to October 18, 1997.

"My client wasn't even in town the week Nicole Strong disappeared," Edwards said. "He was fulfilling his legal obligation for continuing education in Washington D.C. four hundred miles away."

Jake sat down at the table. Malcolm Edwards remained standing.

"Where did you get this?" Jake asked.

"One phone call, Detective Cashen. I called the county bar association. That's all it took. That Federal Practice Seminar has been held at the Watergate for the last forty years. It's one of the biggest ones in the country. Tim Brouchard went to it every other year until he became a county prosecutor."

"Can he verify this?" Jake asked.

"Every Ohio attorney has to report their hours to the state bar, Jake. They're given a certificate of attendance. You think he made it up? It's right there in the packet I gave you. The originals are with the Bar Association. You can subpoena them yourself if you want."

"This was a four-day event," Jake said. "How do you know he was there every single day?"

"Give it up, Detective. Your whole case just fell apart. This completely exonerates my client. He has an ironclad alibi. He had nothing to do with whatever happened to that poor girl. I expect a full and public apology by the end of business today."

"For what? Edwards, if this checks out, then I'm happy for your client. I'm not in the business of arresting innocent people."

"I think you are if it's Tim Brouchard. I think you've loved every second of this. I'm aware of your history with his wife. I think you derived real pleasure from blowing up Tim's marriage."

"Thanks for this," Jake said. "Though Tim could have saved us both the trouble and told me all of this himself."

"Why on earth would he waste a second speaking with you again? Your objectives have been clear from the beginning. You've been hell-bent on destroying Tim Brouchard's reputation and his life. This isn't over. I'll have your badge for this."

"Based on what?" Jake said, rising. He opened the door and started to leave the room.

"We're not done here!" Edwards shouted, making a real show of things.

"Oh, we're done. Your client's the one who lied to the police twenty-five years ago."

"His name never should have been made public!"

"Think what you want. I've got a job to do. I've got a murdered girl whose family has waited a quarter of a century for justice. A girl your client had an inappropriate relationship with. Who, as far as I know, he may have gotten pregnant. He was an officer of the court back then, among other things. And yet he kept his dirty little secret all this time. He impeded a murder investigation. So you can take your speech and shove it up your ass!"

A crowd of sorts had gathered in the hallway. As Jake looked out, several deputies, Sergeant Jeff Hammer, and Darcy the dispatcher quickened their steps to get out of the way.

Jake turned back to Edwards and waved the stack of papers at him. "As I said, I hope this all checks out. I just wish your client had cooperated with the police back when it would have done Nicole Strong the most good. The lies he told have done enough damage. To her and everybody who cared about her. So don't come in here shouting me down about what a fine citizen Tim Brouchard is. Whether he killed that girl or not, his hands aren't exactly clean."

Jake didn't wait for a response. Instead he slammed the door behind him, leaving Malcolm Edwards alone in the room.

TWENTY-SEVEN

Birdie stood at the head of a long table. On it, she had spent the last week organizing all of Nicole Strong's personal effects. Her pictures, books, notes, clothes, trinkets, collectables. All of it. Birdie had managed to make the place look almost like a teenage girl's bedroom, minus the actual bed. She said it helped her get in the right headspace. Jake noticed a new box stacked against the wall.

"What's in that?" he asked.

"Probably a waste of time," Birdie said. "I called in a favor. My mom used to be good friends with Jay Larraby. Do you remember him?"

"Guy used to be a reporter for the *Blackhand Hills Bugle*," Jake said. "They used to send him out to cover the wrestling team. He interviewed Ben and me once or twice. Nice guy. Didn't know a thing about sports."

"That's the one. The *Bugle* only ever had two reporters at any given time. Larraby doubled as his own photographer, too. Anyway, I noticed his byline in a lot of the stories the *Bugle* printed about Nicole when she went missing. I talked to him. He said he saves everything. He had hundreds of pictures he took for different stories he'd done over the years. He gave me what he had on Nicole. There's some from the search parties, a candlelight vigil, even her class's graduation the following year. They did a little memorial for her then. Anyway, I thought it might be worth looking at. I'll start trying to organize it tomorrow. Larraby gave me everything in a giant pile."

"No, that's good, Birdie. Really good. Thanks."

Jake went to the other end of the table where they had a clear workspace. He put the stacks of papers Edwards brought in and spread them out.

"Do I want to even know what that was all about?" Birdie asked.

"That," he said, "was perhaps a torpedo."

Birdie came closer, standing over Jake's shoulder. He couldn't help himself. He gave her a once-over. Birdie had removed her bandage, but still had stitches in her forehead. She'd been cleared of any concussion protocols. Still, he much preferred her spending her time here than out on the street.

"Brouchard claims he was at a CLE in D.C. the week Nicole went missing."

Birdie sat down with the printout. "Can we call the Watergate? Verify that he was a guest? And even if he was, doesn't it seem like a perfect cover?"

"I thought the same, initially," Jake said. "Only he turned in a certificate to the state bar. At least according to the Federal Criminal Lawyers Association, he fulfilled the class requirements such that they gave him six credits for attending."

"Well, you are a former Fed. Do you know anybody at the Federal Criminal Lawyers Association?"

"No, but I'll make a call. Twenty-five years is a long time. But somebody might remember something."

"You've done continuing ed, haven't you? As a detective, as an FBI agent. You've gone to seminars like this, haven't you?"

"Sure," he said.

"Me too. How many of them have you gone to all on your own?"

"What do you mean?"

"I mean … can we find out if Brouchard had a travel companion who can verify being with him?"

"Edwards didn't mention anybody. It would have been in his client's interest to tell me that."

Jake picked up the desk phone and punched in an internal line to Darcy. "Hey, Darcy, it's Jake. Can I ask you for a favor?"

"Another one?" she said.

"Can you see if you can get a hold of someone at the Federal Criminal Lawyers Association based in D.C.? I'm specifically looking for whoever might have been in charge of their Federal Practice Seminar. There's one that ran in October of 1997 I'm particularly interested in."

"Sure. I'll see who I can scare up. You going to be in your war room for a while?"

"All morning probably. Thanks."

"You got it." Darcy clicked off.

"I did some of my own checking at the courthouse," Birdie said. She reached for another stack of papers and slid them across the table to Jake.

"I paid a visit to the Common Pleas and Muni Court clerks. Twenty-five years ago, Brouchard's bread and butter was court appointments. I had the girls pull all the cases he was of record on for the month of October 1997. Then I cross-referenced those with the dockets for that week."

"They still have those records?" Jake asked.

"They do. We're lucky. If Nicole Strong had disappeared two years before she did, none of this would show up anywhere. Worthington County was part of a statewide grant. They started digitizing records the year before Nicole went missing. So ... it only took a few keystrokes to find what I needed. Brouchard was in court the Monday before Nicole's murder, and not again until the next week."

"Which tracks with him not being in town," Jake said, sighing.

"What's the matter?"

"I don't know. I just feel like every time I think I'm getting somewhere with this case, things just keep turning to quicksand. Malcolm Edwards basically accused me of having a vendetta against Brouchard."

"Do you?"

"Of course not. I care about Anya. I've never denied that. I've had a front row seat to how losing Nicole has ripped that family apart. The thing is, so has Brouchard. God. He's been part of that family for a decade. Whether he killed Nicole or not, he knew something. He was involved in her life in a way he shouldn't have been right when she disappeared. And he said nothing."

"He did more than say nothing," Birdie said. "He seduced her lookalike younger sister, Jake. It's weird. It's creepy. And I think it's a little bit evil. If this seminar checks out though ... what else do we have?"

"We have this," Jake said. Last night, before leaving, he'd brought Nicole's letter down and put it in one of the evidence boxes against the wall. He had planned to show it to Birdie this morning. He took it out and placed it in front of her.

"Where did you get this?" she said, picking up the letter. She frowned as she read who it was addressed to.

"Alton Bardo?" she said. "Jake ..."

"Just read it," he said.

She did.

Birdie sat with it for a moment before giving Jake a reaction. She put her hand flat on the table and tapped her fingers.

"Well?"

"Well ... that was one very confused teenage girl. It sounds like she knew she was pregnant. And it sounds like she knew exactly who the father was."

"That's my take too. If I had to guess, they got into some argument about it. She never names Alton Bardo though."

"Right. If he were the father, it seems like she would have been more direct about it. Unless ..."

"Unless what?"

"Well, what if she was worried somebody else was going to get their hands on this letter? Like his family or something. I don't know. It feels like she was talking in code to him for a reason. She had a real concern that maybe their conversation wasn't private."

"Did you find any of Alton Bardo's letters back to her in this stuff?" Jake asked.

"Not a one," Birdie answered. "No journals, diaries, notes, nothing. If she had anything like that, she didn't keep it. Burned them, maybe."

"Maybe ..." Jake said. "Or maybe somebody else got to them before we did."

"Friggin' Brouchard," Birdie said. "Maybe he didn't kill her. But maybe he did enough destruction after the fact to keep anybody else from finding out what she meant to him."

"Yeah."

"That's obstruction, Jake."

"Yeah."

The desk phone rang. The internal line. "Hey, Darcy," he said. "Watcha got for me?"

"The answer to all your problems," she said. "And I made a new friend. Line four. Her name's Norma. She's been the executive assistant for FCLA for thirty years. She's retiring in two weeks. Treat her well."

"Thanks, Darcy," Jake said. "You're the best."

"I know," Darcy said, laughing. She clicked off, and Jake picked up line four.

TWENTY-EIGHT

Within five minutes, Jake knew Tim Brouchard's alibi would probably hold up in court.

"You're sure?" Jake asked. He'd put Norma Byers on speakerphone. Just like Darcy informed him, Norma had been running seminars for the FCLA for almost thirty years.

"Oh, I'm sure," she said. "When I took over this program, it was a mess. The Fed Practice Seminar had a reputation of being nothing more than an excuse to write off a trip to D.C. and spend four days at the bar. Attorneys would sign in in the morning and then go have a liquid lunch on their law firm's dime. I put a stop to all of that. In '95, I instituted a new system. Participants in the seminar have to sign in upon arrival, at the lunch break, and at the end of the day. All four days of the conference. If they want their certificates, it's butts in seats and I'm the one taking attendance."

Birdie caught Jake's eye across the table.

"She's good," Birdie mouthed. Jake knew it. She'd be a defense attorney's dream.

"Do you remember Tim Brouchard coming to those conferences by any chance?" Jake asked.

"I might if you send me a picture," she said. "But I can tell you, I'm looking at my attendance records from that fall right now. I keep meticulous files, Detective. I've got his signature scanned on all days of that conference."

"Mrs. Byers, I really appreciate it," Jake said. "You've been so helpful."

"That's just my job, Detective. But I'm glad if it helped you. Is there anything else I can do for you?"

"Not right now. But I may call you later. If you don't mind me saying, your organization is going to suffer a big loss when you retire."

"Oh I know, believe me. They haven't even hired my replacement. I think they thought I was bluffing."

"Well, you take care," Jake said. He reached over and clicked off the call.

"Wow," Birdie said. "I'd say Tim Brouchard is damn lucky Norma Byers exists."

Jake sat back in his chair. "So that's that. Brouchard wasn't in town when Nicole went missing. We're back to square one except for this."

He tapped his fingers on a copy of the letter Alton Bardo's mother had saved.

"What's your game plan?" Birdie asked.

"I'm going to see if Shannon Weingard can make any sense of it."

"You're not going to show it to Anya?"

"Not yet. I'm not sure Anya is ready to talk to me again."

Birdie pursed her lips. "I'm sorry about that. It's not right for her to blame you for what her husband did. He might not be a murderer, but he's a liar and a creep. Plus ... this line ..."

Birdie reached over and scrolled through the letter. She tapped the line where Nicole begged Alton Bardo to keep writing her letters.

"There were no letters in her things," she said. "Where are they? Brouchard still has to answer for that, maybe."

"Maybe," Jake said. He took the copy of the letter back from Birdie and folded it in his pocket. "I texted Shannon. She's at home right now. I'm gonna head over there."

"You want me to come with?"

"Not this time. Would you mind dealing with these?" Jake asked. He put his hand on the stack of VHS tapes. Darcy had gotten a hold of a TV/player combo and wheeled it into the room.

Birdie grabbed a pen and paper. "I'll take notes and write down any dates or time stamps if I find something interesting."

"I appreciate it. That'll save me a ton of time."

Birdie took the first tape and popped it into the player. Jake held his breath, hoping the thing would actually play after all this time. The storage unit was climate controlled, but the tape was ancient.

The screen filled with static. Birdie fast-forwarded past it. Then the recording began to play.

"Say hi!" A female voice could be heard on the other side of the camera.

"Get that thing out of my face, Nic!" Jake recognized Shannon Weingard. Only she was just a kid. A teenage girl. She wore a black, one-piece bathing suit. She was fit, athletic with toned biceps and her brown hair pulled back.

They were at a pool. Jake remembered Anya's parents used to have one. Behind Shannon, a teenage Shawn Weingard executed a cannonball, aimed right at the girls. Nicole Strong screamed, swearing at Shawn that he'd ruin the camera. Then the picture grew distorted for a second as Nicole must have shut off the recording.

"The time stamp says that's the summer of '96," Birdie said. "Over a year before she disappeared. I've got a lot of these to get through."

"Yeah," Jake said, feeling hollowed out. It was so strange to hear Nicole's voice. He never had before. It was nothing like Anya's. Hers was deeper, almost raspy, with the slightest lisp.

"I'll be back later this afternoon," Jake said.

"Hopefully I'll have something for you," Birdie said.

Jake texted Shannon Weingard, telling her he was fifteen minutes out.

Twenty-Nine

By the time he got to Shannon's house out on County Road Sixteen, there was a familiar car parked in the driveway. Ryan, his nephew, was here. He and Chloe Weingard walked out the front door just as Jake walked up.

They didn't see him at first. Jake caught his nephew giving Chloe a playful swat on the rear end. Jake cleared his throat. Ryan blushed. Chloe's face fell but she recovered quickly, smiling at Jake.

"Hi, Detective Cashen, my mom's in the kitchen. You can go on in."

"Thanks," he said. He gave Ryan a stern look, meant to convey a mild warning. At seventeen, he knew his nephew likely had a one-track mind when it came to his new girlfriend. Ryan had the decency to look sheepish, but took Chloe to his car and the two of them quickly left.

"Shannon?" Jake called out before going inside.

"In here," Shannon answered. He opened the screen door. Shannon stood in the kitchen surveying paint samples spread out on her counter.

"What do you think?" she said, picking up two swatches containing various shades of gray.

"For what?"

"For the kitchen," she said. "I'm getting white subway tile and stainless steel appliances. I want some color on the walls. You like midnight steel, or smoky ridge?"

Jake could discern no difference between the two slate-gray swatches she showed him.

"Uh ... smoky ridge," he said.

"That's what I think too. Shawn's not so sure. The man just wants everything to be white. He's got no vision."

"Thanks for meeting me," he said. "I wasn't sure if you would. I didn't know what Anya might have told you."

Shannon put her paint swatches down. "Yeah. You've screwed the pooch pretty hard on that one."

"Shannon," he said. "I couldn't tell her about Tim. I'm in the middle ..."

"Yeah. Yeah. Ongoing investigation. I get it. Look, she'll come around. Someday."

"How is she?"

"Awful. A complete mess."

"Just tell me she left the house like she said she was going to?"

"Come on," Shannon said. "This is a sit-down conversation. Can I get you a beer?"

"No. I'm still on duty."

"Root beer?"

"I'm good. Thanks."

"Come on. Let's sit out on the porch. It's too nice a day to be cooped up inside."

Shannon led him through the kitchen. They had outdoor couches under a giant pergola. Shawn had installed a gas-powered fire pit. Jake took a chair in the shade. Shannon sat on the couch opposite him. She already had a glass of lemonade chilling on the table beside her.

"Anya's been staying with her parents," Shannon said. "And I'm worried about her. Growing up with Marty and Viv was hell for her. But I suppose you already know that."

"I do," Jake said. "But she's probably better off there."

"Maybe. Tim's trying to get her back. Can you believe that?"

"He can't be serious."

"Oh, he's serious. He wants her to believe you're trying to frame him."

Anger bubbled through Jake. He wished he could have said yes to a beer, or something stronger.

"I know you're not," Shannon said. "For what it's worth, I told her that. Anya's just not ready to forgive anybody yet."

"She's had her world turned upside down. I'm sorry about that. I'm glad you're staying in touch with her. She cares a lot about you."

Shannon nodded. "But you didn't come here to talk about Anya, did you?"

"No. Not just." Jake took the copy of the letter out of his pocket but held on to it. Shannon's eyes widened when she saw it.

"Shannon," he said. "Did you know? Did you suspect at all that Nicole was in a relationship with Tim Brouchard?"

Shannon shook her head. "Not one bit. I didn't think she knew him very well at all. I knew he was an advisor or a mentor or something with that young professionals group, whatever it was called. But Nicole was involved in every school group. You name it. CAA DECA, cheerleading. She was trying to get into a good college. She was trying to get out, you know?"

Jake handed her the letter. Shannon unfolded it. A tremor went through her as she read the first lines. She brought a hand up to her mouth. Blinking hard, she looked at Jake.

"Where did you get this?"

"I can't really tell you that. Do you recognize the handwriting? I know it's a photocopy but ..."

A sob tore through Shannon. "It's Nicole's handwriting. I'd recognize it anywhere. But until this second, I didn't know that. She made those slanted e's. We used to write notes to each other all the time. Stupid stuff."

"Do you still have any of them?"

Shannon shook her head. "I never saved any of that stuff. God. I wish I had."

"But you wrote notes to her? Things she would have kept?"

"I don't know what she kept," Shannon said. "But she was a note writer. Yes."

Shannon sat back, drawing her legs up under her. For a moment, Jake could see the young girl she was in the video tape Birdie had started to play. Her hands shaking, tears streaming down her face, Shannon read Nicole's letter to Alton Bardo. After she got to the last page, she started again. Jake waited patiently while Shannon read it three times. Then, she put it down on the table between them.

"That was written a few weeks before she went missing," Jake said. "What do you think?"

Shannon let out a great sigh. "It's Nic. Just ... typical Nic."

"What do you mean?"

"I never liked how she treated Alton. I'm sorry. I probably shouldn't say that. She's dead. They're both dead. What does it matter?"

"It might matter a lot. Just ... tell me what your gut says. She's vague in that letter. Do you know who she's talking about? What guy did she think Alton was going to rip his nuts off?"

Shannon swallowed hard. She stopped crying. Then, in a voice so small Jake barely heard her, she asked. "Jake ... she sounds like she's maybe pregnant in that letter. Was she? Do you know?"

Jake debated telling her what he knew. In the end, he decided to keep things ambiguous.

"I'm not sure," he said. "It's really hard to say. Did you suspect that she might be?"

"No! God, no. I would have said something to the police if I thought that. I knew ... Nicole was always moody."

"What do you mean you didn't like how she treated Alton?"

Shannon drew her legs up even more, resting her chin on her knees. "Alton was a man, you know? Not a boy. And Nicole was just ... still a girl when they dated. But he was crazy about her. Hell, they all were. I don't think there was a teenage boy in the whole county who didn't have a crush on her. Though I think I've told you that before. Anyway, Alton and Nicole broke up because she tried to give him an ultimatum. She was mad that he was leaving to join the army. She felt like he was leaving her behind. I mean, he was ... but she didn't like the idea of him moving on. Well, that didn't end well. They broke up. Nicole was devastated. I think Alton was a little bit too. But ... he was never gonna stay around here."

Jake stopped himself from telling Shannon that's exactly what Alton's older brother had said. He would keep Rex Bardo's role in this to himself for now.

"This?" Shannon said, pointing to the letter. "This was the kind of stuff she pulled all the time. She played mind games with guys."

"It sounds like in that letter ... Alton knew she was seeing someone else."

"Yeah. That's what I think."

"But you don't know who?"

"No. I don't know anything. That ... that was a weird summer. Nicole was really distant. It was our last summer before starting our senior year. We all knew things were coming to an end, you know? She was starting to pull away a little. And it wasn't all her fault. I'm not saying that. Shawn and I were always together. She was sad about Alton. But she was over him. I really thought she was over him. This letter? It's not where I thought Nicole's head was at. She was getting excited about leaving after we graduated. She wanted to meet some smart college guy. She said she was sick of all the townies and high school boys. That's why I'm saying I had no idea she was seeing anyone else. She told me she was done with the guys around here. Poor Alton. Is she honestly telling him she slept with some other guy but expected him to wait around for her?"

"That's kinda how I read that letter too. But like you said. She was just a kid."

Shannon nodded. "She sounds like ... God. Were we all really ever that young? It's just so hard. So unfair. Nicole's just frozen in time like that. She would have grown up. That's what I miss more than anything. We were supposed to experience all of this together. Getting married. Having our babies. She would have been my maid of honor when I married Shawn. We talked about that. When I got pregnant with Shawn Jr., it was kind of an oops. We were only nineteen. I remember picking up the phone as soon as I found out. It was Nic I wanted to call. She was supposed to be there for me. And Chloe ... I almost named her after Nicole. Shawn was worried that would be too hard for Nic's parents. So it's her middle name. Chloe Nicole. God. I just miss her so much."

"I know," Jake said. He picked up the letter.

"Does she know?" Shannon asked.

"I'm sorry?"

"Anya. Did you show her that letter?"

"No. Not yet. I'm not sure what light Anya could shed on it anyway."

"Yeah. You're probably right. They weren't that close back then. I mean, Nicole loved her baby sister. Don't get me wrong. But I don't think she would have confided in her. She still kind of thought of Anya as a nuisance. That's another thing that is so sad to me. They never had a chance to get close like sisters do when they grow up."

Jake rose. "Thanks for your time. I'm sorry if this upset you."

"Oh Jake, anything. You know that. Whatever I can do."

"Just try and think," Jake said. "If anything occurs to you. No matter how small. Anything you can remember about what Nicole did or said. Something that might help me figure out who this other boy was she was seeing."

Shannon walked with Jake to the driveway. "I've been thinking of nothing else," she said. "In some ways, I haven't stopped thinking about that for twenty-five years."

She came to him. Shannon pulled Jake into a hug, sobbing against his shoulder. He patted her on the back.

"You have to solve this one, Jake. You have to find out who did this to her."

As Shannon finally let go of him, Jake made one more promise he hoped he could keep.

THIRTY

"You're late! Get in here and stir that pot!" Gemma shouted at Jake, giving him her best big sister glare.

"I'm not that late," he said as he walked through the side door and into Grandpa's kitchen. He dutifully took his shoes off and lined them up against the wall. Sunday night was goulash night at Max Cashen's. Normally, no excuse was a good excuse for not attending. But as Jake looked out into the living room, he registered a noticeable absence and was, for once, glad of it.

"Where's Ryan tonight?" Jake asked as he picked up a wooden spoon and started stirring the thick red sauce on the stove.

"He's over at Travis's," Gemma said. "Erica told me he was having kind of a rough day. It's ... um ... Ben's birthday today. I invited them to come here, but she said they just wanted to keep it low key."

Jake stopped stirring. A wave of grief shot through him, making it hard to breathe. "I forgot," he whispered. "Birdie never mentioned anything."

"Why would she?" Gemma said. She reached up and grabbed a huge stainless steel colander from a shelf above the sink.

"Make sure you use olive oil!" Grandpa shouted from the living room. He and Aiden were seated at a table in the corner. Grandpa was determined to teach Aiden how to play chess by the end of the summer. So far, eight-year-old Aiden was having a devil of a time just sitting still in his chair.

"Quit moving that queen so early!" Grandpa shouted.

"But I like moving my queen," Aiden complained.

"Well, there's the right way, and then there's the idiot way. Which one are you?"

"Grandpa!" Gemma shouted. "Don't listen to him, Aiden. There is no idiot way."

Max Cashen mumbled a phrase Jake hadn't heard since he was a kid. If his grandmother were still alive, she would have sailed a wooden spoon across the room with deadly precision and smacked Grandpa in the head with it. The phrase in question was filthy, and Gaelic.

"I should have said something to Birdie," Jake said. "We've just been so focused on this case."

"It's good for her," Gemma said. "I think Erica really likes what she's doing. She's settling in."

"What about Travis?" Jake said. "I haven't seen him much since wrestling season ended. I've been meaning to pop in to one of Coach Purcell's summer conditioning practices. There just hasn't been time."

"He's as all right as he can be," Gemma said. She dumped a steaming pot of pasta into the colander and coated it with olive oil. "Ryan says he's starting to talk more. Starting to hang out with his friends more. He's got a job down at the farm supply store on County Road Fourteen. He'll be working for Lenny Cutler."

"Good," Jake said. "What about Ryan?"

"Get this, he's got himself a job at the Frosty Freeze. He's scooping ice cream. Kid made fifty bucks in tips on a four-hour shift the other night. Chloe got him the job. She works there part time too."

Jake brought the spoon to his lips and tasted Gemma's sauce. It was just right.

"Bring that over here," she said. "There's a ladle on the hook."

Jake did as he was told.

"Buffet style tonight, boys!" she called out. Jake went to the oven. He pulled out two loaves of perfectly toasted garlic bread. Gemma handed him a bread knife. He sliced it, careful not to burn his hands.

Grandpa Max and Aiden filed into the kitchen, helping themselves to heaping plates of goulash. They took them back to the chess table. Grandpa would never quit in the middle of a game, not even for dinner.

Tonight, Jake was glad of it. It gave him a chance to broach a subject with his sister. The two of them went to the kitchen table and took their seats. Even with no one else sitting there, it would never occur to Jake to take any chair but the one he'd used since the days Grandma Cashen strapped a high chair seat to it. And Gemma always sat directly across from him.

"Can you tell me how it's going?" Gemma asked, tearing apart a steaming piece of garlic bread.

"Nicole's case? No. I can't really tell you how it's going."

"Do you really think Tim Brouchard killed her?"

Jake gave Gemma a wide-eyed stare. It didn't matter what he'd just told her. Gemma was never one to take no for an answer.

"Do you remember him being around back in those days?" Jake asked. "He was some kind of mentor to the Future Professional Leaders group. That's apparently how he got into Nicole Strong's orbit."

Gemma shook her head no. "That wasn't my scene or my crowd. I can tell you right now, I would have thought he was a creep. I've always thought he was a creep. Now we just know why. But Anya saw something in him."

Jake dabbed his chin with a napkin when Gemma gave him a dirty look.

"Ya think he raped her?" Gemma asked.

Jake nearly choked on his macaroni. "Where'd you hear that? Is that what people are saying?"

"It's what I'm asking," she said.

"I can't talk about it, Gemma. When I can, you'll be the first to know."

"I just don't get it. He was a lawyer even then. Everyone says he was planning to run for office even back when he was in law school. It was always his ambition. So why would he risk all that getting mixed up with Nicole Strong?"

"When I figure that out, I'll let you know that too."

They ate in silence for a few minutes. Then, Jake took a breath, steeling himself for his sister's reaction to the topic he wished he could avoid.

"So, Ryan and Chloe Weingard."

Gemma looked up from her plate. She'd all but finished. She put her fork down and wiped her mouth with her napkin.

"Apparently so," she said.

"Do you like her?" Jake asked.

"Chloe's a good kid. Shannon and Shawn are all right. But they're really just friends."

"Is that what Ryan told you?" Jake asked.

Gemma narrowed her eyes at him. "What are you getting at?"

"She's his girlfriend, Gemma," he said. "They're dating ... er ... or doing something."

Gemma let out a big, whole-body sigh.

"It's just ... I saw him with her. Out at her folks' place. He wasn't doing anything wrong. Don't worry. It's just ... uh ... have you had a talk with him?"

"What kind of talk?"

"*The* talk."

Gemma looked over her shoulder to make sure Grandpa and Aiden were sufficiently occupied by their chess game. Even so, she picked up her and Jake's plates and walked them into the kitchen out of earshot. Jake followed her. As Gemma began washing the plates, Jake grabbed a dish towel to dry them.

"We've talked," she said. "Ryan knows what my expectations are."

"Your expectations and his hormones are two different things, Gemma."

"We've talked," she said. "My son knows if he does something stupid, I'll cut his weiner off."

Jake laughed. "How'd that go over?"

"He's smart enough to be scared of his mama."

"Gemma, I'm the first to admit you're a scary-ass bitch. But ... at Ryan's age and testosterone level, that's not a big enough threat. Trust me. It won't work."

"Did something happen? Do you know something? Jake, you have to tell me." There was desperation in her voice that Jake wasn't used to.

"No," he said. "But I told you. I saw him with her. He's seventeen. She's seventeen. He doesn't have a dad. If you want me to have a talk with him, well, I'm offering."

"What would you say to him?"

Jake smiled. "That's really between me and Ryan."

"Jake ..."

"Relax. I'll tell him everything I know you want him to hear. I'll tell him how to be careful and respectful, and how to avoid having his mother cut his weiner off, okay?"

She stood at the sink, gripping the side. It was a rare display of emotion from his sister, but when she looked at him, her eyes glistened.

"It's okay, Mama," Jake teased. He put an arm around her. "You're doing okay. He's a good kid. I'll make sure of it."

She nodded. "Okay."

"Okay."

"You're all making it too hard!" Grandpa said. Neither Jake nor Gemma had heard him come into the kitchen.

"You tell that boy to wrap that rascal. Just like I told you!" Grandpa Max pointed a crooked finger right at Jake. Behind him, Aiden walked in.

"Mom, what rascal? Why does it need to be wrapped?" Aiden asked.

Gemma reached down, covered her son's ears, and threw a deadly stare at both Jake and their grandfather.

Thirty-One

Monday morning, Jake surrounded himself with what was left of Nicole Strong's life. Birdie had managed to get a hold of a garment rack and hung all of Nicole's dresses in the corner of their repurposed storage room. Nicole had only worn one prom dress. By the spring of what would have been her senior year, she was already dead. Jake pulled her junior prom dress forward. Black lace with spaghetti straps and a slit that would have run all the way up her right leg. He remembered the night Anya wanted to wear it to their own prom. It had set off that awful fight with her parents. It got so bad her mother threatened to keep Anya from going to the dance at all. So she snuck out that night. Jake picked her up at the end of the lane from her house. She wore a different dress that night and spent most of it crying. It had been one of their last formal dates together.

Jake put the dress back. He pulled another one, a white polyester nightmare with a blue apron over the top of it. Nicole's waitressing uniform from the Paul Revere Diner. Her name badge was still clipped to the front. He ran his fingers across the lettering. Jake knew Virgil had questioned all the regulars at that diner at length.

But Nicole hadn't worked there in almost six weeks before she disappeared. Not after school started in September. The place had long since closed down. Just another abandoned ghost of a business now. And another dead end.

Jake sat at the table. Birdie had left him detailed notes about the videos she'd watched for him. She made cards for every tape, marking the time stamps and events for each event recorded on them. Then, she lined them all up in chronological order.

There were only three tapes, representing eighteen hours of recording time. But there were only about six total hours of recorded video, the rest was just blank static.

Jake picked up the second video in the batch. He popped it into the player and took a seat at the table, grabbing the remote control. He hit play.

It was Anya. He checked Birdie's notes. She would have been just eleven years old. Skinny. Long hair that hung down to her waist. She wore a pink-and-white checkered sundress.

"What do you wanna be when you grow up, squirt?" Nicole asked her off camera.

"A ballerina," she said.

Nicole laughed. "You've got two left feet. And you've never taken a dance lesson in your life. Try again."

Anya stuck her tongue out at her older sister. She sat down on the curb right in front of their house. Anya had scraped knees and bare feet.

"What do you wanna be when you grow up?" Anya asked.

"A fighter pilot," Nicole teased.

"No, really."

"A movie star."

Rolling her eyes, Anya got up. She skipped her way up the lawn, stooping to pick up a dandelion. Nicole zoomed in as Anya puffed out her cheeks and blew its wispy seeds through the air.

The tape cut out. Squiggly lines came across the screen. A moment later, the camera turned back on. Jake tilted his head to the side. Whoever was holding the thing hadn't realized it was recording yet and the camera was pointed sideways, catching nothing but feet. After another moment, the picture straightened. Jake looked at the card Birdie made. This was Nicole's junior prom. The one where she wore the black dress. Jake recognized the backyard of Shannon and Shawn Weingard's home. At the time, Shannon's parents owned it. The fancy fire pit porch wasn't there yet, just an above ground pool in the background.

Nicole recorded Shawn and Shannon Weingard as Shannon's mother took pictures of them. They staged Shawn's placement of Shannon's corsage on the bodice of her pink satin dress. Shawn whispered something to Shannon that made her blush. Her mother's back was turned. Shannon playfully slapped Shawn on the chest. He grabbed her behind then dropped his hands to his side as Nancy Murphy, Shannon's now deceased mother, turned back around.

"Let me get you!" Shannon said to Nicole. She took the camera from her. Nicole stood on the porch. She was stunning in her black lace. Her blonde hair hung straight down her back. She did a little twirl, showing off her impossibly high heels.

"Let's go," Shawn said impatiently off camera. Then the recording abruptly stopped. When it started again, they were at the dance.

Nicole had the camera again. She pointed it at two teachers standing near the gym entrance. Jake recognized Mr. Kramer, the vice principal, and Ms. Schultz, the girls' gym teacher. A few years after this, they caused a minor scandal when each of them left their respective spouses and moved in together. They later got married and recently retired to Florida.

"Smile, Mr. K," Nicole instructed. Ned Kramer gave Nicole a crazy-eyed grin, causing Mandy Schultz to break out in a fit of laughter.

Nicole slowly panned the camera at the crowd of high school students. Some clustered near the punch and snack table, but most were on the dance floor. Couple after couple embraced in that slow, swaying movement that teenagers mistake for dancing.

Jake took a fresh pad of paper and started to make notes. Some of the students, he recognized. Most of them still lived in the area. Nicole herself went stag this night. Alton Bardo was already off at basic training and no longer her boyfriend. She would have met Tim Brouchard already. It turned Jake's stomach to think he'd already made his moves on her.

This was May 1997. Two months later, Nicole Strong would be pregnant.

Jake scanned the crowd, noting every male student Nicole stopped to record and talk to. She moved through the throngs of students and made her way to a table along the wall. Grady Thompson and Brenda Pollack sat together. Brenda was on Grady's lap. Two seconds later, Mr. Kramer came into view and broke them up. Nicole laughed off camera. Grady flipped Kramer off behind his back as Brenda took her own chair beside him.

"Having fun?" Nicole asked.

"He hates it," Brenda answered. Nicole zoomed in on Grady's face. His eyes were glazed over and it became pretty clear he'd spiked his punch or smoked some weed. Maybe both.

"When will you girls be ready to leave?" he asked. "We can head over to my brother's."

Grady Thompson's brother Joel was at least a decade older than him. Jake knew his property well. Joel Thompson had a corn field behind his house that had served as a popular haunt for Stanley High teenagers looking to hook up or get high out of the watchful eye of adults. Grady's cousin Chuck was a member of the Wise Men. He would have been a sergeant then. Jake wondered how well Chuck would have liked knowing his cousin Joel routinely bought alcohol and drugs for Grady and his friends.

"We just got here," Nicole said. "Nobody's even asked me to dance yet."

"Is that all it'll take?" Grady asked. "Come on. I'll dance with you."

Jake watched as Brenda's expression changed. Her smile faltered just a little. Grady took the camera and handed it to Brenda, making Jake a little dizzy as the picture bobbed and weaved until Brenda could refocus.

Off screen, he could hear Shawn and Shannon join the group. Brenda recorded everything as Grady took Nicole Strong out onto the dance floor. It was still a slow song. Grady seemed unsure on his feet. He was a big guy. Six three, probably. He'd been the heavyweight the previous year until Coach Borowski kicked him off the team for smoking weed.

He towered over Nicole. Jake straightened. She was having a hard time keeping a straight posture. It looked as if Grady might be in danger of falling down.

"He's absolutely wasted," Shannon said, her tone angry.

"He'll be all right," Shawn said.

The song changed to something up tempo. Grady and Nicole stayed on the dance floor. Other students got closer to them. Nicole was happy, laughing, spinning around. Brenda widened the angle. For a brief moment, she caught Shawn as he was looking at Nicole and Grady. Then the scene cut out. When the recording picked back up, it was twenty minutes later. The DJ played the Electric Slide. All the girls were on the floor and this time, it seemed Grady had a hold of the camera.

He zoomed in on Brenda's rear end. Then pulled back. Shawn stood next to him, his face hard as he stared at the dance floor. Jake tracked his line of sight.

He grabbed the remote and hit fast forward. There was another hour of footage from the dance. According to Birdie's notes, that's where this particular tape would stop. The next one covered events that happened in the summer.

As Jake watched, all but the last five minutes of the prom footage was taken by either Grady Thompson with his herky-jerky handling, or Brenda. Nicole only took the camera back as the four of them walked back to Shawn's car. He drove that night. If they went to Thompson's corn field, Jake had no idea.

Jake rewound. He watched Nicole and Grady make their way to the dance floor again. Then he watched as she danced with other girls. At one point, she was in the arms of a boy he didn't recognize. Birdie had covered that too though. He read her notes. His name was Rick Wolverton, another member of the Christian Athletes Association who wore a chastity pin. They kept at least a foot between each other. Clearly just friends.

But in the corner of many of the frames, someone kept watching her. He'd spent so long looking at it, Jake couldn't be sure he wasn't just seeing things.

"Sorry I'm late!" Jake jumped, startled as Birdie walked in and flipped on the lights. He hadn't even realized how dim it was in the room before then, he'd been so transfixed by the video.

"Four car pile-up on County Road Eleven. Nate Stinson fell asleep at the wheel again. Wrapped his F-350 around a telephone pole."

"Is he okay?" Jake asked.

"He'll live. But he clipped two other cars on the way. It was a mess. No fatalities though so that's a blessing."

"You did amazing work with all of this," Jake said, gesturing to her detailed note cards.

"I've asked IT to digitize all those tapes," she said. "I'm worried about them degrading with all the fast forwarding and rewinding. We'll have best evidence with the tapes if we ever go to trial, but for our purposes, we can watch on a laptop."

"Good thinking," Jake said. "I want to run something by you. I think I might be going crazy."

"What's up?" Birdie said. She came around the table and took a seat beside him.

"Maybe nothing," he said. "I'm maybe looking for something that isn't really there. Or I've watched these so many times they've stopped making sense."

"Show me," she said.

Jake rewound the tape to the bit where Grady Thompson took Nicole to the dance floor.

"She looks a little jealous, I thought," Birdie said, pointing to Brenda.

"Maybe," Jake said. "Only she's the one who keeps recording. If she were angry, wouldn't she just go out to the dance floor and peel Grady off of her?"

"That's what I would have done, yes," Birdie said.

"But look." Jake froze the tape. Birdie squinted at the figure on the screen. Jake advanced it a little more, catching another angle. Nicole was dancing the Electric Slide next to Brenda and Shannon.

"See that?" Jake said. Grady was recording now. For a second, he had Shawn Weingard in the frame. Jake froze the recording again. Birdie got up.

"He looks angry," Birdie said.

"There are two more," Jake said. He fast-forwarded. Birdie sat back down.

"Do you see it?" Jake asked. "Am I wrong?"

Birdie shook her head. She took the remote from Jake and replayed the four bits of footage Jake had focused on.

"Shawn Weingard," Birdie said. "He's not looking at Shannon. Christ. Jake. He's looking at Nicole the whole time."

She fast-forwarded up to the scene where Nicole danced with Rick Wolverton. Shawn stood just a few feet away from them. Shannon was next to him but her back was turned talking to Brenda and Grady. Birdie paused the playback. She caught it perfectly. Shawn Weingard was staring hard at Nicole Strong. A glare. A flash of anger, maybe. But he appeared not to like seeing Wolverton's hand as it rested just above Nicole's rear end.

"Is it something?" Jake asked.

"It's noticeable," she said. "It's not just you. I was so focused on writing down time stamps and people's names. I never really watched facial expressions and body language. But yeah. Whatever was going on that night, Shawn Weingard is paying a lot of attention to Nicole. He's everywhere she is. What do you want to do?"

"I'm not sure yet," Jake said.

"If we're picking up on it off a twenty-five-year-old videotape, don't you think somebody who was there, who knew them, might have been clued into it too?"

"That's what I'm thinking too," Jake said. "I think I'll start with Grady Thompson. He and Brenda Pollack were there at the bowling alley the night she disappeared as well. I'll be subtle. But ..."

"Yeah," Birdie said. "Do you want me to reach out to Brenda? She's moved to Cleveland, but I was friends with her younger sister."

"That'd be helpful," Jake said. "Thanks."

His pulse racing, he grabbed his phone and made a call to Grady Thompson, who answered on the first ring.

Thirty-Two

J ake met Grady Thompson on his lunch hour the next day. There was a little burger place just outside of Stanley on Grace Church Road. As Jake pulled in, he realized it was directly across the street from what used to be the Blackhand Hills Bowling Alley. The place had closed down over ten years ago and had fallen into disrepair. Weeds grew through the cracks in the asphalt where the parking lot used to be.

A coincidence, Jake knew. They picked the restaurant because Jake wanted some place out of the way, dimly lit, and quiet. Still, it was hard not to think Nicole's spirit was somehow guiding him today. But Jake didn't believe in ghosts. He shook off the chill and went inside.

Grady Thompson had the benefit of having looked like he was forty since the day he hit puberty. Thinning hair, a bulging midsection, and a thick, lumberjack-style beard. Minus a few gray hairs here and there, the man looked exactly like his yearbook picture.

"Cashen," he said, smiling. It seemed a bit odd as Jake never knew him back in the day. Thompson predated him on the wrestling team by five years. Thompson wasn't one of the alumni who worked out with the team beyond high school. Still, he gave Jake a firm, meaty handshake. A young server showed them to a booth all the way in the back of the restaurant. It had high seat backs, the kind you couldn't see over. It meant no one would know they were there besides the waitress.

Good.

They made small talk. Grady asked what Jake thought of the varsity team's chances at State this upcoming season. In the background, a Tigers game played on a screen above the bar. There were only two men at the bar, seated on the far end out of earshot.

Jake ordered an iced tea and a cheeseburger. Grady ordered the same but stuck with a water. Jake had noticed a "One Day at a Time" bumper sticker on Grady's truck when he walked in.

After their food came, Jake pulled a thin stack of papers out of his leather bag and set them on the table.

"I really appreciate you making some time for me today," Jake said.

"Oh sure. I figured you'd be calling. I talked to the cops a lot around the time Nic went missing."

"That's what I wanted to talk to you about ..."

"She was banging Tim Brouchard though? No shit?"

"That isn't ..."

"I had no idea," Grady said. "I'll tell you that right off the bat. She was nuts for Alton Bardo. Like ... classic psycho crazy chick nuts."

"What do you mean by that?"

"He wasn't into her like that," Grady said. "Alton was a good guy. A great guy. Intense as hell. Real serious. But you knew he wasn't gonna stick around Blackhand Hills because of some girl. Nic used to play head games with him."

"I've heard that," Jake said.

"Oh yeah. They were on and off again for a couple of years before she went missing. They were off when he left for basic, you know. Before she vanished. But before that, the times they'd break up, Nic would pretty much throw herself at other guys whenever Alton was around. Trying to make him jealous. Then when it worked, when he started calling her again, she'd go cold. Make him chase her. He got pretty sick of that after a while. It backfired on her. The last time they broke up, I don't know what she thought, but we all knew he wasn't coming back for her."

"That tracks with what I've heard," Jake said. He laid his hand flat on the papers. "You mind if I ask you about the last time you saw Nicole?"

"Sure." Grady took a big bite of his burger. Mustard dripped down his chin. He fumbled for his napkin.

"What can you remember?"

His mouth full, Grady answered, "Isn't it all written down there?"

"It is," Jake said, taking his hand off the stack of papers. "But just ... sitting here, what do you remember?"

Grady put his burger down. "It was just a normal night. It was me, Shawn Weingard, Shannon ... she was Murphy back then. And Brenda. We were still going out then. Broke up just before graduation. We went over to Blackhand Hills Lanes. Geez. That's right across the street. Small world, man."

"Small town," Jake said.

"Right. Anyway, we bowled a couple of games. That was it. The girls wanted to turn in early because they were taking the SAT or the ACT, one of 'em."

"You didn't take the test?"

"Nah. I wasn't going to college. I had a job lined up at the mill."

"Sure. About that night …"

"It was just normal. I remember I wanted to leave and hang out at Brenda's. Her parents were out of town. And well … you know … I was seventeen. I was hoping to get some. That's what was most on my mind. I was just a dumb, horned-up kid. Right? I wasn't paying a whole lot of attention to anybody else. I think I told the cops all that back in the day."

"You did," Jake said.

"Lemme look though." Grady reached for the statement. Jake let him take it. He didn't immediately start reading it, he seemed far more eager to talk. It's what Jake hoped for.

"I took Brenda home. We were the first ones to leave. Like I said, I had a one-track mind."

"Was Nicole still there when you left?"

"No," Grady said. "She drove herself. I remember that. That's the thing they kept asking me. But Nic left early. Brenda and I left right after she did."

"I don't want to get too personal, but just so I have a clearer picture where everybody was, did you end up at Brenda's house after the bowling alley?"

"Yeah. For a little while. Her sisters were home so things didn't pan out for me, you know? Brenda was worried they'd rat on her. I remember we got into an argument about it. Not a bad one. Just …

I was pissed when I left. I remember all that because the next day, when the news about Nicole came out … I just remember thinking how glad I was that I saw Brenda home. Like I made sure she got inside. I waited in the driveway until she opened the front door. I wondered what might have happened if I hadn't."

"That's understandable. But … do you remember who Nicole left with?"

"Nobody. She was on her own as far as I know."

It was then Grady began leafing through the photocopy of his twenty-five-year-old witness statement. But he only skimmed through from what Jake could see. Jake waited, letting Grady absorb what he could. Finally, Grady handed the papers back to Jake and resumed eating the last two bites of his hamburger.

"You got any idea who did this?" Grady said while chewing.

"There have been some promising leads," Jake said. "But I can't really get into that."

Grady took a drink. "Yeah. I figured you'd say that. It sucks this all getting stirred up again. I hadn't talked to Brenda in, I don't know. Ten years. She called me out of the blue the other day. She's a paralegal or something at some law firm in Cleveland. She's married now. Got a couple of adult kids. We're still friends even though it didn't work out between us. We share this thing, this awful thing, what happened to Nicole. She just wanted to know how I was doing with all of it since they dug up Nic's body."

"That's a good friend," Jake said. "If you have a current phone number for her, do you think she'd mind if you shared it?"

Grady took out his phone. "I know she wouldn't." He pulled up his contacts and flipped the screen so Jake could see the number. Jake quickly wrote it down. Birdie was working on tracking Brenda Pollack down. In case she had any trouble, this would help.

"Grady," Jake said. "There's been something bugging me. I've had a lot of people spreading a lot of rumors about how things were back then. Most of it I assume is total garbage. But there's one thing I think you might be one of the only people who know something about."

"Shoot," Grady said.

Jake rolled the dice.

"I got the impression there might have been something going on with Nicole and Shawn Weingard."

Jake waited, held his breath, and studied Grady's reaction. He sat with his elbows on the table, hands folded. He scratched his chin on his knuckles then put his hands in his lap.

"Who's been telling you that?"

"I'm sorry. I can't say."

"What are they saying was going on between them?"

"It's been vague rumors and innuendo. I was hoping you could set it all straight. You were close to that whole group. You and Shawn are still buddies, aren't you?"

It was a tiny thing. Just the tightening of Grady's gaze. But Jake saw tension go through Grady. If he had to name it, it seemed like anger.

"She's dead, Grady," Jake said. "I can't give details. You understand. But it was brutal. Violent. Nicole suffered before she died. And that's something I need to know you can keep quiet. I can't have her family finding that out."

Grady winced. He looked like he was about to vomit. Then he recovered except for the fire in his eyes.

"It's true, isn't it?" Jake said. "There was something ..."

"I don't know," Grady snapped. "I never saw them together like that. Shawn never told me anything like that. Neither did Brenda."

"You never speculated with her? Or she … she never asked *you* if there was something going on between you two?"

"Me and Nicole? Hell, no. No way. She was never my type. Too skinny. Too much drama."

His type. Jake knew Grady Thompson had never married.

"You said Nicole liked to play head games with guys. Was she doing that that night? At the bowling alley? Do you remember anybody she might have flirted with?"

Grady let out a heavy sigh. "She wasn't flirting that night. She was agitated. She barely talked to anybody. I told you. The girls were all nervous about that college exam the next day. It was not a fun evening."

Grady's entire posture had changed. No longer relaxed, he sat straight up, not touching the seat back.

"What is it?" Jake said. "You can tell me."

"You have to promise me it won't leave this table," Grady said.

"I can't do that. I'm investigating a murder, Grady."

His shoulders dropped. "I guess I can respect you're honest at least. Look, it was nothing. Probably nothing. But yeah. Nicole was angry about something that night."

"More than just pre-exam nerves?"

"I think so. She … dammit. It's nothing."

"You don't think it's nothing, or you wouldn't bring it up," Jake said.

"I saw them. Shawn and Nicole got into some kind of argument. They were over by the restrooms. Those were tucked in a little alcove past the game room. Behind the pinball machines. I was on my way to the john and I saw them."

"What did you see?" Jake kept his tone flat.

"Shawn was pissed. His whole face was red. The way he was standing. Clenched fists. There was like steam coming out of his ears."

"What did you do?"

"I backed off right away. Didn't want to interrupt. Didn't even let them know I saw."

"Where were Shannon and Brenda during this?"

"Sitting at the table in our lane. They were on the other side of the building. They didn't see. Only me."

"Could you hear what Shawn or Nicole was saying?"

"No, man. No. I only saw Nicole from the back. She was standing in front of Shawn. I could see his face, not hers."

"But you're sure it was Nicole?"

"Yeah. She had on that pink sweater and jeans. Nic wasn't somebody you confused with anyone else. She … she grabbed him."

"What do you mean?"

"She thumped her hands on his chest and kind of grabbed his shirt, you know, bunching it up."

"What did Shawn do?"

"He backed off. Put his hands up, like in a surrender. I kinda ducked behind one of the pinball machines. Whatever was going on, I sure didn't want to be in the middle of it."

"What happened next?"

"That was it. Nicole just turned around and stormed off."

"Did she still look angry?"

"She wasn't crying or anything. She was just ... moving fast. She blew right by me. Went out to the lane where Brenda and Shannon were."

"What about Shawn?"

"He waited a second or two, then went over there too. I went to the john. When I finished, I went back and told Brenda I was ready to leave if she was. They said Nic already took off. Brenda said she was ready to go so we said goodbye to Shannon and Shawn and we left."

"Did you mention what you saw to Brenda?"

Grady shook his head. "Wasn't my business. And everything seemed okay again when I came out of the bathroom. Nobody seemed mad. They were all laughing again so I didn't think anything of it."

"But you said Nicole took off. It didn't bother you that she seemed angry. And you never told the cops this, Grady. You're telling me that Shawn Weingard got into a heated argument with Nicole Strong just hours before she went missing and this is the first anybody's heard of this."

"Because Shawn didn't do anything," Grady said. "I know he didn't. We were friends. They were friends."

"Did Shawn ever talk to you about Nicole? What did he think of her?"

"He thought she was a hot mess, you know? We both did. But we loved her. She was part of our friend group."

"She went missing, Grady. Did you ever ask Shawn what the argument was about?"

Grady looked down. "No. This thing broke us. All of us. Those few days after Nic went missing. It was awful. Hell on earth. And searching for her in the corn fields. Knowing she was probably dead. It was ... one of the worst things I've ever been through. I think in some ways, it was the beginning of a lot of trouble I had in the years after that. I drank a lot more than I should have. And Shawn was broken up too. It gutted him. I just know he couldn't have had anything to do with what happened."

"So why tell me? Why now?"

"Because I think you already know," Grady said. "You said someone's been telling you something was going on between them. So ... maybe that was it. I can't believe it, but maybe she was playing mind games with him too. And Shawn? I wouldn't say we're friends anymore so who cares."

"What'd he do to you, Grady?"

Grady's eyes flashed. "He's not my friend. Okay? He hasn't exactly had my back over the years so why should I care about his. You should ask him what he and Nic were fighting about. Let him explain it. Leave me out of it."

"How did he not have your back, Grady?"

"There were just little things. They add up."

"Like what?"

"We worked together at the mill right after high school. He wasn't gonna stay. It was just a summer job for him, but it was my livelihood. I didn't have my daddy leaving me a restaurant. My dad kicked me out two days after graduation. And I got through that by the skin of my teeth. Shawn got me fired from the mill. They accused me of drinking on the job. I wasn't. I swear to God. But when they called Shawn in to question him about me, he didn't tell the boss where to stick it. He didn't tell him no way would I do something like that."

Jake resisted the urge to ask Grady Thompson whether the allegations against him were true back then. It didn't matter anymore.

"I wish you would have told Virgil Adamski what you just told me, Grady."

"Yeah. I wish I had too. It still doesn't mean I think Shawn had anything to do with this."

There was a bigger problem with Grady's story. He'd just admitted to having an ax to grind with Shawn over whatever happened at the clay mill.

Still ...

Jake threw down a fifty-dollar bill and thanked Grady Thompson for his time. His head pounded. If Grady was telling the truth, and Jake's gut told him he was, Shawn Weingard had gotten into a heated argument with Nicole Strong. He wasn't imagining the looks he saw Shawn give her in the videos they watched. Nicole was pregnant the day she died.

If Shawn was the father ... it would have given him the perfect motive to silence her.

THIRTY-THREE

He waited.

Jake stood in the adjoining observation room as Shawn Weingard settled himself in the interview room behind the one-way mirror. Shawn looked mildly annoyed, maybe a little impatient, but otherwise comfortable. Birdie had brought him a cup of coffee. The two of them shared some small talk. He asked her how Travis was doing, expressed awkward condolences for her brother, even though he'd seen her several times since his passing last year. But now, Shawn sat sipping his coffee from a paper cup.

Waiting.

Birdie came into the observation room. She had a notepad with her. She would pay attention to Weingard's body language while Jake conducted his interview. He was glad to have the extra pair of eyes.

Twenty minutes. Just enough time to let Shawn grow just a little more uncomfortable. He started tapping his heel, checking his watch.

"I'll be back," Jake said to Birdie. She gave him a quick thumbs up, then settled herself into the chair closest to the window.

Jake walked into the interview room.

"Hey, Shawn. So sorry to keep you waiting. Had a meeting that should have been an email run a little longer than planned. You know how it goes."

Jake reached across the table and shook Shawn's hand. Jake smoothed his tie and took a seat opposite Shawn.

"It's not a problem," Shawn said. "I was just surprised you had me come down here. I could have met you for lunch or something."

"That would have been a good idea." Jake smiled. "I figured I'd have you in and out this morning. I really am sorry about screwing up your day."

"It's okay," Shawn said. "I can move some things around. This is important."

Jake set his file down on the table and opened it. Like Grady Thompson's, Jake had printed a copy of Shawn's formal statement to Virgil from twenty-five years ago. He put a hand on it.

"I'll have you look at this in a few minutes. But before you do, I want to ask you a few questions. Just have you think back without feeling confined by what you said here. It's been a really long time."

"Sure. Sure. Whatever you need. I told you from the beginning. Whatever Shannon and I can do to help."

"Right. I appreciate it," Jake said. "If you don't mind, I'm going to record our interview. It'll save me a bunch of time. It's just a formality."

Shawn waved a hand across the table. "Of course. Like I said. Whatever you need."

"Okay. Okay. So can you just tell me what you remember about the night Nicole disappeared again?"

Shawn shifted his weight in his seat. "I've told this story a million times. For a million years. But of course. We all went to the bowling alley. Me. Shannon. Grady Thompson. Brenda Pollack. There were a few other kids we knew there. Some from Stanley. Some from St. Iz."

"And Nicole drove with you and Shannon?" Jake asked, knowing she hadn't.

Shawn shook his head. "Nope. She had her own car. None of us were drinking that night. At least … I know Shannon and I weren't. Nicole hardly ever drank and she wasn't that night. Brenda wasn't. Grady? I didn't see him drink. But I can't say for sure."

"How did you and Grady get along? Was he who you considered your best friend?"

"We were close back then, sure. But mostly as a double date situation. Shannon and Brenda were better friends. Grady and I didn't hang out a lot, just the two of us. It was just kinda convenient, you know? Shannon and I were a couple. Grady and Brenda were a couple. When Nicole was dating somebody, we'd double with them too. But it had been a while since that was true."

"She went stag to the homecoming dance that year, right?"

"Yep."

"And prom the spring before?"

Shawn squinted, as if he were trying to call up the memory. "I think so. Yeah. Yeah. That would have been after she and Alton broke up for the last time."

"You're sure they were broken up?"

"Shannon would know better than me. But as far as I know. Yeah. I didn't see him around her that year."

"Not even during the summer? Do you know if he came back or had a leave?"

Shawn gave Jake a blank look. "I don't know. I wasn't friends with Alton."

"How'd you feel about Nicole dating him?"

"Feel? I didn't feel anything."

"Well, I mean, he had a reputation. Or his family did. Did you ever worry it might get Nicole into trouble?"

"I didn't think she'd really end up with him," Shawn said. "I knew that one wasn't long term."

"Why do you say that?"

"I don't know. Alton was just ... different. Too serious. We knew he wasn't gonna stick around here."

"What about Tim Brouchard? I haven't had a chance to talk to you about him. Did you know she was seeing him?"

Something changed in Shawn. He stiffened a bit. He'd been sitting with his hands casually folded on the table. At the mention of Brouchard, he drew them back out of view.

"I didn't know anything about that."

"She was kind of a flirt though," Jake said. "That's the thing I've been hearing most from people. My sister even ... she said those chastity pins you were all wearing in the Christian Athletes club photo, that it was an inside joke. Nicole was … well … you know, I hate this part of the job. Here we are, having to dissect the sex life of a teenage girl who's been dead for twenty-five years. I just want you to know, I don't enjoy this."

"I get that."

"Look … Shawn … between you and me … I've become pretty alarmed with some of the stuff that's come to light. Can I trust what I say here … that you'll keep it between you and me?"

"Of course."

"Good. Listen. I think you're wrong about Alton Bardo. I've gotten some pretty irrefutable information that the two of them were intimate again as late as the summer before she died. I don't think she told anyone. I wonder if Shannon even knew."

"She was screwing Bardo?" Shawn asked.

"It looks that way. Yeah. And then there's Tim Brouchard. As far as I can piece together, that was still going on that summer as well. That's what's making my job so difficult. And it's terrible. These aren't things I can exactly share with her family. So, I'm really glad to have the chance to talk to you about this. You know. Guy to guy."

Everything about Shawn Weingard read tension. Jake sat back just enough so he could see partially under the table. Shawn had his fists balled on his thighs. His lips pursed into a bloodless line.

"I believe there were others," Jake said. "I talked to Grady Thompson. He …"

"Grady? She was hooking up with Grady?"

Jake said nothing. He did a slight head shake and let out an exaggerated sigh. He wouldn't say the words Shawn wanted him to. He would simply let Shawn's anger or his paranoia read what he wanted to in Jake's expression.

"There was this video," Jake said. "Nicole's family kept all her things. There was some footage from the prom dance for your guys' junior year. I got kind of suspicious because Grady seemed to be paying a lot of attention to her that night. I mean, I know it's a million years ago … but did you ever suspect?"

Shawn jerked backward, slamming his body against the chair back.

"Yeah," Jake said. "You knew something was going on, didn't you?"

"No," he barked. "But like you said. Nic was a flirt. She liked having the attention. I don't know how Shannon put up with it."

"There's a word for it," Jake said. "A man-eater."

"Yeah. Yeah," Shawn said, leaning forward. He brought his hands up, resting his fists on the table.

"It never ends well for girls like that," Jake said. "I've seen this time and again. Now … don't take what I'm saying the wrong way. She didn't deserve what happened to her. God, no. It's just … you play with fire long enough, right?"

"You think Tim killed her?"

Jake studied Shawn. It could have seemed like an innocent question, but Jake knew it wasn't.

"No," he said. "Tim didn't kill her. But again, that's between you and me, okay? I'm not ready to let the public know that yet."

"I get it, I get it."

"Shawn, I gotta ask you something straight out. The thing about my job. When I'm investigating a murder like this. The hardest part is trying to get inside the head of the victim. You have to do that. You have to try and reconstruct what was going on in their lives at the end. What I know? It's like I said. I think this girl was playing with fire. I think she'd been heading for trouble for a really long time. I think she played all these guys off each other. I could see it in those videos. I'm telling you, you can actually see it."

Jake opened the laptop between them. He cued up the digital copy of Nicole's prom video. Birdie had spliced bits of it together showing Nicole dancing with Grady Thompson. Jake let it play.

Shawn watched, no expression on his face. That alone seemed odd. This was footage Shawn himself hadn't seen in over twenty-five years.

"There," Jake said. "See that?" He paused the playback. Grady's hands had slipped down Nicole's back. It was an innocent enough gesture. He was so much bigger than she was. And he was clearly under the influence, swaying on his feet. Only it was the kind of thing that could make another guy jealous if he wanted Nicole for himself.

Jake pressed play. A second later, the camera caught Shawn's face staring intently at the couple from the corner of the dance floor. Jake paused the video there.

"Shawn," Jake said. "There's something else I need to tell you. I really do need your word that it won't leave this room."

Shawn sat frozen, staring at the paused image of his younger self on the screen.

"Shawn?"

He snapped his attention back to Jake. "Yeah. I mean, yes. You have my word."

"Great. Listen. There's something I've been keeping back. Something the press doesn't know about. Something Nicole's family doesn't even know about."

Jake pulled out two pieces of paper from the file folder. One was a blown-up picture of a tiny set of bones. The other was a photocopy of a portion of Nicole's letter to Alton Bardo.

Jake let the stillness fill him. No sound except for the constant, faint buzz of the overhead lights. His own breath. Shawn's.

He slid the picture of the bones in front of Shawn.

"What is this?"

"It's what we found with Nicole's remains. Shawn ... those are fetal ear bones. The picture's blown up so you can see."

"It looks like nothing," Shawn said, perhaps not truly understanding what Jake was saying.

"Fetal ear bones," he said more slowly. "As in ... from a fetus. Nicole was pregnant when she died, Shawn."

Nothing. Not a flicker. Not so much as a blink. Though he couldn't read his mind, Jake knew in his soul this news came as no surprise to Shawn Weingard.

"And this," Jake said, putting the second piece of paper in front of him. "Do you recognize it?"

Shawn didn't pick it up. Instead, he slid it closer. Jake detected just the slightest tremor in Shawn Weingard's hand. Jake had taken a single paragraph from Nicole's letter to Alton Bardo and blown it up. Shawn read it.

I'm scared for you. Terrified, actually. And I'm scared of what he'll say when I finally get brave enough to tell that asshole the thing that will change his life forever too. Thank you for not overreacting.

Thank you for not going over there and ripping his nuts off. There was a part of me that wanted you to.

Shawn's jaw clenched as he met Jake's eyes.

"She wrote this?"

"She was writing to Alton Bardo, " Jake said. "She poured her heart out to him just a few weeks before she died, Shawn. I believe she told him she was carrying someone else's baby."

The color leached from Shawn's face.

"Shawn?"

"Did she tell him whose it was?" Shawn asked. "Did he know?" He shook his head. Slowly at first. Then faster. Too fast.

"Shawn. There's more in that letter. I can show it to you. But ... she confided in Alton Bardo. That letter? His mother gave it to me. She never read it. Can you believe that? All these years. She kept it but couldn't read it. She said it was too painful for her. She lost her son too. But ... Nicole confided in Alton, Shawn. She told him everything." Another bluff.

"No. No. No!" Shawn bolted up from his seat. He started to pace. Started to tear his hands through his hair.

"The bones?" Jake said. "From the baby? There's testing we can do. DNA. Can you believe that? They can get it from the marrow after all this time. It's going to show me who the father of Nicole's baby was. It's going to confirm scientifically what she wrote in her letter to Bardo."

"No. No. That slut. That ... bitch!"

"She told you it was yours, didn't she?"

When Shawn Weingard turned to face Jake, raw hatred filled his eyes. "She was sleeping with half the county. I knew it. I *knew* it."

"Shawn, people saw you arguing with Nicole the night she disappeared. At the bowling alley. It got pretty heated, didn't it? Tell me what happened. Now's your chance to set the record straight. It's you and me. Let me help you."

Shawn kicked a chair. It bounced off the far wall.

"She's a liar. I told her. She's a liar. I knew she was boning someone else. I thought it was Grady at first. But I knew it. It was Bardo. Or Tim. Half the football team."

"Tell me what happened, Shawn."

Shawn was sweating. It poured down his temples. Dark patches formed under his arms.

"She was going to ruin everything. Everything! It was my fault. Oh God. It was all my fault. But she was all over me."

"She threw herself at you," Jake said.

"Yes! You don't know how she was. She just ... I should have just walked away. I should have told Shannon. I should have ... I don't know."

"You had a moment of weakness, is that it?"

"Yeah. It was only gonna be the one time. We felt so bad afterwards. But then ... it felt ... good. You know? Shannon and I were going through some stuff. Nicole was just ... easy."

"Sure."

Shawn began to sob. He slid to the floor in the corner of the room and buried his face in his hands.

"What did she tell you that night that made you so angry, Shawn?"

"My fault. You don't understand. It was all my fault. If I hadn't ... If I'd have just ..."

"You were angry," Jake said. "Anyone would be."

Shawn began chewing his nails.

"Shawn. Come sit down. We can talk about it. It's understandable that she would have made you angry. But you have to tell me what happened."

"No," he said. "You don't know. We're not friends, Jake."

"No. We're not. But that doesn't mean I don't want to help you. I can't do that if you don't tell me the truth. What did Nicole tell you that night? Why were you arguing? I told you. Witnesses have come forward. They saw you together."

"What witnesses? Grady Thompson? You ask him why he's all of a sudden so eager to talk shit about me? That guy's had a chip on his shoulder since high school. Thinks I owed him a job at the End Zone after they fired him at the mill. Or owed him risking my own job for him. He's a drunk. He was a drunk back then. I told you. He was probably drinking that night at the bowling alley."

Jake knew he'd just stepped into quicksand. Shawn was smart enough to hit on the very thing that would call Grady Thompson's credibility into question if this ever got in front of a jury.

"Grady wasn't the only one at the bowling alley that night, Shawn."

Jake rose from his seat. Slowly, he walked over to where Shawn sat. "Get up. Sit at the table. You're not this guy. The walls aren't closing in."

Shawn glared at Jake, but he got to his feet. He grabbed a different chair and sat.

Jake had the file folder in front of him. It was empty now, but Shawn didn't know that.

"It's amazing what they were able to find out at the lake, Shawn. No soft tissue. Just bones. Soon enough we'll be able to prove who the father of her baby was. She told you it was you though, didn't she?"

"Yes," he hissed. "She said it was mine."

"I'm going to need a DNA swab. It's better if you give it to me willingly."

"She was a liar. A manipulator."

"I know."

"She didn't care whose life she wrecked."

"Shawn. I need the truth. I need it to come from you. But I already have the science. I told you. It's amazing the kinds of things we can find out now. So many years after the fact. I'm going to be able to reconstruct what happened out there. We found more than bones, Shawn."

He started furiously shaking his head again. Shawn's face had grown ashen. "You can't. You can't. You can't."

"I can. Now's your chance. You can level with me. If you don't, I'll get what I need." Jake placed his hand on the empty file folder. He started to rise. "When I walk out that door, I can't help you anymore."

He turned. Took two steps.

"It's my fault!" Shawn shouted. "It was all my fault. All of it. If I hadn't … if she weren't … I did it. Okay? I did it."

Jake froze. He still had his back to Shawn. Squaring his shoulders, he turned around.

"You did what?"

"It was me ... It was my fault. All of it. It's what I did."

"What did you do?"

Shawn kept on shaking his head. Jake didn't dare breathe.

"I killed her," Shawn whispered. "I did it. I killed her. I killed Nicole."

Jake took two steps back toward Shawn. He grabbed the legal pad and pen from the center of the table.

"Shawn, this changes things. You understand. You aren't free to leave. I need to read you your rights."

Shawn nodded. He kept on nodding as Jake recited his Miranda warning.

"Do you understand?" Jake asked.

"I understand. I killed her. I need you to know that I killed her. I killed Nicole. I'll sign anything you want. Just ... I want this to be over. It's been twenty-five years. I need it to be over."

Jake sat down. He slid the legal pad over to Shawn.

"Shawn. Listen to me very carefully. I need you to write it down. Everything that happened. In your own words. All of it. Write down what you did."

Shawn grabbed the legal pad. His hands were steady as he picked up the pen.

"Take your time," Jake said. "I'm going to go out and get you some water. Are you hungry? Do you need ..."

"No. Nothing. I don't want anything. I just want this all to be over."

As Shawn began writing, Jake stepped out of the room. He went next door. The observation room had filled. There was Birdie, still scribbling her own notes. Sheriff Landry stood beside her. Ed Zender showed up. Word had spread through the building like wildfire. It had only taken a few minutes.

Twenty-five years and a few minutes. Jake looked back at Shawn Weingard through the one-way mirror as he wrote out the story of how Nicole Strong lost her life.

THIRTY-FOUR

Her car would have been just there. Parked to the side of the driveway almost in the grass so her parents could get out of the garage. As Jake drove past Marty and Vivian Strong's old house, Shawn Weingard's words, his confession replayed in his mind.

I just wanted to talk. That's all. Just talk. She told me she was going to tell Shannon. She told me she was going to tell everyone about the baby if I didn't help her make it right. I told her I'd find a way to fix it. I told her I'd do whatever she wanted. She wouldn't listen. She just wouldn't listen.

Jake slowed his car in front of Nicole and Anya's old house. Different people lived here now. They'd taken off the black shutters, painted over the giant "S" on the garage door. But the house looked so much the same. How many times had he come here to get Anya? To take her away from the chaos and drama that was always just a moment from exploding.

Jake kept driving. The Strongs' new condo was just two miles down the road. They never wanted to move far. In the grief-hardened corners of Vivian Strong's heart, she wanted to be easy to find if Nicole ever came home.

I asked her to go for a drive with me. Someplace quiet. It was her idea to go to the lake. So I took her. She got out of the car. She never stopped yelling at me. I told her she was going to ruin both of our lives. I didn't love her. I'm sorry about that. I'm sorry about everything.

When Jake pulled into the driveway of Marty and Vivian's new condo, he could see Anya through the front window. She had her back to him. She was running the vacuum. She never stopped. Always the caretaker. She would work herself to the bone to make sure her parents had what they needed.

It just got out of hand. She lunged at me. Slapped me. I just wanted her to lower her voice. We were alone, but you never know. She was hysterical. It got out of hand. It just ... got out of hand.

Jake shut his car door and began to walk up the sidewalk. Anya still didn't see him. She had her back to him.

I don't know. I just ... I snapped. I must have just snapped. I grabbed her. I didn't mean to hurt her. I swear to God I never meant to hurt her. But she was screaming and crying and she slapped me. The things she was saying. She was going to ruin my life. Before I knew what was happening, she was on the ground. I was on top of her and she was on the ground. She wasn't breathing. I knew it. I saw it. She wasn't breathing. She was dead.

Jake raised a fist and gently knocked on the front door. He had to knock more than once. The whir of the vacuum cleaner drowned out the sound.

"How did you kill her, Shawn? What did you do?"

I didn't mean to kill her. It just got out of hand. It got out of hand. I snapped. I must have snapped. She slapped me and I must have snapped. Before I knew what was happening, she was on the ground. I was on top of her and my hands were on her neck. She was dead. She was dead. My God. She's dead because of me. It's my fault. It was always my fault. She's dead because of me.

"Jake!"

Marty Strong's voice startled Jake. He came around the side of the house, holding a bag of potting soil.

"Hey, Marty. Is Vivian home too? Can we go inside?"

"Sure," Marty said. He put the bag down, dusted his hands off on his jeans, moved past Jake to open the front door. The moment he did, the vacuum cleaner stopped. Anya turned. She had earbuds in and pulled one out.

She knew. Jake locked eyes with her. She read his expression and she knew.

"Mom?" she called out. "Can you come out to the kitchen for a minute?"

Vivian Strong appeared. She was wearing an old, faded Stanley High School sweatshirt. She was cold. Jake remembered the woman was always cold. It was seventy-eight degrees outside.

Anya took her mother by the shoulders and led her into the kitchen. Her father followed close behind.

"Can I get you something to eat?" Viv asked. "I made lasagna last night. We have some leftovers. It's always better the next day, I think. I remember that was one of your favorites."

"Thanks. But no. Have a seat, Marty."

It was then Marty Strong's posture changed. His shoulders sagged. Slowly, with shuffling steps, he took a seat at the kitchen table beside his wife. Jake stood in front of the sink. Anya stayed against the wall, her arms folded around her waist, protecting herself.

"I wanted you to hear it from me. We've made an arrest in Nicole's case, Marty. We've caught the man who killed your daughter."

Vivian's hand flew up, covering her mouth. Marty's eyes misted over, but he kept Jake's gaze.

"Tim," Anya whispered.

"No," Jake said quickly. "No. This is going to be hard to hear. But ..."

"You pulled my baby out of the ground," Marty said. "You've already told us the worst there is. Now tell us what happened."

So Jake did. All of it.

"She was pregnant," he said. Waiting for that news to settle in the minds of Nicole's shell-shocked parents. Anya stayed strangely quiet. As far as he knew, she'd not heard that information either. Not from Jake. But who knew what Tim Brouchard had been telling her all these weeks. What lies. What excuses.

"She was in a relationship with Shawn Weingard," Jake said. "It didn't end well. Shawn was afraid she would tell Shannon and everyone else about the baby. He came to your house and asked her to go for a drive. They ended up at the lake. And ..."

"He killed her," Viv said. "My baby. He killed her. You're saying it was Shawny? He killed my baby?"

"Yes," Jake said. "He confessed. To all of it. He's being booked as we speak. It's over. We know what happened now. We know who did this."

"She was going to have a baby," Vivian whispered. "No. No. No. No."

Marty Strong went eerily quiet. Only a small shudder through his body gave a window into the silent storm brewing in him.

"Thank you," Anya said. She was calm. Rod straight. Jake knew this. She was taking it all on. She was preparing to manage her parents. She would not let herself feel anger or grief or sadness. Not yet. And she would only do that alone.

A car pulled up. Jake heard a car door slam. "Is there anything I can do for you right now?" Jake said. "I'm going to send a social worker to the house. And a couple of deputies. There will have to be a press conference. You don't have to be there unless you want to. If any reporters come to the house, the deputies will deal with them for you. But I'm going to be here for you, okay? I'm going to help you get you through this."

A door opened. It was the side door through the garage. On instinct, Jake's hand rested on the handle of his service weapon.

Vivian started to rise out of her chair.

"Are you expecting somebody?" Jake asked. Then heavy footsteps fell on the tile floor in the mudroom.

Jake turned just as Tim Brouchard strode into the kitchen. For an instant, he didn't see Jake. The refrigerator partially hid him from Tim's view.

"Anya," Tim said, breathless. "It's over. It's over. I told you it wasn't me. It's over."

Two things happened at once. Jake stepped into view. Tim's face turned ashen as he saw him. Then filled with quiet rage. Marty Strong got to his feet.

"You!" Marty said, his voice quaking with fury. "Get out of my house! Get out of my house!"

"Marty?" Jake said.

But Marty Strong was a father first. And he knew Tim Brouchard had exploited his little girl. It didn't matter that he hadn't killed her. With a strength and quickness that surprised Jake, Marty flew across the room and launched himself at Tim.

Tim was bigger. Younger. Stronger. But Marty threw a punch that made Tim's left eye explode.

"Marty!" Viv yelled. Jake moved. Tim raised his hands, ready to push Marty off him in a move that might have broken the older man. Jake got between them, pulling Marty away.

"You son of a bitch," Tim's voice boomed. "You did this. You fucking ruined me."

"Daddy!" Anya cried. Jake turned and faced Tim Brouchard.

Tim took a swing. Jake let it land right across his jaw. But he felt no pain. One punch. It was all he needed.

Jake landed a right uppercut to Tim's chin. The pair of them stumbled into the living room. Jake was in control. He wrestled Tim to the ground then put him in a double arm bar, pressing his face into the carpet until he gagged.

"Give it up, Tim. Next shot's gonna make you shit your pants."

Tim grunted, tensed, and tried to throw Jake off him.

"Enough!" Jake said, spit flying. "You've done enough to this family. Now you're gonna get up and you're gonna walk out of here."

Vivian Strong sobbed in the kitchen. Marty's rage had left him. He held his wife. Anya stood in the middle of it all. Still stoic. Shocked, maybe.

"Leave," she said. "Tim, just leave. Don't come back here."

Jake pushed himself off Tim. Tim straightened his shirt. Jake could see the fight hadn't quite gone out of him. But he got himself to his feet.

"Come outside and talk to me," Tim said. "I just want to talk."

I just wanted to talk. Shawn Weingard's words thundered through Jake's mind. Talk. Just talk.

"Outside," Jake said. "Now. She doesn't want to talk to you."

"And that's just what you've been waiting for."

"Tim, stop!" Anya said. "Get out. Go home."

"It's your home too," Tim said. "I didn't kill Nicole. I had nothing to do with it. Stop letting other people tell you what to think."

"I suggest you start moving," Jake warned.

Tim gave him a hate-filled look, but walked back out the way he came. Jake followed him. He was done punching Tim in the face for now, but they were by no means done.

Anya stayed inside with her parents. Jake shut the garage door. When he was reasonably sure they were out of the Strongs' earshot, Jake grabbed Tim and pushed him against his own car door.

"Take your damn hands off me," Tim hissed.

"Don't come back here," Jake said.

"She's my wife," he said. "They're my family. And I've broken no laws."

"Yeah? You may not have killed that girl, but you're not innocent in this. You tampered with evidence. You lied to the police. You obstructed justice."

He let go of Brouchard. The man straightened, ran a hand through his hair.

"And if you could prove any of that, you'd have arrested me by now. That's what you've wanted all along. I know who you really are now, Jake Cashen. And we're not done, you and me. Not by a mile."

"Good," Jake said. "So we understand each other."

A patrol car pulled up. It was the two deputies Jake had requested to sit by the Strongs' house. Jake gave them a look, wordlessly conveying that he had things under control. For now.

He had more to say. His fingers itched to throw another punch. To drive Tim Brouchard's lying face into the dirt. If he'd told the truth to Virgil all those years ago, might it have made a difference? Maybe not. But in his soul, Jake believed Brouchard took something from Nicole's room. A letter. A photograph maybe. Something that would have exposed his relationship with Nicole. Only now they would never know.

Jake's phone vibrated. Tim chose the wisest path. He got into his car. Jake took a step back. He answered the call.

"Yeah, boss," he said.

"Have you informed the family?" Meg Landry asked.

"Yes."

The family. The wreckage.

"Then I need you back down here. We have to make a statement. Do the Strongs want to be here for that?"

Jake looked back up at the house. From the window, he could see Anya consoling her family. Always putting them before herself.

"No," Jake said. "They've been through enough for one day. I'll be right in."

"Listen," she said. "Tim Brouchard might be headed that way. This thing is already starting to leak and he's got plenty of ears in the building still. He knows Weingard is under arrest for the murder of Nicole."

"Copy that," Jake said, staring back at Brouchard as he slid behind the wheel of his car. For now, Landry didn't need to know he and Brouchard had already confronted each other.

"Can you stop by my office as soon as you get back here?" Landry said. "I want a quick briefing before I step in front of another microphone."

"You got it," Jake said. "I just have one more stop, then I'll be there within the hour."

"Hurry," Landry said.

Behind him, Tim Brouchard kicked up gravel, spraying it in front of Jake as he sped off. Jake pocketed his phone. He ordered the deputies to stick close to the Strong family. Then he made his way out to the lake.

THIRTY-FIVE

I t wasn't Tuesday. It wasn't an official meeting of the Wise
Men. But Jake found Virgil Adamski fishing off the end of
his dock with Chuck Thompson and Bill Nutter. He was
glad about that. It was good Virgil wasn't alone. This news would
give him closure, sure. But it would also deliver a blow to his solar
plexus. The kind that could trigger things in Virgil he'd spent a
lifetime trying to fight.

As Jake came around the back of Virgil's house, the men spotted
him right away. Chuck and Bill waved. Virgil simply reeled in his
line and laid it in the back of his fishing boat.

He knew. Of course he knew. The other men sensed a change in
their friend's demeanor. They each reeled in their lines and
followed Virgil up the dock to meet Jake.

"Come inside," Virgil said. He took slow steps. It almost seemed
like he was trying to stretch the time. As if closure wasn't at all
what he was after. He would blame himself, perhaps. Question
whether there was a lead he didn't follow. Some signs he didn't
read. But Jake knew there wasn't.

Virgil took a seat in his battered recliner. Chuck and Bill stayed in the kitchen, seating themselves at the table. Ready to close in around their friend if it seemed he needed it.

Jake took a seat on the couch opposite Virgil. Virgil stared straight ahead, not meeting Jake's eyes.

"Shawn Weingard confessed to killing Nicole this morning," Jake said. "They were having an affair. He says she told him the baby was his."

Slowly, Virgil Adamski closed his eyes.

"How?" Virgil said. "How did you get there?"

"Chuck?" Jake said. "You need to hear this too. It involves your cousin Grady. Seems he lied to you, Virg. Said he saw Shawn and Nicole arguing at the bowling alley that night. Said it was pretty heated."

Chuck hung his head. "He lied."

"He withheld the truth," Jake said. "Left out a critical detail. I had a hunch is all. Something didn't sit right with me about Shawn. After I confronted him about what Grady said and told him we'd be able to get the baby's DNA from the bones, he admitted to it all."

"You can do that?" Nutter asked.

"No," Jake said. "But Weingard didn't know that."

"I didn't see it," Virgil whispered. "I talked to that kid a dozen times. More. Grady too."

"I'll kill him," Chuck said. "That stupid son of a bitch. Why? Why now?"

"Grady says there's some bad blood between him and Shawn now. They were kids back then. Teenagers. He thought he was looking out for his friend. Even now when I questioned him again, he swore Shawn wasn't capable of murder. He doesn't know Shawn's been arrested yet, as far as I know. No one does except his family and Nicole's. I wanted you all to hear this from me. Virg, Landry's giving a press conference in about an hour. You should be there. This is still your case."

Virgil shuddered. "I should have seen it."

"Virg," Chuck said, coming in from the kitchen. He stood beside Virgil, putting his hand on his shoulder. "Don't. Just don't."

"You had no body," Jake said. "You had no idea she was pregnant. No idea how she was killed."

"I should have seen it! I told you, I talked to that kid. Looked him straight in the eye. Not once did I ever get a bad vibe. He was never on my radar for this."

"It'd be great if it worked like that, Virg," Jake said. "You can't read minds. Back then? He didn't have two and a half decades of guilt eating him up. Every hour, every day that went by without anyone finding her body, he figured he was going to get away with it."

"What will you charge him with?" Virgil asked. "Can you prove premeditation?"

"That'll be for the grand jury to decide. He claims he snapped. That he never had any intention of hurting her. Just talking. He'll say it was a crime of passion. It might just be enough to keep a needle out of his arm. But that's not our call."

"The Strongs," Virgil said.

"They're a wreck," Jake said. "Tim Brouchard showed up just as I was breaking the news. It went a little sideways. But I think he knows to stay away from that family for a while. Hopefully forever."

Virgil nodded. "Was this my fault?" For the first time, he locked eyes with Jake. Jake could see every bit of the last twenty-five years in the lines on Virgil's face. The weight of it. The regret.

"No," Jake said. "This was Shawn Weingard's fault. And Tim Brouchard's. Grady's a little bit. And Alton Bardo's too. He had a letter from Nicole. She told him she was seeing somebody. Implied she was pregnant though didn't come right out and say it. But Alton might have known who the father was. He never came forward either to tell you he'd been in communication with her. If he had, it might have broken this case for you. But he didn't. I wish I knew why. And none of that matters anymore, Virg. So come with me. Stand by my side at that press conference. Let's put this case to bed once and for all, you and me."

Virgil smiled. He got up from his chair and walked over to the window. He looked out at the lake, at the far shore where Nicole Strong's body had lain. Then, he turned back to Jake.

"I don't think so, kid. This case is yours now. So's the credit. I've done my job. I did the best I could. Maybe Nicole and I both can finally rest in peace."

Jake tried once more to persuade Virgil. In the end, he went back to town alone. He hoped Virgil was right. That Nicole could finally rest easy. That Virgil could. In his heart, Jake knew the Strong family might never achieve that goal.

THIRTY-SIX

Fifteen seconds into the Q&A of Sheriff Landry's presser, Jake changed his mind. He was glad Virgil Adamski was nowhere near this. Ever since Tim Brouchard's lawyer started giving his own press conferences, the case garnered wider and wider attention. Mercifully, in just a few short weeks, as soon as Jake handed everything off to the visiting prosecutor, he could at least pretend this was no longer his circus.

"Sheriff, Shawn Weingard has lived and worked in this community his entire life. You're saying for twenty-five years, your detectives ruled him out?"

"Murderers tend to not wanna be caught," Meg said, in a rare show of public sarcasm. Maybe the pressure was starting to get to her a little too. "Mr. Weingard enjoyed the benefit of time. Luckily, secrets as well as bodies don't always stay buried."

"What was the motive?" another reporter asked.

"I can't comment on that," Landry said. "Or any further details about this case other than what I've already said. An arrest has been made. Ms. Strong's next of kin has been informed. But I hope that you'll all give them their privacy during this difficult time. This could be a long process. Mr. Weingard is of course innocent until proven guilty by a court of law."

"Did his wife know?" another reporter shouted.

"Was the victim pregnant?" another reporter asked. Jake bristled; that detail had not been released to the press and wouldn't be. It would come out at trial if the case went that far. He hoped this particular vulture was just taking a lucky guess. Landry's jaw tightened, but she, like Jake, kept her poker face in place.

"Will your office be issuing a public apology to Tim Brouchard?" another reporter asked. Jake didn't recognize her. Odds were, Malcolm Edwards had planted her there. She was probably his paralegal or something.

"Mr. Brouchard is still under investigation by this office as well," Landry said. "There may yet be charges brought for his conduct during the investigation of this case. But I cannot comment further on that either. To your original question though, no, we'll not be issuing an apology to Mr. Brouchard. It isn't warranted. Next question."

There was more of the same. Jake stayed still as a rock. Trying not to show the slightest emotion at all the wild theories and innuendo thrown out about Nicole Strong's character. No matter what happened next, it seemed Anya's sister would be killed more than once before this was over. With any luck, Weingard would do the smart, decent thing and plead this sucker out to second degree. Only it meant he could still get out and be a happy grandpa someday. At least Marty and Viv wouldn't likely live long enough to see it.

"Detective Cashen, can you speak to how your predecessor, Detective Adamski, handled this case?"

"I'm gonna stop you right there," Jake said, leaning into the microphone. "Detective Adamski did tremendous work on this investigation. He went as far as he could with the information he had at the time. I'd like to thank Commissioner Arden, who was instrumental in the discovery of Nicole Strong's remains. Without his discovery, this case might never have been solved."

Landry poked Jake in the ribs. Uncle Rob was in the room, standing just off to the side. His face was beginning to turn purple. But just as Jake hoped, a few reporters turned and started throwing questions at Arden. It gave Jake and Meg a few seconds to breathe. But only a few.

The next question, directed to Sheriff Landry, blindsided them.

"Sheriff," Jim Stone from Channel Fourteen held his cell phone up. He read from something on the screen as he crafted his question. "As of four fifty-seven p.m. this evening, so roughly ninety minutes ago, we've received word of a murder at the federal correctional facility in Elkton."

"That's not my jurisdiction," Landry said, starting to gather her notes to leave the lectern.

"The victim has been identified as Thomas Cypher."

Jake went cold. Landry shrugged. "Okay?"

"Well, you're aware that Tom Cypher was a prime suspect in Nicole Strong's murder in the weeks after she disappeared. And today he ends up stabbed to death in the infirmary at Elkton Prison. Are you saying that was just happenstance?"

Meg looked at Jake, her eyes wide with confusion. He could offer her no help. Tom Cypher. Stabbed to death. Jake needed to get to his phone.

"Those are questions for the warden at the prison," Meg said. "As far as I'm aware, there is absolutely no connection between these two cases. And that is all. Thank you."

Landry turned away from the lectern. A wave of new questions came at them, but Jake held the door for her then promptly slammed it shut behind them, drowning out the noise.

"What the hell was he talking about?" Landry asked.

Jake had his phone out. He pulled up Gable West's contact and fired off a text.

"You heard it the same time I did," Jake said to Landry.

"How long's Tom Cypher been incarcerated?"

"Something like five years," Jake said. "He was exonerated in Nicole's murder. The guy had an alibi. He was out of the county the night she disappeared. It's just a coincidence. Don't worry about it."

Meg nodded. Neil, her media liaison, was waiting for her down the hall.

"I'm not worried," she said. "Because I trust you to do any follow-up necessary. Good work, Jake. I know how hard this one has been."

Jake's phone buzzed. Gable West texted back.

> I've got nothing. Just heard myself. I'll find out what I can. Talk later.

Jake slid his phone back in his pocket. As he made his way back to his office, he went through a gauntlet of well wishes, back slaps, thumbs up, and general congratulations. Though Jake didn't at all feel victorious. How could he?

He practically collapsed in his desk chair. His head was pounding. His hip ached from the constant weight of his sidearm. And he knew he wasn't done. He pulled out his phone again and shot a text to West.

> Can you do me another favor? I need to pay a visit to a certain inmate. Tomorrow morning if I can.

He stared at the three blinking gray dots on his phone. Then Gable texted back.

> Your tab is getting pretty large, Cashen. I'll see what I can do. You better make sure neither one of us regrets it. I hope you know what you're doing.

> Thanks

Jakr hoped he knew what he was doing too.

THIRTY-SEVEN

King Rex Bardo wasn't expecting Jake. He wasn't expecting any visitors at all. They pulled him from the yard, in the middle of his morning weightlifting routine. He strode in sweaty, his curly brown hair pulled back into a tie. He was fierce. Formidable. His frown would terrify lesser men. But when Rex saw who had dared show up to disrupt his routine, his frown melted into a deadly grin.

They met outside today. Surrounded by a chain-link fence, guards along the perimeter, and sitting alone at a long picnic table in the center of a row of forty.

Rex came to him. Jake didn't rise. He fixed a stony stare at Rex. It only made Rex smile wider as he sat down, straddling the bench, one leg on either side.

"Better be good, Cashen," he said. "I don't care about that razor wire. I don't jump for any man. Sure as hell not you."

"You heard I got a collar in the Strong case," Jake said. It wasn't a question. Of course Rex was keeping tabs on him. "And you know

I did what I said I'd do. Nothing's landed on your family. I kept my word."

"I expect you to keep on keeping it. These things have a way of going sideways at trial."

"Alton had nothing to do with what happened to her. People knew that before. They'll know it even more if this thing goes to trial."

"So we still understand each other. That makes me glad, Cashen."

"Do we? Understand each other?"

"What I understand is that this puts you in the debt column with me."

"I did what I said I'd do," Jake said. "Here you are. Out in the yard. Enjoying the sunshine on your face."

"Let me ask you," Rex said. "This collar? You wanna tell me if the gift I sent you helped you with that?"

Jake took a breath. He could have lied. Said it was a coincidence. Told Rex Alton's letter had no bearing on the case. But it did. Jake knew without it he wouldn't have had enough leverage to flip Shawn Weingard. He might not have confessed.

"Yeah," Rex said, reading Jake's face. "That's what I thought. Thanks for stopping by. I don't need anything from you right now. I'll let you know as soon as that changes. Because you know it will, Cashen."

Rex started to get up. Though Jake had called this meeting, Rex meant to end it.

"Sit down," Jake said. It earned him a flash of anger from Rex's eyes.

"You got something else to say to me, boy?" Rex asked. It wasn't about the two of them. Rex was no doubt aware of all the witnesses. He could never appear weak in front of the guards.

"Tom Cypher," Jake said. Rex froze, then sank back down to the bench.

"Tragedy," Rex said. "Heard they sliced him crotch to throat. Shame. We deserve better security around here."

"Look at me," Jake said. "You know exactly who ordered the hit, don't you?"

It was a stupid question, Jake knew. Rex would never admit to anything. But that wasn't Jake's point. He wanted to see Rex's face, his eyes as he denied the accusation.

"I think it's time for you to go," Rex said.

"Those girls in Hancock County. The sisters Cypher was accused of assaulting," Jake said. "Cypher was a pedophile. I think he hurt those girls. And maybe a few others. Was this prison justice? You let the word get out on that, didn't you?"

Rex shrugged. "Guy was a creep. A loner. Who knows who he might have pissed off. Bikers, Crips, Bloods, Aryan Brotherhood, the Mexicans. They might not like each other, but they live by the same code. He was a pedo, Jake. I ain't losing sleep over him. Neither should you."

"You used it," Jake said. "Leveraged information I gave you. It could have gone south, Rex."

No answer. Just those cold eyes. But it was all Jake needed. He knew. King Rex had handed down Tom Cypher's death sentence. He was good enough, his killer would never be found. The security cameras inside would be conveniently out of order at the critical moments, perhaps. No one saw anything. No one would say anything. And the scourge that was Tom Cypher was just wiped off the earth.

"See ya, Cashen," Rex said. He started to rise again.

Jake stared straight ahead. "See ya, Rex."

Rex straightened his broad shoulders, turned his back on Jake, and strode back to the gate, his dark hair gleaming under the sunlight.

Someday. Somewhere. Jake knew there would be a reckoning between him and Rex. He'd sealed his fate the first time he sat down at a table with him. A part of Jake couldn't wait.

THIRTY-EIGHT

"It's always so ... depressing, what we get reduced to," Birdie said. She stood in the middle of storage room number seventeen. Within a few hours, it would become that again. The war room would be dismantled. They'd spent most of the morning repacking everything left of Nicole Strong's life.

"I mean, I'm used to it. You move around so much in the military. And it was always just me. For fifteen years, I've kept my life ordered so I could pack everything on a moment's notice."

They'd made four distinct piles. The largest encompassed all the items that would be turned over to Roger Bernicki, the visiting Marvell County prosecutor. He was building what he needed to take Shawn Weingard's case to the grand jury in a few weeks.

The second-largest pile would make its way down to the bowels of this very building where it would be held in the department archives, probably for the rest of eternity or until the building crumbled. There was another group of things that could be returned to the Strong family. Nicole's clothing, mostly. All the odds and ends recovered from Anya's storage unit. He had no idea if she'd take them back there, or let everything go for good. Finally, there were those items that would go back to their owners. Most of that encompassed what Birdie had collected from Jay Larraby of the defunct *Blackhand Hills Bugle*.

"We were lucky though," Jake said. "I don't know if I could have solved this one if Nicole's family hadn't kept what they did."

He found himself standing in front of the garment rack one more time. Drawn to that simple black dress Nicole Strong wore for her last big high school dance. He could see Grady Thompson's dinner-plate hand sliding down her back as the punch he spiked worked its way through his bloodstream. That simple act. One he probably hadn't even realized he'd committed. But it had been enough to trigger Shawn Weingard's jealous eye. And it had made all the difference.

"Do you think he'll let this thing go all the way to trial?" Birdie asked. She sat down at the table. Somewhere, she'd found a label maker. One by one, she stuck the tape to the various boxes, then slid them in each of the four sections.

"He's got himself a public defender," Jake said. "Josie Woodbine."

"Oh geez," Birdie said. "She's been around forever. Well, that's good, I guess. Josie doesn't strike me as someone who'll sugarcoat things for her clients. Shawn's facing the death penalty if he gets indicted for first degree."

"My guess, Josie's gonna try to broker a guilty plea for second," Jake said. "It'll have him out in probably twenty years. Young enough he could still be around for his grandkids."

"That doesn't feel like justice," Birdie said. "Marty and Vivian Strong won't get to see theirs. They'll maybe never have them. And in a weird way, that's because of what Shawn did too. Tim Brouchard can profess his innocence all he wants, but you can't tell me he wasn't obsessed with that girl. That her memory didn't have something to do with him going after Anya. It's just ... sick."

"Bernicki's got that case too," Jake said. "For now anyway. It'll be up to him to figure out whether he's got enough to charge Tim with anything. Either way, his dreams of being a judge or achieving any higher office are over. His best play is to retire as a prosecutor before they force him out."

"I hope he does," Birdie said. She sat in front of the last box. It was filled with newspaper clippings and hundreds of photos from Jay Larraby's B-roll. Birdie pulled out one of the articles. The front page of the *Blackhand Hills Bugle*, three days after Nicole went missing. The headline read, "Search Party Expands to Shepherd's Hollow in Case of Missing Teen."

Jake looked over Birdie's shoulder. The picture showed a human chain of searchers, covering the trail leading up to the Devil's Eye Gorge.

"Look at that," Birdie said. She stabbed her finger above the image. Shawn Weingard was in that line, standing shoulder to shoulder with two other classmates.

"Gives me the chills," Birdie said.

"Virgil wondered," Jake said. "He figured there was a chance one of the searchers knew more about Nicole's disappearance than he was saying. He kept at least one member of law enforcement with every group." Sure enough. Jake spotted a much younger Chuck Thompson in the background of the same photo.

Birdie folded the article and put it back in the box. "I'll take this over to Larraby when my shift ends," she said.

Birdie pulled out a stack of photos from the box. These were the images he shot that didn't make it into the paper. More pictures of members of the search party. Virgil had combed through these twenty-five years ago. In another box, he'd kept detailed lists of every face in the crowd. His instincts were right, he just didn't have the information he needed to put it all together. Shawn Weingard had made sure of that.

Birdie sifted through the photos. She separated out any that Shawn appeared in. "Do you think Bernicki will need these?"

"I'd rather he have more than what he needs instead of less. I know it's a lot, but if you could make a list."

"Already started," she said.

There were other pictures in the box. Birdie laid them out. All these young faces. Filled with worry and grief. Parents. Friends and classmates of Nicole. Volunteers from other branches of law enforcement in the surrounding counties. The whole time, the killer had been among them.

Birdie pulled out the last set of discarded photos. These were from the candlelight vigil held just a few days after Nicole's disappearance. Shawn was in those as well.

Jake picked one up. Shawn stood holding a small candle with a paper cup under it to catch the wax. Just a kid then. Skinny. Tall. His face ashen. Shannon stood beside him, her head against his shoulder, hiding her tears.

"Did he ever tell her?" Birdie asked. "About any of it?"

"I don't know," Jake said. "He confessed to everything but that."

Birdie held another yellowed newspaper. The exact picture Jake had in his hands appeared on the front page below the fold. It was the beginning of "the forgetting," he knew. There was only so long the people of Worthington County could hold Nicole Strong's tragedy at the forefront of their minds. Over the weeks and months and years, their memories had faded. Or in Grady Thompson's case, were never revealed at all.

"I can get Larraby's things back to him in one box," Birdie said.

"Thank him again for me," Jake said. "For Bernicki too. Tell him he might yet get contacted by the prosecutor if Bernicki ends up wanting to introduce any of the photos from the search parties into evidence. In fact. Let's put all of those in Bernicki's box."

"What about this one?" Birdie asked, pointing to a small black bag still sitting in the corner.

Jake looked at it. "I'll take care of that one myself. Those are Shawn's personal effects. His wedding ring. Wallet. Watch. I told him I'd make sure Shannon got them."

Ed Zender walked by. He stopped, leaning into the storage room.

"Good work," Zender said, tapping the door frame. "You'll probably get another plaque for this one, Jake. We're gonna have to ask for a bigger office so you can display it all."

As usual, Ed had a smarmy tone. But Jake knew he was at least partially sincere.

"Thanks, Ed. And thanks for picking up the slack on everything else while I worked on this one. It made a huge difference."

Ed smiled. There was laughter down the hall. Day shift was getting ready to clock out. Jake knew he should too. Ed waved at Birdie and headed for the stairs.

"I hate to ask," Birdie said. "But how much help was he really?"

Jake smiled. "He does what he can."

"How much longer does he have until he can retire?"

"He keeps moving the goal post. At this rate, odds are I'll be out of here before he is."

Birdie put a few pictures back in the box for Jay Larraby. She had a dark expression.

"Ed helped," Jake said. "But I couldn't have done this one without you, Birdie. You've got a knack for organization that is pretty impressive." He spread his hands out, gesturing to all of the items in front of them. It would have taken him weeks to get this far if left to his own devices. Birdie had whipped this room into shape in a matter of days.

"I'm just glad you solved it," she said, but her voice trailed off. She still held a few photographs in her hand. Jake went to the corner and picked up the bag he'd promised to take to Shannon. He could do it later tonight after dinner with the family. He checked the time. He was already late for that. He pulled out his phone and dialed Gemma, bracing for her wrath.

"Sorry," he said as soon as she answered. "I'm just tying up a few loose ends at the office. I'll probably be another hour. Just put a plate aside for me. You don't have to wait."

"It's okay," she said. "I was just about to call you. I got a little waylaid myself. Chloe Weingard is here at the house. She spent the night actually."

"In Ryan's room?" Jake asked, incredulous.

"No, dipshit. On the couch. But she's in pretty rough shape. I've brought her over here to Grandpa's. She, uh … she's gonna stay for dinner. It's okay if you're late. If you're …"

"I get it," Jake said. "Look, it's fine. I'm glad Chloe has support. I'll stay away for tonight."

"You sure? I feel bad."

"It's fine," Jake said.

"Jake?" Birdie said. She was staring sideways at one of the pictures in her hand, seemingly unaware he was on his phone.

"Gemma," he said, sensing something odd. "I'll talk to you later. Maybe I'll drop by for leftovers when you tell me the coast is clear." He clicked off with Gemma and headed over to Birdie's table.

"Take a look at this," Birdie said, handing him one of the photos. It wasn't one he remembered seeing before. It was taken at the candlelight vigil. A bad shot. The lens was angled sideways, almost as if Jay Larraby snapped it by mistake. Brenda Pollack was in it, standing beside Shannon Weingard. Shannon's face was in profile, staring in the distance. There was a shadow across the left side of her face.

Birdie handed him another photo. This one must have been taken no more than a second or two after the first one. Shannon looked up at something. The same shadow darkened her face. Jake looked closer. He realized it might not be a shadow at all.

"Look," Birdie said, handing him a third photo. Shannon again. She had her hand up, combing her fingers through her hair, pulling it down over that side of her face.

Jake went to the box of pictures. He began pulling them back out, one by one. In the photo that was published in the paper, Shannon rested her head against Shawn's shoulder, obscuring the left side of her face. In four others, where she was captured more straight on, she wore her hair parted to the side, also covering her face. He picked up the three random photos where her hair was pulled back.

"Jake," Birdie said. "Is that a bruise? It looks like she has a bruise?"

Jake held one of the photos up, looking at it in a better light. He compared it with the two others showing the left side of her face. It wasn't a shadow at all.

"What do you think?" Birdie asked.

"I don't know. I'm not sure."

Birdie's radio squawked. "Unit 110. Are you still in the building?" Birdie took the radio call and stepped out into the hall.

Jake put the pictures down. He pulled out Virgil's full report. The witness statements were tabbed in the back. He thumbed through to Shannon's. He read back Virgil's observation.

"Witness was questioned at her parents' home. She was quite distraught. Almost hysterical. Crying through most of the interview. I let her mother be present."

"Crying," Jake said, his mind lost in thought. "Your eyes can look swollen when you cry hard enough."

He pulled out the report from Dr. Coleman, the forensic anthropologist, quickly scanning for the one line he knew might matter. When he found it, his heart turned to stone. Jake pulled out his phone and called his sister. He started talking before she could even say hello.

"Gem, do me a favor. Keep Chloe there as long as you can."

"Um ... sure. What's up?"

"Is her brother in town, do you know?"

"Shawn Jr.? No. He left yesterday. He had to get back to work. Chloe said he's planning on taking a leave of absence once his dad's trial starts. If it starts. You know ... I'm not sure how ..."

"Gemma, just keep Chloe there for me. Okay? Don't let Ryan take her back home until you hear from me."

"Sure. Fine. But why?"

Jake let her question go unanswered. He clicked off the call.

Birdie walked back into the room. "I'll be back in an hour," she said. "Deputy Rathburn needs backup in front of the courthouse. A drunk and disorderly. When I get back, we'll sort through the rest of this?"

Jake nodded. "Take your time. Be careful." But he knew he'd be long gone before she got back. As soon as Birdie rounded the corner toward the stairs, Jake grabbed Shawn Weingard's personal effects and headed for the parking lot.

THIRTY-NINE

T he house was dark. At first, Jake didn't think anyone was home. He stood at the front door, his fist poised to knock. Then, he heard something. Running water. He peered through the glass block window to the side of the front door. Though he couldn't make out details, he saw a shape moving.

"Shannon!" he called out, finally knocking. "It's Jake Cashen. Can we talk for a few minutes?"

She shut off the water. Through the thick glass block, he saw Shannon's blurry shape turn and freeze.

"I'll be right there, Jake," she called out. Her voice was muffled through the door so Jake couldn't really gauge much from her tone. He waited. It took almost a full minute before Shannon Weingard opened the door.

She looked different than he'd ever seen her, wearing a pair of loose-fitting jeans and a gray sweatshirt with water spots down the front of it. Her hair was a tangled mess.

"What do you want?" she said.

"Just talk. Do you mind if I come in?"

"Why?"

"Well, unless you don't care if your neighbors see you talking to me. Mrs. Bowden across the street is a gossip."

Shannon peered around his shoulder. "Come in. I'm making dinner. Chloe should be home soon."

"I think she's actually staying over at my grandpa's for dinner," Jake said. "I talked to Gemma about an hour ago. Ryan invited her."

Shannon walked down the hall and made a right turn into the sunken living room. The television was on. Some game show. Shannon grabbed the remote and clicked it off. The house was in disarray. Dishes in the sink. Garbage overflowing. Shannon took a seat in the corner of one couch and pulled a blanket around herself.

"They won't let me see him," she said. "Shawn's been in lockup for three days, Jake. They won't let me see him. Can you do something about that?"

"I'm not sure. I can tell you he's all right."

"He hasn't asked to see me," she said, more insistent. "I don't know what's going on. Nobody will tell me anything."

"He's got a lawyer now. Have you talked to her?" Jake asked.

"I don't know what's going on. Nobody tells me anything."

Jake hadn't yet taken a seat. She hadn't invited him to. Jake stood in the living room holding the black plastic bag with Shawn's personal effects inside. He held it up.

"I promised Shawn I'd bring all of this to you. It's his wedding ring. His wallet. His belt. Just the personal items he had with him when he was booked."

Shannon made no move to take the bag from him. Jake set it on the floor. Shannon merely stared straight ahead. Jake took a seat on a chair in front of her. "I know this has been tough for you. I know your whole world's been turned upside down. But maybe you can help me understand a few things. Things that could help your husband."

Shannon's eyes snapped to Jake's. "You think I'm stupid? You're not here to help Shawn. You're not here to help me."

"I am. I know your family got ripped apart. But so did Nicole's."

Nothing. No emotion.

"Chloe's been spending a lot of time with Ryan," Jake said. "I know he's worried about her. Shannon, if you need some help around the house ... Gemma would be glad to ..."

"I don't want her here. I don't want anyone here. Just leave us alone. Chloe is fine. We're all fine. Except Shawn. I told you. I don't know how he is. He won't talk to me. His lawyer won't talk to me."

"Maybe that's for the best," Jake said. "I'm sure Shawn doesn't want to put you in an awkward position."

Still nothing from her. Just a cold stare into the distance.

"Shannon. We can do this down at the station if you'd like. But I thought maybe you'd be more comfortable here. I can come back another time. It's just ... there are a few things I need to clear up about what happened. Some things Shawn said ..."

It was then she met his eyes. "What did he say? Tell me? No one will tell me."

Jake wrung his hands. He waited for a beat. "They got into an argument," Jake said. "Things got heated. It was to do with the baby she was carrying. Shannon, that's what I'm trying to understand. You didn't know she was pregnant? She was your friend. Surely she would have confided something like that to you."

She didn't answer.

"They got into an argument that night," Jake said. "That's what Shawn said. Grady Thompson saw them going at it at the bowling alley. I believe Nicole gave Shawn some type of ultimatum about the baby she was carrying. She said it was his. But ... I gotta be honest. I'm not sure."

Still nothing.

Jake shifted in his chair. "Shannon, there are some things I need to say. Things I hope you don't share with anyone else. Between you and me. It's ... been hard. I know that. Nicole in death has become a martyr, really. God. Anya has certainly suffered under the shadow of that. I know you have too. But this girl? She was just that. A girl. A kid. One who made a lot of mistakes in her short life. And I know she hurt people. I know she hurt you."

Shannon stared at him. Her nostrils flared but she kept silent.

"She tried to destroy Shawn's life. That's going to come out if this goes to trial. He was your boyfriend. I can't imagine how tough this is for you. Finding out your best friend and your boyfriend ... your husband ... were having an affair behind your back."

She let the blanket fall from her lap. Shannon reached down and picked up the black bag with Shawn's things inside of it.

"You didn't deserve that," Jake continued. "You didn't deserve any of it. In the next few weeks, or months ... you're going to have to relive it all. The grand jury. The trial if it goes that far. And even if it doesn't, even if Shawn is offered some kind of plea deal …"

"Will he? Have they offered him something? Has he said anything?"

"I can't speak to that. But maybe. My point is, even if that happens, Shawn's going to prison. He's going to have to stand in court and tell a judge what he did. That'd be a condition of any sort of plea deal. And then the Strongs would have a chance to speak at his sentencing. It's just … it's a lot. Even in the best of circumstances, your family is going to have to face a lot. So I'm sorry for that. I wanted you to know."

Shannon looked beyond Jake; turning her head, she stared out the window. A light drizzle had started, leaving tiny beads on the glass. Over her shoulder, Jake saw the porch chairs stacked up against the side of the house. A few of them had fallen over.

"She wasn't what everyone thought she was, was she?" Jake said.

Shannon looked back at him.

"She was cruel," Jake said. "Vindictive. That's the thing I can't say to Anya. But I've spent the last few weeks looking through all of Nicole's things. Her notes. Letters. She was playing mind games with Alton Bardo. And Tim. Then she moved on to Shawn, didn't she?"

Shannon drew her knees back up, resting her chin on them.

"I can understand how Shawn would have gotten angry with her that night. Sitting here, Shannon … I can't tell you if Nicole really was pregnant with Shawn's baby. There were at least two other possibilities. Maybe more."

There. Just a flicker. But Jake saw something pass through Shannon Weingard's eyes. Contempt, if he had to name it.

"She craved attention. Fed off it. That's what everyone was afraid to say. It had to have been very hard to be friends with someone like that."

Shannon squeezed her eyes shut. "Is he going to get the death penalty?" she asked.

"That's not my decision. But ... if he was provoked. If what Shawn did was in the heat of the moment. Josie Woodbine is a decent lawyer, she can maybe make a deal for second degree murder. Or ..."

"Or what?" Shannon asked.

"Are you angry with him?" Jake asked. "I mean, you weren't married at the time. But it has to still feel like he cheated on you."

"He did," she said, her voice so quiet Jake had to strain to hear it.

"They both did," Jake said. "Your best friend and your boyfriend. That's ... that's a lot."

Jake slipped his hand into his breast pocket and pulled out the picture Birdie found. It was the one at the candlelight vigil that showed Shannon's face the clearest.

"If she instigated the violence," Jake said. "If she ... hit Shawn."

He stood up and came closer to Shannon. She looked up at him.

"What is it?"

"Nothing. Probably nothing. It's just ..." He handed her the photograph. Shannon took it. He couldn't read her expression as she looked at it. She handed it back to him.

"Why are you showing me this?"

"Do you know when that was taken?"

Shannon shrugged.

"Do you remember a vigil for Nicole at the school?"

"There were a lot of vigils."

"Right. But this one was three days after Nicole went missing. You were there with Shawn. Your picture was on the front page of the paper. Not this one. But from that same night."

"I don't remember," she said.

"Take another look." He held the photo out. She glanced at it but didn't take it.

"Shannon. Your face is bruised."

She looked at Jake, but wouldn't look at the picture. Instead, she threw the blanket off her legs and stood up.

"Nicole had a very specific injury, Shannon. It's called a boxer's fracture. On her right hand. She punched someone that night. She punched someone after she left the bowling alley. I mean, she couldn't have bowled with a broken hand, could she? The type of wound she had could only have been made one way."

Nothing. No reaction.

"You have a black eye in that photo, Shannon. Your left eye."

Stony silence.

"It was you she punched, wasn't it?"

Shannon wouldn't meet Jake's stare.

"I'm trying to help you, Shannon, whether you believe me or not."

"I need a glass of water," she said. "Can I get you one?"

"Sure," he said. She moved past him. In her bare feet, she padded to the kitchen. She stepped out of view as she went around the fridge and opened a cupboard. He heard a drawer shut, then the clinking of glasses. Shannon stood in front of the refrigerator now. But she wasn't pouring any water.

Jake walked toward her.

"Shannon," he said. "You can tell me. I probably know Nicole better than anyone now. I've had to try and live inside of her head. I know she hurt you. Did she hurt you that night too? Did she punch you? Did she provoke you?"

Shannon just stood, facing the refrigerator, one hand at her side, the other resting on the countertop. He couldn't see her from that side. The fridge obscured his view of her right arm.

Jake took another step toward her, the hairs rising on the back of his neck.

"Shannon. It's okay. If she provoked you. If you got into a fight ..."

Shannon took a staggering step backward. When she did, she brought her right hand up. In it, she held a small pistol.

"Shannon!" Jake yelled. His own hand went to his service weapon.

"You think I really believe you're here to help me?" she said, tears beginning to roll down her cheeks. "No one can help me. I'm on my own. I've always been on my own."

"Shannon," Jake said. "Put the gun down."

She held it up to her own temple.

"Shannon, don't do this. I told you. I can help you."

"Don't take another step," she said. "I'll blow my brains out right here. Then maybe he'll understand how badly he's hurt me. He's *been* hurting me."

Jake's whole body tensed. He kept one hand on the holster of his weapon. He took a small step forward. Shannon took a step back.

"You're right," she said. "Nic wasn't a martyr. She wasn't a saint. She wasn't this sweet, innocent person. She was a taker. A user."

"Right," Jake said. "I see that now. I told you."

"No. You don't. You're saying these things because you think it'll make me trust you. I don't trust anyone. Not ever. Everyone lies to me. Shawn lied to me. He was fucking my best friend behind my back. They laughed about it. About me."

"I know," Jake said. He took another tentative step forward, eyes on Shannon's right hand. Her fingers shook but she held the barrel of her gun flat against her right temple.

"This won't help," Jake said. "You dying won't help."

"It'll help me!" she said. "He still loves her. All I got was his guilt. And she didn't love him! She was screwing Tim Brouchard. She was still in love with Alton. She didn't even want Shawn. She just wanted whatever I had."

"It's okay," Jake said. "We can work all of this out. It's going to be okay … if you were provoked."

"You should have seen her," Shannon said. "Strutting around in a tight sweater and jeans. She just had to have them looking at her. All the time. Grady. Shawn. Every guy in Stanley. He was mine! She could have had anybody else she wanted."

"I know," Jake said, taking another step forward. This time, Shannon moved back. She sobbed. Her whole body began to shake, but she kept the gun pressed against her temple. "This isn't the way, Shannon. You have to believe me. Think about Chloe and your son. You can't leave them. Chloe's only seventeen. Shannon, I know what it's like to lose a mother like this."

"You know what she said to me that night at the lake?" Shannon said. "She said it was too easy. She said she barely had to try. That Shawn had been following her around like a puppy since they were ten years old. She said it wasn't her fault that he loved her more than me. I couldn't take it. I wanted her to shut up. I just wanted her to shut up! I made her shut up!"

Jake went very still. She had just admitted she was at the lake but didn't seem to realize it yet.

"But that's not true, what she said," Jake said. "Shawn does love you. He did this for you, didn't he? He was willing to spend the rest of his life in prison for you."

"He owes me," she said through tight lips.

"Yes. He owes you. And he knew it. All these years. He knew, didn't he? It was the deal, wasn't it?"

"I fixed his problem. I made Nicole go away. I always clean up his messes. The bar? The expansion was my idea. My family gave him the money to do it. He'd have nothing if it weren't for me. He would have let Nicole ruin everything."

"Did he help you that night?"

Shannon let out a haughty laugh. "He never helps me. It's always been the other way around, Jake. Always. But he knew. Believe me. He knew. I made sure of it after we got married."

"You told him you cleaned up the mess he made with Nicole."

"Yes! The night Shawn Jr. was born. That's when I told him. He didn't want to hear it. He just wanted to go on, not a care in the world while I was here, doing everything. Taking care of the house. Taking care of the kids. Working myself to the bone at the bar when he couldn't afford to hire anyone else. It was me. I've kept this family afloat. I've done it all. This? Him in jail? It's the least he can do, Jake. He deserves it. You think Nicole would have put up with any of this?"

My God, Jake thought. Shawn Weingard had carried the secret for over twenty years. Shannon had waited to tell him until she knew Shawn would never go to the police. Until after she was his wife and the mother of his son.

Shannon's eyes went wild. "She took! Nicole always took! I couldn't have other friends. I couldn't be too popular. She would find ways to tear me down. Since we were little kids. We were going to get married right after high school. We were gonna get out of here. Move to California or Florida. And she couldn't go! Her parents were never going to let her go. She was stuck here. So she wanted us to be stuck here with her. She trapped him! I wouldn't let her. I wouldn't let her! She doesn't get to win! She doesn't get to have him! She doesn't get to win!"

There! A split second. A twitch of her shoulder. Maybe she lost her resolve. Maybe it was the weight of the gun. But Shannon Weingard's hand shook and for a moment, her arm began to lower.

Jake leaped forward, crossing the distance between them. He grabbed Shannon's wrist and wrenched it straight up. She screamed. She squeezed the trigger. But the shot went into the ceiling.

There would not be another.

Jake twisted Shannon's arm backward, putting pressure on her wrist. She loosened her grip on the gun and Jake tore it out of her hand. He pushed her into the counter and got cuffs on her.

"No!" she screamed. And she kept on screaming. Her voice became a raspy horror as she yelled at a dead girl who couldn't defend herself.

"He's mine. He's mine. He's mine!"

Shannon sank to the floor as Jake recited the words he knew by heart.

"You have the right to remain silent …"

FORTY

At Jake's urging, Sheriff Landry sent two female deputies and a county social worker to Grandpa Max's house. Jake would later learn they arrived just as Gemma brought dessert out to the table. Chloe Nicole Weingard learned of her mother's arrest for the murder of the woman she was named after on the front porch over strawberry shortcake and Grandpa Max's freshly squeezed lemonade. By the time Jake got there, Chloe walked zombie-like toward the social worker's car.

Gemma stood on the porch step, her arm around Ryan. Grandpa Max had taken Aiden into the house and occupied him with the television.

Jake walked up to Chloe. She looked just like her mother. He hadn't really noticed before, but now that he'd spent so much time looking at photos of a seventeen-year-old Shannon Murphy, the resemblance was striking. It chilled him in a way. She was just a kid. Shannon had been just a kid. But she'd made the decision to strangle the life out of Nicole Strong and covered it up all these years.

"I'm sorry, Chloe," Jake said. It seemed wholly inadequate. But he had no other words for her.

"I know he didn't do it," Chloe whispered. "I knew he didn't do it. When can I see him? When will my dad get to come home?"

No questions about her mother. No apparent shock, even.

"It might take a little while," Jake said. "And it might not be up to me."

"He didn't do anything," Chloe said. "He didn't kill that girl. I knew he didn't kill that girl. I knew you had it wrong. My mom ... she's just ... she turns sometimes. She gets ... angry."

"Detective," the social worker said. Her name was Regina Watson. Jake had worked with her on a case or two over the last year. "I don't think it's a good idea for you to question Miss Weingard right now."

Jake put a hand up in a surrender gesture. "That's not my intention. Chloe, I just want to know you're okay. Ms. Watson will take good care of you."

Chloe gave Jake a numb nod. "I just knew my dad couldn't have done this," she whispered as Regina helped her into the front seat of her car. Regina reached over and snapped Chloe's seatbelt into place. She gave Jake a quick wink as she came around to the driver's side. Jake turned and faced his family as Regina drove Chloe down the hill.

"You okay?" Gemma asked. Ryan let her keep an arm around him. That alone was a rare enough event. It pained Jake to think of what had transpired when the deputies delivered the news of Shannon's arrest.

"It's been a day," he said. "Is there any fried chicken left?"

"I saved you a plate," Gemma said. "But you're not out of the woods yet, baby brother."

Jake gave his sister a quizzical stare. Then, the deputies he'd asked for came out onto the porch. Mary Rathburn and Birdie. Birdie's glare cut straight through him. He could only guess at what turned her face to stone.

"Come on," Gemma said. "Let's leave the cops out here to do their cop thing." She started to lead Ryan back into the house but his nephew dug his heels in. He shrugged off his mother's embrace.

"Uncle Jake," he said. "Is Chloe's dad getting out of jail tonight?"

"I honestly don't know," Jake said. "He lied to the police, Ryan. Gave a false statement. He may be charged with obstruction. Like I told Chloe, that isn't my call to make. But I think there's a good chance he won't do time even if he is charged. You understand that's not a promise I can make. Not to you. Not to Chloe. What her parents did ... it's serious, Ryan. I hate that it all had to happen this way, but I'm afraid that girl's childhood is over now. Do you understand?"

Ryan's jaw twitched. Pain furrowed his brow. But he nodded.

"She's going to need her friends around her," Jake said. "And she's going to need space to grieve. There's a good chance her mother is going to spend the rest of her life in prison."

"Come on," Gemma said to her son. "There will be plenty of time for questions later."

This time, Ryan let his mother coax him inside the house.

"Good work, Detective," Deputy Mary Rathburn said as soon as Ryan was out of earshot. She patted Jake on the arm. "We heard you had some excitement at the Weingard house. Heard she pulled a gun on you."

Birdie stood leaning against the porch post, her eyes flashing fire.

"Not on me," Jake said. "She pointed it at herself. For a minute there … I was pretty sure she was going to pull the trigger. But it's over. She's safe."

Mary looked back at Birdie. She seemed to sense something brewing. "Well, my shift is just about over. I'm gonna clock out and head home. See you in the morning, Erica, Detective."

Jake waved goodbye. Rathburn got in her patrol car and drove off, leaving Jake alone with Birdie.

He was tired. Bone-weary. Jake sat down on the porch steps. If Birdie was going to unload on him for something, he figured he might as well get comfortable before she did it. He was dead on his feet.

Birdie stomped down the porch steps and turned to face him. "That was really stupid, Jake."

He rubbed his forehead. "Birdie, it's been a long day. I'm sure I've done at least five stupid things just in the last twenty minutes. You wanna narrow it down for me?"

"Why did you go over to the Weingards alone? Why didn't you tell me or anyone else you were going? When I left the office, I told you I'd be back in like an hour. You should have waited for me. You needed backup."

He arched a brow as he looked up at her. "Birdie …"

"She pulled a gun!" Birdie said. "Christ, Jake."

"You heard me tell Rathburn. She wasn't aiming at me. She was …"

"You know how that could have gone. That woman was cornered. Desperate. She could have decided to commit suicide by cop. I'm not mad you couldn't handle yourself in that situation, I'm mad because you shouldn't have been in it. Not like that. Not without backup. And I was the person you should have taken out there. We were working on this case together. And you could have ..."

Jake put his hands up. "Uncle ... okay? I give up. You're right. I'm sorry. I didn't think ..."

"No. You thought. You didn't have me come out there with you because you *knew* this thing might get dicey. You didn't want me in the middle of it. You want me at a desk. Organizing files in the bowels of the station. I know why. I know you've got this pigheaded idea that it's your job to keep me out of trouble. That's twice now you've let this bro code you think you have with my dead brother get in the way of me doing my job."

"Birdie ..."

"I don't need you to protect me, Jake. I need you to treat me like a grown-up. I need you to quit doing stupid stuff like putting Deputy Denning into walls. Okay?"

Jake opened his mouth to argue, but as Birdie stood there, hands on her hips, cutting straight through him with her words and her killer stare, he knew he had very little cause.

"Okay," he said. "I'm sorry. Truly."

The air went out of her a little. Maybe she hadn't expected Jake to agree with her. But he did. He didn't like it. But she had a point.

"Okay," she said. "And ... great work, by the way."

"You too. That photograph of Shannon, that was a brilliant catch. An innocent man could have spent the rest of his life in prison if you hadn't found it, Birdie."

Jake got to his feet. He held a hand out to Birdie. "Fresh start?"

She chewed her bottom lip. "You're sure you're really okay? That had to have been rough with Shannon."

"I'm fine," he said. "And I do appreciate you asking."

Birdie nodded. Keeping one arm wrapped around her middle, she held out her other one and shook Jake's hand. "Fresh start. See you at the office tomorrow."

With that, she picked up her hat off the porch, dusted it off, and headed back to her cruiser. Jake sat back down on the porch steps. He waved as Birdie drove off.

Behind him, the front door opened. Both Gemma and Grandpa Max came out. Birdie gave a quick tap on her horn before she rounded the curve and drove out of view.

"I told ya," Grandpa said. "I like her. She sure told you."

Jake looked back at his grandfather. "I was just trying to keep her out of trouble."

Gemma snorted. "How'd that work out?"

Jake grunted.

"Yep," Grandpa said. "Chewed your ass out but good, grandson."

"Baby brother," Gemma said. "Aren't you beginning to notice a pattern yet?"

Jake stared up at his sister, mystified. Gemma rolled her eyes. "Jake … while it's really noble of you to want to protect all these women in your life, maybe you should just quit it until one of us asks you to."

Behind her, Grandpa Max just let out a soft chuckle. Jake was too damn tired to argue anymore with either of them.

"Come on," Gemma said. "Get in here and eat this chicken while it's still warm, hot shot."

Jake heaved himself to his feet. He knew the easier path would have been to just march himself back down the hill and into his cabin alone. But Gemma's fried chicken smelled delicious. Plus he probably would have felt his sister's gloating and heard his grandfather's laughter at his expense all the way through the woods. At least now he could face them on a full stomach.

FORTY-ONE

Two weeks later

This time, when Jake drove up Virgil Adamski's winding drive, he found the old man's RV out of the barn and hitched to the back of his truck. Virgil himself had just stepped out on his front porch and was locking the door behind him.

"Looks like I got here just in time," Jake said, shielding his eyes from the glare of the late June sun. It was the official first day of summer. Not the time for lake dwellers to be hitting the road.

Virgil smiled. He took a step toward Jake then tossed his keys straight at him. Jake reacted just in time to catch them before they hit him in the chest.

"You sure did. You think you could hang on to those for me? Check on the place once or twice a month?"

Jake had a small brown package in his free hand. He tucked it under his arm and walked up to Virgil.

"Where you headed?"

"I got a niece who lives up north. Near Traverse City. Thought I'd camp up there for a few weeks. Then my brother lives out west. Phoenix. I've been promising for years to spend some time there."

"Summer's just starting, Virg," Jake said.

Virgil nodded. "I just ... I don't know. I don't feel like staring across the lake right now. I need a change of scenery."

Jake went very still. He understood.

"Shannon gonna plead out?" Virgil finally asked.

"Bernicki's not offering right now. He thinks he can make first degree murder. She lured Nicole into her car that night. Drove her here."

"What about Shawn?"

Jake sighed. "He's out on bond. But he's gonna get charged for obstruction. He knew, Virg. All this time. He knew Shannon was the one who killed Nicole."

Vigil nodded. "I didn't see it. I just didn't see it." His voice cracked at the end.

"Neither did I," Jake said. "Not at first. I was ready to believe Shawn Weingard's confession was true."

"Why?" Virgil asked. "Why'd he do it?"

"Guilt," Jake said. "Then he kept her secret out of some sick sense of loyalty. We're hearing from both of their kids that Shannon has always run the show in that relationship. Shawn has been doing Shannon's bidding since the day Nicole died. Penance, I guess. He's saying he felt like what happened with Nicole was his fault, even if he wasn't the one who killed her. His actions are what set off this whole chain of events. And Shannon

... she was far more manipulative than anyone gave her credit for."

"But he knew?" Virgil said. "All these years?"

"Yeah, Virg," Jake said. "He knew. That's how he was able to give me such a convincing confession. He says Shannon confessed to the murder well after it happened. She calculated. Manipulated. Told him the night their son was born because she knew by then he wouldn't...couldn't turn her in. He didn't know what to do."

"He could have told the damn truth!" Virgil said, his lips quivering.

"Yeah. Yeah."

Jake took the package out from under his arm. It was the real reason he came out here today.

"Marty and Viv," he said. "They asked me to give this to you. They were hoping you'd be at the last press conference. They would have given it to you then."

He handed Virgil the flat, rectangular package. Virgil met Jake's eyes. He held the package to his heart for a moment. Then he slowly peeled back the paper.

Even Jake hadn't known what was inside, though he suspected. There, in a new gold frame, was a black-and-white photograph of Nicole Strong, laughing at the camera, her hair lifted away from her face by the breeze. She was beautiful. Happy. Full of life.

Virgil turned the frame over. Viv Strong had written a small note. "We want you to remember our Nic like this. It's who she was. Thank you. We know you came to love her too." Vivian had taped a gold St. Christopher medal beside the note. Virgil carefully tore it off and squeezed it in his palm.

A tear slid down Virgil Adamski's face. He quickly wiped it away.

"They didn't have to do this," he whispered.

"They know," Jake said. "And I think maybe they did. They wouldn't want you to stop enjoying the lake, Virg. They don't want people to think of it as the place Nicole died."

Virgil nodded. "I know. And maybe someday, I won't anymore. This will help." He clutched the photograph, cherishing it.

"Don't stay away too long," Jake said. "We like having you around. Plus, somebody's gotta help me keep the rest of the Wise Asses in line."

Virgil smiled. "Thanks, Jake. For ... all of it. The keys to my fishing boat are on that chain too. Maybe bring Max out here some afternoon."

"He'll like that," Jake said.

Virgil nodded. He put a hand on Jake's chest. Then he let go and headed to the driver's side door of his truck. Jake watched him put Nicole's picture on the seat beside him. She'd ride shotgun all the way up north. Jake hoped in time, it would help Virgil exorcise her ghost. Then, Virgil hung the St. Christopher medallion off his rearview mirror. It made Jake smile.

When Virgil left, something made Jake drive around the lake one last time. As if he needed to say his own goodbye to Nicole.

It was just a quick, five-minute drive to the southeast end of the lake. As he rounded the curve, he left the tranquility of Virgil's place behind. Jake came to a stop just before the entrance to the new Arch Hill Estates. Last week, construction had been allowed to move forward. The utility crews were out digging lines for the water and sewer hookups. Great big trucks chugged through the dirt, shattering the quiet.

Jake watched for a moment. The developers had scrapped plans to build the showpiece home in the lot where Nicole was found. Instead, they moved it further south. Nicole's burial site would now be part of a cul-de-sac. They'd plant a flower garden there, someone said.

Jake was about to drive away when he saw her. For a moment, his heart seemed to erupt into his throat. Her blonde hair flapped in the breeze. Those luminous eyes. He blinked hard, thinking he was cracking up and seeing an actual ghost.

Then Anya turned and started walking down the road away from him. He got out of his car and called out to her.

Anya startled, then her step faltered as she recognized Jake past the glint of the sun. Hands in his pockets, Jake walked up to her.

"Seems we had the same idea," Jake said, looking out at the construction crews.

"I don't know if I'm ever going to be able to come out here again after this," she said. "That's why I came today ... to ... to see if I could. What it would feel like."

Jake turned to her. She looked pale. Tired.

"I just came from Virgil's," he said. "I gave him the package from your mother. Tell her it mattered."

Anya nodded. "It was a big step for her. It's the first thing my mother's done that was, I don't know. Final. Accepting. She's started talking about my sister in the past tense."

"What about you? How does it feel, Anya?"

She considered his question for a moment. "Shawn and Shannon ... they were part of how we coped, Jake. She tried to be like a sister to me. I don't know how to feel yet. But to be honest, I'm angry."

"That's understandable. Shannon killed your sister, Anya. She ..."

"No," Anya said, cutting him off. "I'm angry at Nicole. I mean, of course I'm angry at Shannon. Anger ... it's not strong enough of a word for how I feel about her. But I'm so damn mad at my sister too. It was all just so unnecessary. She could have made better choices. She could have asked for help. She could have fought harder."

"I think it's natural to feel all of those things."

"Everyone I leaned on. Everyone I thought I was close to. They all lied to me, Jake. Shannon Shawn. Tim. They all knew my sister better than I did. They all used her. Abused her. I let them in. I gave them pieces of myself. And it's like Nicole is up there. Her spirit. She knew these things about people that I loved. None of it was ever real. I hate her for it. I know it doesn't make sense. My God. It wasn't her fault. She died for it. She trusted the wrong people and got killed because of it. But she left me. Jake ... she still left me."

As she sobbed, Jake pulled Anya into an embrace. He let her cry against his chest for a moment. Finally, she came back into herself and pulled away.

"I should have left with you," she said. "I should have gotten as far away from Blackhand Hills as I could have. I should have done what Nicole set out to do. I would have ... Jake ... I would have waited for you."

He turned to the lake. "I know." There was an unspoken question in her words. Would he wait for her now? In the end, he said nothing. He knew his answer wouldn't be what she wanted to hear and he refused to causer her more pain today.

"And I'm mad at you," she said, letting the moment pass. "I know I have no right to be. But I am. I'm mad at you because you came back when you told me you wouldn't. I'm mad at you because ... and I know it's not fair and it's crazy. But I'm mad at you because if you hadn't come back ... things would just be how they were before. God. I know that's insane. And it's not fair. But ..."

"But I came back and blew up your life," Jake said. "I'm sorry. I really am."

Anya let out a sort of cry-laugh. "You gave my sister back to us. I just never knew how much that was going to cost. I know I'm not being fair. But I just need to be mad for a little while longer. I'm ... I'm leaving."

"You're leaving Tim?"

She shook her head. "Well, yes. But I'm leaving Stanley. For a little while at least. I haven't taken any time off in years. I worked it out with Melissa at the restaurant. I don't know when I'm coming back. But ...I just have to go."

"It's good," Jake said. "You should. You've been holding too many other people together for far too long. Go. Figure out who you are. You don't have to be Nicole's sister anymore. I don't think she would want that for you."

She turned and looked out at the lake with him. The heavy trucks had stopped. It was lunchtime. All the crews were taking a break. To the east, he saw two doves peeking out from behind a thicket. Behind them, Jake saw their two small chicks. Soon enough, they would venture out together, claiming this portion of the lake for their own.

For a moment, peace settled over the lake once more. By the end of the year, this entire landscape would change. New houses. New people. New life. New dreams. Nicole Strong's bones were long gone. He knew it would take far longer to exorcise her spirit. For Anya. For her parents. For Virgil. And for himself.

As Jake turned, the smaller of the two dove chicks took flight and disappeared into the trees. A moment later, their parents called to them in that warbling way doves do. When the wind went still and Jake closed his eyes, it almost sounded like cries echoing across the lake.

One-Click Red Sky Hill - Jake Cashen Book 4 so you don't miss out!

Turn the page and keep reading for a special preview...

Interested in an exclusive extended prologue to Murder in the Hollows?

Join Declan James's Roll Call Newsletter for a free download.

Special Preview of
Red Sky Hill

Red Sky Hill
Jake Cashen book 4

Three months later ...

They called it the Golden Hour. Just before six in the evening on the first day of fall. Gemma Cashen Jarvis Stark Gerald could barely contain her excitement as she drove up the winding drive that disappeared into the woods. She went slow, no more than ten miles an hour, as she approached the sloping curve that led up to the house. A mix of gorgeous, century-old hardwoods lined the drive. Still in full bloom, the maple leaves formed a canopy then broke away, revealing the sprawling farmhouse at the top of a small hill.

Gemma still got goosebumps when she saw it. The white picket fence. The wraparound porch. The cheery cedar shutters and flower boxes against the newly installed slate-gray siding.

She pulled her car to the side of the house so it wouldn't be the first thing anyone saw when they drove up. Her palms were sweating as she opened the car door and walked over to the lush green berm at the center of the circular driveway. She straightened the sign sticking out of the ground there. Dusting off a clump of grass that had stuck to the "G" in her first name. Her hands were shaking as she stepped back. Her own headshot smiled back at her from the top of the "For Sale" sign.

This was it, she knew. The listing that could change her and her sons' lives forever. At $999,999 and likely to end in a bidding war, Gemma was looking at her very first million-dollar sale. The commission would be enough to cover her oldest boy's college tuition and room and board for the next two years. With good planning and a lot of luck, she could get him through debt free.

"It's only the beginning," Gemma said. She walked up to the house, fluffing the pillows on the custom-built swing bed on the north side of the porch. A late addition to the staging at Gemma's suggestion. She'd seen one just like it on her favorite home and garden show.

Tires crunched on the gravel behind her. They're early, she thought. It was a great sign.

Gemma waved a hand over her head and went to meet her buyers. Karl and Daphne Birdwell. Both in their mid-thirties, Karl was the newly hired weatherman for WBLK News. But that wasn't how they could afford this house. No. The Birdwells ran a YouTube channel with nearly ten million subscribers. Their niche was sustainable living and from what Gemma could tell of Daphne, being fit and pretty.

The passenger door opened. Daphne Birdwell, her blonde hair pulled back in a shellacked bun and mirrored sunglasses on her face, rose from her seat. Her jaw went slack. She slowly peeled off her sunglasses, her expression of awe reminding Gemma of the paleontologists in *Jurassic Park* when they saw living dinosaurs for the first time.

"It's amazing, isn't it?" Gemma said.

Karl Birdwell came around to his wife's side. He stood with his hands on his hips, waiting for Daphne.

"The pictures are fabulous," Daphne said. "But this ... it's like a magazine."

"Eighty acres," Gemma said. "The pond is through those trees on the east side of the property. It's three acres, natural spring fed and stocked with bass, bluegill, crappie, and catfish."

"He knew what he was doing," Karl said. "Whoever built this place. The porch faces west."

"That's right," Gemma said. "You can enjoy the sunset as it sinks behind Red Sky Hill. In about twenty minutes, you'll see how it got its name."

Gemma had planned it just so. She wanted the Birdwells sitting on that swing bed with a glass of freshly squeezed lemonade in their hands as the sky turned crimson and gold.

"Come on," Gemma said. "Let me show you inside."

She punched her code into the lock box as Karl and Daphne crowded in behind her. Daphne wrapped her hands around her husband's waist. For his part, Karl kept a bit of a scowl in place. Gemma knew he'd want to seem skeptical. But the moment Daphne walked into the foyer and took in the original slate flooring, built-in oak coat rack and bench, and hummingbird-patterned stained glass, even Karl's eyes went wide.

Daphne broke away from him and ran down the hallway into the kitchen.

"This sink!" she squealed. "Gemma, is it original to the home?"

"It is," she said. "The owner had it reglazed along with the clawfoot soaker tub up in the primary suite."

Daphne ran the water. Above her, copper pots hung on hooks. Karl moved in, running his hands along the butcher block counters.

"Every detail is its own showpiece," Daphne said. She had her phone out and started recording video. Gemma tried not to sound giddy.

"It really is," she said. "You've got twenty-five hundred square feet in the main living space. Five bedrooms upstairs. Two with en-suite bathrooms. You've got a guest bath right around the corner built in under the stairs. There's another fifteen hundred feet of living space in the basement. Mr. Albright installed a full kitchen down there. With the sixth bedroom and bath, you can use it as a mother-in-law suite if you'd like. There are so many options."

She stood back, letting the Birdwells explore the property on their own. Each ooh or aah from Daphne made Gemma see dollar signs. Instinct told her, Karl would have no choice but to write an offer right here at the kitchen table. And Gemma had four other showings right after them. She had four unanswered texts from other realtors with clients ready to write their offers sight unseen.

"Those dormer windows!" Daphne shrieked as she ran back downstairs to find Gemma. "I just can't get over the detail put into restoring this house!"

"It's one of a kind," Gemma said. "Modern amenities with a farmhouse feel."

"The land though," Karl said. "I just can't get over it."

"You could get instant value out of the back forty acres if you wanted to log it out," Gemma said.

"My God. No!" Daphne said. "I wouldn't let you touch a single tree, Karl."

"And you don't have to," Gemma said. "Mr. Albright didn't hunt himself, but he made quite a bit renting it to a couple of locals. That would stop, of course. If that was your preference. Albright has been pretty happy here running this place as a hobby farm for the past few years. There's a fenced-off paddock behind the barn for horses or goats, whatever you want. I can't wait to show you the custom-built chicken coop next to the barn. I've been saving that for a surprise."

"Are there chickens now?" Daphne clapped her hands under her chin.

"There are," Gemma said. "Come on. Let me show you my favorite part of the entire property."

As they went out the back and walked toward the giant red barn, Gemma saw Karl Birdwell's poker face slip for good.

"How big is it?" he asked.

"60x80. Forty-eight hundred square feet. Mr. Albright wanted the ultimate man cave and workspace for himself. He's walled off the back section and had the place wired for his home office. He liked watching the horses graze right from the window."

Gemma unlocked the barn padlock and swung open the door. Daphne ran forward. It was dark inside. Gemma fumbled for the lights.

"All the office furniture can stay," she said. "Albright's got a custom-built desk, leather furniture, a large flat-screen television.

He had the bathroom addition put on just last year. He wanted it so he'd never have to leave the barn."

Gemma switched on the light. Craig Albright's vintage cars were still parked inside. A candy-apple red 1964 Mustang GT and an emerald-green 1970 Plymouth Roadrunner. Karl ran his hands along the side of the Roadrunner.

"There's plenty of room for all your toys and then some," Gemma said. "You can finally get Daphne that Airstream she's always wanted."

Gemma found the last key on the ring and walked to the back wall of the barn. She unlocked the office door and swung it open, knowing it would seal the deal as soon as Karl saw it.

She let Karl and Daphne go in ahead of her. The sun was just starting to set. Gold light spilled through the large window on the far wall.

"As I said, Albright's willing to include all the furniture with the sale," she said, waving away a fly as it buzzed near her ear. "Karl, have a seat at the desk. Picture yourself working out here while Daphne's tending to the garden and the chickens."

Gemma put a hand on the leather seat back and swiveled the thing around.

Or tried to.

First the smell hit her. Then, her heel slipped in something slick and wet.

Craig Albright was still sitting in his desk chair. His lips were blue. His eyes bulged open. A fly landed on his mottled nose. As Gemma took a step back and dropped her hands, Albright's head fell to the side. He'd been sliced from ear to ear, his white shirt stained through with dried blood.

Daphne Birdwell let out a blood-curdling scream.

A shocking discovery at the foot of the infamous Red Sky Hill will send Detective Jake Cashen on a harrowing hunt for a brutal killer. Don't miss Red Sky Hill, Jake Cashen Book 4 in the Jake Cashen crime thriller series. Click the book cover or go here to learn more. https://declanjamesbooks.com/red

About the Author

Before putting pen to paper, Declan James's career in law enforcement spanned twenty-six years. Declan's work as a digital forensics detective has earned him the highest honors from the U.S. Secret Service and F.B.I. For the last sixteen years of his career, Declan served on a nationally recognized task force aimed at protecting children from online predators. Prior to that, Declan spent six years undercover working Vice-Narcotics.

An avid outdoorsman and conservationist, Declan enjoys hunting, fishing, grilling, smoking meats, and his quest for the perfect bottle of bourbon. He lives on a lake in Southern Michigan along with his wife and kids. Declan James is a pseudonym.

For more information follow Declan at one of the links below. If you'd like to receive new release alerts, author news, and a FREE digital bonus prologue to Murder in the Hollows, sign up for Declan's Roll Call Newsletter here: https://declanjamesbooks.com/rollcall/

ALSO BY DECLAN JAMES

Murder in the Hollows

Kill Season

Bones of Echo Lake

Red Sky Hill

With more to come...

Stay in Touch with Declan James

For more information, visit

https://declanjamesbooks.com

If you'd like to receive a free digital copy of the extended prologue to the Jake Cashen series, sign up for Declan James's Roll Call Newsletter here: https://declanjamesbooks.com/rollcall/

Made in the USA
Monee, IL
24 August 2024

64511573R00210